Praise for
The Robin & Marian Mysteries

"When it comes to creating an authentic atmosphere for the historical mystery, Clayton Emery ranks with the best in the genre..." **Janet Hutchings, *Ellery Queen Mystery Magazine***

"The atmosphere is vivid, the writing sharp, and the puzzles neatly constructed... all set against a backdrop at once familiar and freshly reimagined." **Steven Saylor, author of the Roma Sub Rosa series starring Gordianus the Finder**

"Clayton Emery's little mysteries are well-conceived and well-written. Give Emery a mystery, and you can be sure he'll solve it in a reader-pleasing way." **Mike Resnick, author of SOOTHSAYER, IVORY, and THE CHRONICLES OF LUCIFER JONES**

"Few authors could do justice to the legend of Robin Hood, but Robin and Marian are in good hands with Clayton Emery. Emery blends the best of the classic mystery with all the heroism and romance one would expect in Sherwood Forest. What a pleasure it is to return to Merry Old England in Emery's stories!" **Rick Riordan, Edgar® Award Winner for the Tres Navarre series**

"Robin and Marian are ideal sleuths and Emery gives them a whole new lease on life." **Mike Ashley, editor of THE MAMMOTH BOOK OF HISTORICAL WHODUNNITS and other MAMMOTHs**

"Clayton Emery's lively Robin and Marian tales of historical crime, misdeeds and gallivanting are like a breath of fresh air, and bring a much-needed sense of enjoyment to the erstwhile legends of Sherwood Forest. Forget the green tights and Errol Flynn mustaches and savor the romantic reality that should have been." **Maxim Jakubowski, editor of MURDER THROUGH THE AGES and other anthologies**

Mandrake and Murder

Mandrake and Murder

The Robin & Marian Mysteries

by Clayton Emery

Merry Man Publishing

Mandrake and Murder

Dedicated to Janet Hutchings,
Editor of *Ellery Queen Mystery Magazine*,
without whom there would be
no Robin & Marian mysteries.

Mandrake and Murder: The Robin & Marian Mysteries
The POD Edition
ISBN 978-0-9815317-6-2
© 2009 by Clayton Emery

First appearances
"Dowsing the Demon", *EQMM*, November 1994.
"Floating Bread and Quicksilver" as "A Loaf of
Quicksilver", *EQMM*, October 1995. "Grinding the
Ghost", *EQMM*, March 1995. "Shriving the Scarecrow",
EQMM, Sept/Oct 1997. "Flushing Scarlett", *EQMM*,
March 1998. "Abjuring Justice", *EQMM*, August 1998.
"Tilting the Tournament" *EQMM*, July 1999. "Squaring
the Circle", *Crimestalker Casebook*, Winter 1999.
"Fathoming Fortune", *EQMM*, July 2000. "Plucking a
Mandrake", *Murder Most Medieval*, edited by Martin H.
Greenberg and John Helfers, 2000. "Flyting,
Fighting", *Murder Through the Ages*, edited by Maxim
Jakubowski, 2006. "Robin Hood's Treasure", *The
Fantastic Adventures of Robin Hood*, edited by Martin
H. Greenberg, 1991.

Merry Man Publishing
515 Pelican Avenue
Gaithersburg, MD, 20877
claytonemery at claytonemery dot com
www.claytonemery.com

Learn more about Robin Hood at claytonemery.com.

Cover art by NC Wyeth from THE BLACK ARROW

Other Ebooks by Clayton Emery

ROYAL HUNT: A Robin & Marian Mystery
ROBIN HOOD AND THE BEASTS OF SHERWOOD
ROBIN HOOD AND THE BELLS OF LONDON
PALE GHOST: A Joseph Fisher Colonial Mystery
JUMPING THE JACK with Earl Wajenberg

Contents

Mandrake and Murder

Dowsing the Demon

"Murder! Help, for God's mercy! It's murder and witchcraft! Help!"

Hammering on a door rang on and on. Robin scrambled off his pallet, fumbled for his bow and sword, found neither, settled for his hat. Marian scuffed on her shoes and combed fingers through her dark hair. The outlaw wrenched the bar from the inn door and they dashed outside.

The morning sun slanted long shadows down the sleepy streets of Lincoln. The faces and shuttered windows of one- and two-story houses were etched in darkness. April was already warm. Dew spiraled from the trashy street. Four doors down from the inn, a young man pounded on the door of a small house.

His cries of "Murder and witchcraft!" had people congregating from all sides. His wails were infectious. One man shouted, "Open the door then, by the rood!" Another yelled, "It's barred tight!"

Robin shoved through the crowd and jiggled the wooden latch, thumped the door with his shoulder. It bent at top and bottom but not the middle. Barred. As he smacked the door, smells spurted around the edges. Brimstone. And blood.

He whirled on the shrieking lad. "Hush. All of you. Whose house is this?"

The youth plucked his thin beard with both hands. He wore a smock of rich blue with an embroidered collar, a belt with a silver-hilted dagger, yellow hose, good shoes of oxhide, a brimmed black hat. "It's the house of Jabin, my father, but something's plaguey wrong! The house stinks of blasphemy!"

Robin had to agree. The smell that wafted from inside was enough to knock a man flat. "Is there a back door?"

"No, only the window, and it shuttered! And the chimney!"

Though still befuddled by sleep, Robin felt hairs prickle along his neck. What devil's work had the occupants gotten up to?

"The door it is, then. You and you and you, come with me." From the crowd of workmen, wives, and idle children, Robin picked out a porter with a tump line and a pair of masons in stone-dusty aprons. While Marian minded the door, the four men hopped down the street to a house under construction, hoisted a square beam, and trotted back. Three lusty blows at the middle right cracked the door and bashed loose the inside bar.

The reek of brimstone made their eyes water, the smell of blood gagged them. Holding his breath, Robin slipped inside and fumbled open the shutters to the one window on the street.

Dawn's light filtered through a yellow haze. Revealed was a scene from some pardoner's chapbook of Hell.

The house was only one room. Four whitewashed walls, a worn wooden floor, smoke-stained rafters, a stone chimney, a saggy rope bed, a red chest against the wall, a table and two stools, a cabinet for a larder, pegs on the walls where hung clothing. Spare, dingy, but tidy. A short broom of rushes stood propped against the fireplace.

On the floor lay an old man stringy and naked as a plucked chicken, and white as one. His throat had been hacked away, his belly from ribs to crotch torn open, as if he'd been rooted to death by boars. His eyes were wide open, filmy and white as boiled eggs. By the bed, tangled in blankets, lay a goodwife in a pool of tacky blood, she stabbed so many times her skin and organs hung in shreds. The gore looked all the more offensive for having violated the woman's clean floorboards.

Marian bit a knuckle. Robin blocked the door with one brawny arm as the crowd pushed for a look. Yet the young merchant, the son who'd raised the alarm, squeezed between him and Marian with the strength of the hysterical.

He flopped to his knees alongside the dead man. "Oh, father, father! Who's done this? Who?" Old Jabin didn't answer, only stared wide-eyed at his son as if in accusation. Unmindful of blood, the lad touched his father's face.

"Sir, wait," piped Marian. "We needs look in his eyes."

But the son clawed closed the thin eyelids. "I can't stand his gaze. As if it were my fault. Had I gotten here only an hour earlier −" He broke into tears, sobbing.

Robin rubbed his beard as he surveyed the room. Shocking though this macabre spectacle was, he'd seen worse, though not usually this early in the morning. And his famous curiosity, an itch he could never scratch, prodded him like an ox goad. His wife, too.

Marian lit a stick of candlewood at the smoldering hearth. Gingerly, she picked across the room, leaned over the dead mother. She peered deep into the woman's eyes.

"Anything?" Robin asked.

"No," Marian sighed. "Nothing. She must have closed her eyes when the knife struck."

Robin grunted. Something by the fireplace had caught his eye. He stooped, swirled his fingers through white grit, the only dirt in the room. Streaks of it pointed to the chimney. Feeling around, Robin tugged loose a stone big as a loaf. Behind it was a cool darkness. Squatting, he mumbled to Marian, "There's a hole here big enough for my head. Nothing in it, though."

"The hole or the head?" Her lame jest was just something to break the silence. Marian left the dead mother, put her hand on the red chest against the wall, tried to lift the lid. It clinked and stayed put. "This chest is locked. My thumbs are pricking, Rob... And look here."

Robin's wife knelt at the fireplace, leaned low and sniffed, picked out some charred scraps of leather that stained her fingers yellow-brown. "What think you of that?"

"It's not something they had for supper. Let me see this door..."

Waving the crowd back, Robin shoved the battered door shut. It groaned in protest. Twin iron brackets had held the bar solidly across the posts. One bracket was broken, the fracture gray against blackened iron. Behind the door, the other bracket was twisted out of shape. The stout bar trailed from it to the floor. The door itself was oak, thick, and battened so neither wind nor knife blade could infiltrate. It was dark behind the door but, bending, Robin found jots of yellow gunk smeared on the battens. He scraped them like old cheese with his fingernails. He sniffed, held his fingers to Marian.

"Why, it's sweet. It's —"

The door slammed Robin in the face as it was kicked open. The outlaw hit the wall. A splinter nicked his nose and it bled.

"Stand fast, you thieving blackguard. Don't you move."

Filling the splintered doorway was a sheriff of Lincoln in a red smock and gray hose, with a sword at his belt as badge of office. He hefted a long club with the head drilled and filled with lead, hoisted it to keep Robin on the defensive.

At his other hand, Marian shifted. The sheriff whirled on her, then froze when he spotted the bodies on the floor. "God's fish and teeth."

Behind the sheriff came a younger version of himself, a deputy, obviously his son. But the lad whirled and dashed into the street to puke. The crowd parted for him.

Still on bloody knees, the young merchant keened. "Witches and demons have descended and murdered my parents." He waved his hands around the room. "Smell the brimstone from their passing? Satan's minions have savaged them and drunk their blood."

The sheriff commanded the room with his presence, his club, and his broad belly, though his son's retching spoiled the effect somewhat. He studied the bodies calmly. "If that's so, they didn't drink much. You're Peter, ain't you, the wool merchant? This couple's son? Well, I'm sorry, lad."

He stretched his club and thumped Robin's breastbone. "And who are you, standing knee-deep in crime and picking lice out of your beard? I never saw you before. Think you to rob the dead?"

Robin's temper sparked. His hands clenched for the sword he didn't have. He squelched his ire. He and Marian were in town to buy cloth, both Lincoln green and red, for spring clothes for the Sherwood band. Too, it was a holiday after a winter cooped up in the Greenwood. They wore disguises plucked from the common chests in their cave, red woolen smocks and hose and soft round hats, the garb of minor merchants. Robin felt naked without his sword and longbow, only a long Irish knife.

Robin showed the sheriff the top of his head, hangdog and humble. "I'm Robert of Farnesfield, sir sheriff, near Ealden Byrgen. This is my wife, Matilda. She knows some herbalism. We thought we might help if someone was hurt."

The sheriff glared, still suspicious. Behind him, in the doorway, the porter raised his voice. "He speaks true, Martin. He came out of the inn and we all broke down the door. He couldn't have murdered no one, and he was just looking around while she there checked them dead folk."

Watching Robin with one eye, Martin the Sheriff asked the porter, "What mean you, broke down the door? How could the door be barred if all within were murdered?"

"That's what I was wondering," Robin supplied. He wiped blood from the sting on his nose. The outlaw usually took every man as he met them, without prejudging, but this sheriff had two counts against him already. "On the backside of this door —"

"You belt up," the sheriff told him. "Keep out of the way and keep still."

Robin leaned back against the wall. Marian, calm as a cloud, seated herself on the red chest.

The sheriff squatted over the dead man, prodded the wounds with his club. The young merchant, face stained with tears, raised bloody hands. "Sheriff, who could have done this? My father was a good, honest man. He had no truck with necromancers. Yet he's been struck down by sorcery. It was no man born of woman could have done this."

The sheriff expelled a gust flavored with rye bread and beer. "I don't know, Peter. Wights and phantasms can't touch iron, but I'd say this ungodly mess was from a steel knife, or I'm a bugger for a Jew. Still..." He pointed his beard at the shattered door.

"Hoy!" called a voice from down the street. "Hoy! Come to save the day, I have!"

The crowd perked up. By now a hundred or more people crowded the street, all gawking at the sensation through the doorway and one window. Most had been quiet, as if at a funeral, but now giggles and whispers broke out. Robin peeked out the door over heads. Jogging and puffing their way was something the outlaw had seen only at fairs.

Skipping like a milk-fat puppy bounded a man burly and jowly as Friar Tuck. Wild red hair fluttered. A parti-colored smock, red on one side, blue on the other, circled the man with a broad yellow girdle, and one hose was green and one black. Behind him scampered a dog brindled and golden as a butterfly, but incomplete, being three-legged and one-eyed. This fat man, or tournament marshal or mummer, waved a dowsing stick like a giant wishbone.

Robin caught comments from the crowd. "Oh, Lord, look who's coming. He'll know what to do. Aye, collect his fee and run. He cured my mother of the boils. Boils go away on their own, fool. He'll make us laugh, if nothing else."

"Make way, make way." The fat man puffed amidst them. "Denis the Dowser's on the job. Let me through. I needs see — Saint Benno's keys and fishes."

His pop eyes bugged even farther at the sight of the ravaged bodies. Robin noted the man had soft skin, a weak chin, and little beard. He wondered if the dowser were a eunuch, and if that contributed to his power — if any. The crippled dog stuck his head between the dowser's knees and drooled.

"Denis, you big bag of wind." The sheriff stood over the body, club hanging. His sheepish son had crept in behind him. "What are you doing here with your infernal stick? I know you can find water with that thing, but there's no way you can track —"

"Ah, but I can, Martin. I can. By the tongue of Saint Genevieve I can. I needs only wave my stick around the room and I'll track your murderers — demonic or no — to the ends of the earth. Shall I try? Dare you I try?"

The sheriff slapped his heavy stick against his thigh. "And you'll collect a fee from the city if you're successful, I suppose."

The fat man smirked and spread his hands. "If you catch your murderer, what care you? Have you any clues to proceed from now?"

The sheriff blew through his mustache, surveyed the hearth, the window, the door. Then he swept his club towards the corpses. The crowd buzzed.

Gimpy dog at his heels, Denis the Dowser minced inside, skirted pools of blood, positioned himself between the dead husband and wife. Striking a pose, the dowser dropped his head as if in prayer. He grasped the dowsing stick tight, thumbs pointed towards his chest. Robin noticed a red thread tied around the fork as a charm against witches. He imagined the stick was rowan wood, mountain ash, probably cut under a full moon with a blade of copper or brass. Robin wasn't certain whether he believed in dowsing or not. Certainly this clown —

Denis moaned. The rod's tip began to vibrate. People at door and window gasped. The dowser's body vibrated along with the stick. He crowed, "By the stones of Saint Stephen, by the arrows of Saint Sebastian, by the flames of Saint Lawrence, show me the way, oh Lord, lead me to the traitors who've committed this dastardly act and spilled these innocents' blood!"

Robin stared as the dowser howled, jerking his head back and forth as if struck by invisible blows, writhing as if trying to free his feet of mud. Meanwhile, the mangy dog limped around the room, sniffed at the bodies, lapped at blood, lifted his leg against the bed post. Evidently the mutt had seen it before.

Denis shivered, calling on every saint Robin knew and many he didn't. "By the cross of Saint Helen! By the visions of Saint Hildegard! By the monster of Saint Cuthbert —" Louder he yelled, until people outside moaned in ecstasy with him. Even the dog barked, sharply, twice.

Denis snapped open his pop eyes, grimaced with horror and haunting. Then the dowsing stick lunged for the doorway like a spear and Denis was towed behind it. People squealed and shrilled and dodged. Denis, his dog hot behind him, cantered off down the street, barely able to keep up with his own dowsing rod. "Saint Thomas à Canterbury, send me grace! Saint Gregory, send me wisdom! Saint Ambrose —"

Sheriff Martin hollered to his son to guard the house, and took off after Denis. Marian hiked her skirts and followed. Robin grabbed his knife hilt and ran along, with the young merchant right behind.

People stared as the dowser plunged by, head down and stumbling, stick outright as if it were an arrow and Denis tied to it. The crazy dog skipped along in its queer gait, first at one heel, then the other, until Robin wondered how the man didn't step on the poor creature. The crowd would have followed, but the sheriff waved them back with his club. When Marian drew alongside, skirts dancing and cheeks flushed, Sheriff Martin waved his club at her. But she flashed him a winning smile, lighting up the street, and he let her be. Robin trotted behind the sheriff, out of sight.

Magician he might be, but fat Denis was no marathon runner, and he spent what breath he had calling on saints, so it wasn't long before he fell to a trot, then a brisk walk. They neared the end of the street, where the houses were all two stories, homes of more prosperous merchants, then struck the marketplace. Dotted around the big square were stalls of winter vegetables, sheaves of salt hay, paddocks with skinny horses and oxen, blacksmiths whanging on anvils, and tables and tables of bolts of cloth, including the fabled Lincoln green and red. Everyone interrupted business as the dowser entered the square.

Denis waggled the stick in a half-circle before him. He gabbled, "Saint Hugh, protect your people! Saint Wolfgang, heal our sorrow!" Between his heels, the dog sniffed the ground and drooled, began to cock his missing leg against his master's ankle and then recanted, jigged sideways, sat down.

"They make a good pair," Robin hissed to Marian, "both being afflicted with Saint Vitus's Dance."

His wife puffed her red cheeks. "Hush."

Slowly, eerily, Denis waved the stick around. The rod stopped as if arrested by an invisible hand. "Thanks be to Saint Norbert, and Gregory the Seventh! Thy wills be done!"

They were off. On the far side of the marketplace were the mills, all kinds, grinding, sawing, and many fulling mills, for here the River Witham took a right angle in the middle of town. Across a stone bridge they clattered, four people watching the dowser and the dowser watching the stick before him. With the dog skipping under his feet, Denis stumbled off the bridge and down the embankment, to stop where the mucky bank dropped into the brown river. Rotten hulls and scraps of rope and trash dotted the mud.

"By Jonah. The dastards entered a boat."

"Boat?" echoed the sheriff. He banged his club on an overturned hull in frustration. "Then we've lost them."

"Not if," Denis panted, "we can get a boat too."

"You can't follow them across water, can you?" asked Robin. He still wasn't sure if he believed in Denis's dowsing ability or not. Things were happening too fast.

"By the eyes of Samson, I can follow anywhere if we get a boat."

The five of them looked down the river. Two men in a low skiff heaped with saplings were building a fish weir. Robin cupped his hands and hollered, "Fishermen! A crown for your trouble!" Digging in his purse inside his shirt, he held aloft a coin.

"What's a beggar like you," puffed the sheriff, "doing handing out crowns like they was groats? What'd you say your name was?"

"Robert." The outlaw looked him in the eye. "Of Barnesdale."

The sheriff's eyes narrowed. "You said Farnesfield before."

Robin blinked.

Marian put in, "I hail from Farnesfield, good sheriff. My family lives there. We're occupying their loft until we can buy a house. But I fear my scalawag husband is too free with our coins. Would he were a sensible man like yourself, wise in the ways of the world and blessed with an exceptional memory." Her smile warmed the space under the bridge.

The sheriff shook his head in exasperation.

The boatmen had drawn close enough to catch the coin. Five passengers and one dog clambered aboard and perched on the sweet-cut saplings. The boatmen pushed back their hoods and poled into midstream.

Denis aimed his stick along the west bank, for the east was too steep to land a boat. Beside him, the dog teetered on his one back leg and drooled overboard. The animal sniffed at the wind, bubbles in the water, glooping fish, flecks of drifting grass. As the trail grew colder, Denis hollered so his saints might better hear. "Saint Giles, be our friend! Saint Wenceslaus, the betrayed, guide us to the perpetrators of —"

Denis prattled on as the bank slid by. Robin realized he was hungry. He'd missed his porridge and beer. He heard Marian's stomach rumble and smiled at her. "Once this foolishness has run its course, we can —"

The dog barked, twice, sharp, interrupting his master's reverie. Denis shook his head, stood upright in the boat, almost tipping them all into the Witham. The stick quivered like a hunting dog's nose. "That way, by Saint Paul! The heathens await!"

The boatmen stroked, bumped the muddy shore. Denis leapt out and splashed them all. His dog dove like a seal, shed water from matted fur, scampered up the bank leaving three muddy footprints. Robin hopped out, wetting his boots, caught a giggling Marian by her waist, and landed her dryshod. Peter and Sheriff Martin slopped along behind.

Here the streets were narrower, the houses more tumbledown. Denis dilly-dallied like a drunkard, his muddy dog at his heels. Priests and fishwives and masons, shabby and ragged, turned to watch the parade. Around corners and down alleys they went, till they threaded a twisted shambles. The entourage had to weave around garbage, ash heaps, bones, and the emptying of chamber pots. Robin noted people here lurked in doorways and peeked from windows to satisfy their curiosity.

All along the dowser wailed his litany of saints until he was hoarse. Robin figured he'd run out of breath soon, and they could drop this nonsense. It was obvious the sheriff's temper was fraying. He'd raised his club for a halt when Denis stopped.

The house had once been large, with a solid stone lower floor, but a fire had gutted it and collapsed the roof. A rotten door leaned in a warped frame.

Denis puffed, rested a hand on his dog's wet head, waved to indicate they'd arrived. The sheriff hoisted his heavy club and rapped the crooked door. Nothing happened, though Robin thought he heard a rustle inside. He realized they might suddenly come face-to-face with vicious murderers, and loosened his staghorn knife in its sheath.

The sheriff raised a big shoe and kicked the door flat.

The interior stayed dark. The fallen door raised dust at the foot of — a pale maiden in a ragged gown. Barefoot, she crept closer to the light as if it pained her. Under her stringy hair, her face was lined and strained.

The sheriff barked. "Mary? Ach! Where's your good-for-nothing brother —"

A roar like a lion's drowned him out. Flashing from the dark came a larger dark. A huge form shaggy as a werewolf bowled the pale girl aside and leaped full in the sheriff's face. The official's club was slapped aside. Steel flashed and the sheriff dropped with a howl, stabbed and spraying blood. The monster raised his bloodied knife to stab overhand.

Robin stiff-armed Marian so hard she bounced in the road a dozen feet away. Lacking time to draw his own knife, Robin simply jumped at the attacker. The blooded steel scythed down at him, but he ducked under the blow. The monster's arm slammed on his shoulder hard enough to break the elbow. The knife clattered into the street.

Hampered by the stinking body, half-tripping over the prostrate sheriff, Robin could only ram a fist into the monster's belly. The mighty frame shook, but then a shoulder smashed his jaw. He slammed on his back, the monster atop him. Two mighty hands found his windpipe.

With a shock the outlaw realized this wasn't a monster. It was a man — dirty, hairy, with a wild beard and tangled dark hair, in clothes so filthy they looked black. But the biggest shock came with another roar, a windy gabble. Staring down the man's throat, Robin saw his tongue was gone, cut out, leaving a waggling stump. He kicked to get free, swung at the man's ears, in vain. His vision tinged with blackness...

A shadow above blacked out more light. The monster gasped, gargled blood that splashed on Robin's face. The outlaw pushed free of the collapsing form and struggled up, rubbing his throat.

The monster, the man, was dead, pierced through the heart by a silver-hilted dagger. Peter stood above him, pale as if he'd been strangled himself. His sheath was empty, his hands slack.

Marian bent over the dark man, looked to her husband, then tended the sheriff. His forearm had been skinned to the bone.

"I should have known it'd be Nicholas, our town wastrel," the official growled. Marian cut strips off his smock for bandages. "He's served enough time in the stocks and at the wheel for robbing and beating folks. It was a circuit judge ordered his tongue cut out when the swine cursed him to his face. I'll probably get blood poisoning. Christ."

He barked at the slim girl cowering in the doorway. "Mary, you damned slut. You're as guilty as him. You'll pay for this."

"Hush," Marian tied off a rude bandage and made the man wince. "The poor thing's scared witless. A beast like that would terrify Saint Columba. You know this girl and her travails, you're wise enough to see her sorrows, aren't you?"

She addressed the trembling girl. "Pray, fetch what your brother brought home and we'll depart. We shan't harm you. I give my word."

The girl disappeared, like a ghost in the sunlight, and reappeared lugging an iron strongbox. She set it on the threshold and prized open the lid. Inside was a handful of silver coins and several dozen copper. "I didn't know," the girl squeaked. "I didn't know what he'd done. I — I didn't — know." Marian laid a hand on her arm to shush her.

Leaning against the door frame, the sheriff groused, "That stinking changeling bastard butchered those old folks for this paltry sum? Damned little for two lives."

"Three," said Marian. "How's your throat, Rob?"

Robin massaged his Adam's apple and waved. Every swallow burned, but he could breathe better than the monster Nicholas. He moved to pick up the strongbox.

"I thought your name was Robert," the sheriff grunted.

The outlaw rasped. "I go by many names. Sometimes I get confused myself."

The sheriff sniffed. "You saved my life, too. I won't forget that."

Robin nodded. "And Peter saved mine." The boy didn't look up. He stood facing up the alleyway, eager to be off.

Through all this, Denis the Doswer had stood to one side, his fat frame like a haystack, his lopsided dog panting between his feet. To him, Robin said, "You've shown your skill, dowser. Your —" he gestured, "— stick led us true. No doubt you'll fetch a reward from the town elders."

Somber for the first time, the magician mumbled, "Would the saints could raise up the dead and erase this day. Then would we all be paid."

Marian caught Robin's eye, nodded towards his middle. Without letting the sheriff see, the outlaw tossed some silver pennies into the depths of the ruined house.

Limping, grumbling, cradling their wounds, the party and the dog tottered towards the river. They left the dead murderer where he lay, and his sister weeping over him.

Rather than hunt up a boat, they threaded the mucky streets and crossed the bridge, filtered through the marketplace. Robin caught his wife's elbow and spoke low. "There's much left unexplained. I can guess how he closed the door and barred it, but how did he open it?"

"He didn't, but it opened," Marian whispered. "I've figured that out. But how he closed it —"

"Well, I can — he didn't open it but it opened?"

"Hush. You'll see."

The house came in view, with the sheriff's son deputy and curious crowd before it. With them was

an exasperated priest eager to deliver a prayer for
the dead, but the boy obviously feared the wrath of
his father more than the wrath of God. The boy
looked relieved to see his father, then dismayed at
his bandaged arm and cross expression.

As they stopped before the house, Robin said.
"My curiosity may kill me yet, but I can vouchsafe
some answers. I know how the door was barred."

The sheriff raised his hand to rub his chin and
winced. "Get on with it, then. I needs get drunk
soon. This wound burns like the pit."

Robin shoved the door open. The bodies
remained undisturbed. Flies buzzed around their
dead faces. The outlaw plucked the bar from
behind the door and brought it out into the
sunlight. He pointed to yellowish smears dotted
down one side. "Beeswax. Someone kneaded lumps
of it, pressed them against the battens, stuck the
bar to them. When the door was banged shut, the
shock dropped the bar into the iron brackets. So the
murderer left the house locked behind him."

The sheriff frowned and thumped his club in
the street. "P'raps. May be. I don't think Nicholas
were clever enough to think on it, and I can't see
why he'd bother. And how'd he open the door in the
first place?"

"He didn't," Marian said. "I can explain that.
Rob, step inside and bar the door, please."

"The brackets are broken."

Marian smiled sweetly at her husband.
"Pretend to bar it, then. Dear."

Shrugging, Robin stepped into the charnel
house and closed the door. He was alone with
corpses and flies. Shuddering, he propped the bar
against the cracked door and called, "Right. It's
barred. Now what?"

Marian's voice came through the window. "Oh,
Rob. I forgot something. Come out again, please."

Mentally scratching his head, Robin took down
the bar and opened the door. "What is it now,
Marian?"

The sheriff scowled. "Not Matilda?"

The wife only smiled. "Notice I got the door

open. All I did was ask."

"But..." said most of the men. The sheriff grumbled, "Jabin wouldn't open the door for a stranger. And Nicholas couldn't talk anyway. He had no tongue."

"Exactly," said Marian. "Somebody else —"

"Catch him!" shouted Robin. He jumped but was too late.

Peter pelted down the street and careened around a corner.

"Them alleys are all twisty!" shouted the sheriff. "He can go a hundred different ways. Get after him, Berthold. Use your legs!"

Robin snagged the piebald sleeve of Denis the Dowser. "Come on, man. You needs track like you never tracked before."

Surprised by the sudden turn of events, gulping for air, Denis was tugged along, his dog treading under his feet. The sheriff's son tromped ahead of them.

Robin took the corner Peter had passed, stumbled up a short alley towing Denis like a barge, and came to a crossing. Peter would know these alleys, he realized, but he didn't have a clue. The trashy floor was impossible to read. The deputy Berthold took off down one alley, but Robin wouldn't risk running blind. "Denis. Find his trail."

Manfully, Denis hoisted his dowsing stick before him. "By Saint Germain, the hunter, find this felon —"

Robin slapped the dowsing stick out of his hands. "Balls to that, you fat fraud. Get moving!" And he half-flung Denis before him.

Denis sighed and then whistled. "Come, Turk, track him, boy!"

The dog barked twice and took off skittering down an alley as if shot from a catapult. Robin was hard put to keep up with him, crippled or not. They tore down a short alley and then around a corner, down another straight-away where the houses almost touched, and on. Robin let his legs stretch and ran full out. He splashed in puddles, slipped in garbage and manure, ducked jutting beams and drying laundry.

They rounded a corner. Ahead he glimpsed the fleeing Peter.

"Halloo, the fox!" The outlaw put on a burst of speed. Within five heartbeats he caught up to the winded boy, and five paces beyond that, crashed full into him. The two tumbled headlong down the filthy alley. Robin scrambled up first, shedding dirt and debris, and smashed both knees onto the lad's back. With a sob, Peter crumbled. The dog cocked his head, happy and confused.

As Robin jerked him upright, the boy began to cry. Robin only shoved him down the alley. He panted, "It's about time – you cried. I've no doubt – your parents – cried over you – many a time."

Back in the main street, the first thing he saw was Marian, her eyes shining.

It wasn't long before the sobbing boy was trussed and guarded. The deputy strapped the door bar across his shoulders and tied his hands to it – an appropriate punishment, Robin thought. He asked, "What will happen to him?"

The sheriff hiccuped. He'd been plying himself with brandy from the inn for his wound. "He'll needs tell us where he's hid the rest of Jabin's money, for one. What Nicholas had in the strongbox probably wasn't a tenth of the old man's wealth. Then... usually we hang murderers. But this one's killed his own parents like some cold-blooded viper. Probably he'll burn." The boy, pale and pained, gave a moan and fainted.

"But there are still some things I don't understand," the sheriff added. The others agreed, but together they figured it out.

The sheriff offered, "Peter must'a gotten tired of working for his skiving father, who wouldn't give a groat to the Pope. He lived in this hovel next to a strongbox bursting with silver. He must'a decided to collect his inheritance early and hired Nicholas to do the killin'. In the dead of night, he called his father to unbar the door. Nicholas hacked the parents to pieces."

23

Marian took over. "Peter went straight to the chimney and extracted the strongbox. Robin found grit on the floor. The thief had to know its hiding place, for the red chest was locked. A stranger would have breached it first. And I suspicioned Peter when he rushed into the room and closed his dead father's eyes. Everyone knows the image of the murderer lingers in the victim's eyes. Peter feared his own image would be etched there, rather than Nicholas's."

Robin added, "He chucked a leather bag full of brimstone on the fire to release the stench of witchcraft. Then he affixed the beeswax so the bar would fall when he closed the door. Thus only a supernal being could have exited. But the wax was stickier than he thought. When Peter returned in the morning, he found the door open – the wax still held the bar. So he banged the door to crack the wax and drop the bar. He woke the street with his pounding and shouting."

The sheriff commented, "He was quick to backstab Nicholas too, once he was cornered."

"But," Robin finished, "we never would have found him without the aid of Denis the Dowser. Sir Fraud of Lincoln."

The fat magician aped a pained expression. Without his dowsing stick to play with, he fiddled with his fingers. "Not so much a fraud. Half a fraud, perhaps. I did take you straight to Nicholas's door."

"You did no such thing," Robin retorted, but he smiled to draw the sting. He patted the dog on his scruffy head. "T'was your hound did all the work. Your foolish howling to the saints and dancing like a March hare was nothing but a blind to keep people watching you and not that animal. It's true, you've trained your dog to track a scent from behind you rather than in front, and you watch him between your feet, but still – what's the point of all that foolishness?"

Denis gave him a pitying look, then shook his head of wild hair. "I see you know nothing of magic, Sir Robin of Wherever You Hie From. A man

with a trained dog is just a clever man. Or a clever
dog. But a dowser – ah!"

Floating Bread and Quicksilver

"Rouse, rouse!" Pounding at the door shook the cottage. Moaning on the sea wind came the doleful cry. "A boat's come back empty! Rouse!"

Robin and Marian were off their pallets instantly – sleepy outlaws didn't live long – with bows in hand. Their host, the fisherman Peter, unbarred the door. Sea wind, cold and salty, swirled in their faces and made the fire in the hearth gutter.

"What's happening?" asked Sidony. A barrel-shaped woman with a face like a dried apple, she was bundled in wool with a scarf over her head. Five sleepy-eyed children clustered around. "Whose boat?"

"Gunther's! Both him and Yorg are missing!"

"Oh, my." The fishwife put a gnarled hand to her mouth. "And Lucy and Zerlina so young to be widows."

Robin Hood shrugged on his quiver, an instinct when trouble portended. He and Marian were dressed alike, in tattered wool of Lincoln green, laced deerhide jerkins, and soft hats sporting spring feathers. The outlaw chieftain and his wife stepped outside the tiny cottage.

With food lean in the Greenwood and a long winter over, they'd taken a holiday of sorts, walked from Sherwood east and then north, followed a Roman road through Lincoln, across the Humber, to the high cliffs at Scarborough, which Marian had never seen. They'd dawdled on the way back, followed the coast dotted with black wrecks, out to buy dried herring for Lent and "to smell the salt air".

They had salt air aplenty, for the wind never quit. It pulsed and blustered and boomed and tickled, never still. Sea and wind and clouds were half the world for tiny Wigby, sixteen cottages almost overwhelmed by wide Humber Bay, roiling with waves driven from the turbulent North Sea, called the German Sea hereabouts. Behind the village lay sandy dunes with grass atop, and a forest, The Wolds, like a fog bank in the distance. A long way to haul firewood, the outlaw thought.

Against a cloudy red-streaked sunrise, villagers clustered at the high tide mark, an undulating wave of seaweed. Men and women were almost identical in salt- and scale-streaked smocks, shabby wool hose, and pitchy half-boots. Hats were tied under chins to confound the wind. Amidst the fisherfolk slumped two new widows, teary but resigned, as if they'd expected this day. Children clung to their skirts and stared at an empty dory.

As the fishing family and their guests straggled down the shingle, Sidony muttered. "It's their own fault. 'If two relatives go out in a boat, one will drown.' And sneaking out in the middle of the night."

"Sneaking out?" Marian listened close, for the local accent was guttural and garbled. The last phrase resembled "sneegin' gout".

"Aye. Gettin' a jump on the herrin'. You're not supposed to go ahead of the rest, t'ain't fair. You wait, pass your boat through the rope circle, get the blessing of the deacon. It's custom goes back forever. And they sailed under a full moon, too."

The party squeezed in to examine the dory, floated in on the tide and hauled up from the surf, but there was little to see. The boat was a dozen feet long with a tombstone stern and flat bottom, broad-beamed and high-walled to ride blue water. Around the mast was a lateen sail of coarse yellowed linen. Nets were folded in heaps across the waist. A large rock in the bow served as anchor. The oars were missing while a worn boot had been left behind. Many villagers echoed Sidony's admonitions about tempting fate and taking advantage.

Robin Hood's keen eyes were busy. Peering, he handed Marian his bow and clambered over the gunwale, careful to tread on ribs and not the bottom planks. Still someone warned, "Not supposed to step in a boat ashore. S'bad luck." Robin rubbed his hand along the ribs, swirled his hand in the bilge slopping in the bottom. It might have been tinged red, but his calloused hand came away clean.

A toothless elder sighed and let go the gunwale, then did the others, as if letting go the lost fishermen. "Enough grievin'. Tide's makin'. Time to get the fish in." Instinctively people scanned the wind and waves and sky, turned to breakfast and ready their own boats lined along the strand.

Robin and Marian lingered, as did their hosts. The outlaw scanned the dory from stem to stern as if he'd buy it. He used his Irish knife to poke the outer hull, felt the sea moss and barnacles. Then he stood back stroking his beard. Marian knew that sign: his curiosity was piqued.

They walked with Peter's family back to the cottage for chowder and ale. Sidony muttered, "Knew it would happen some day. I'm just surprised it took this long."

"What?" asked Robin and Marian together.

The fisherfolk looked at them, still unsure of their status. These were the famous outlaws of Sherwood Forest, they knew, and supposedly lords. They'd descended on Wigby uninvited, seeking lodging and paying in silver. Their hosts were unsure how to address them, but fishermen were a hardheaded lot who feared only God and storms. Husband and wife let the silence drag to underline their independence. Robin added, "Please. We're strangers hereabouts. Why are you not surprised?"

Peter remained silent, let his wife talk for both. "Well... The good Lord knows we lose enough men to plain accidents. There's more ways to die on the swan's road. Strike a rock, or a whale, a rogue wave, a sea serpent. But if anyone went hunting grief it was Gunther and Yorg. They were brothers and forever fighting. They even fought over who owned that boat when both helped build it. So squabbling's been the death of them, I'd say."

The outlaw nodded absently. "'Most of our troubles we bring on ourselves.'"

The family stamped up the shingle. Marian lagged behind. "You're pensive, Rob. What's your guess?"

Robin turned and scanned the sea. "I'm a simple man given to simple explanations. There's no sign the boat struck anything: no planks stove in, no barnacles scraped off, the moss intact all over. The boat might've pitched them overside, but the nets are still folded neat. And there's that boot."

"Yes?.."

"I don't know... It's rare that ghosts or selkies or serpents pluck a man into the sea. Men bear enough evil we needn't blame the feys for murder."

"And?.."

"Perhaps nothing." Robin shrugged. "I don't wish to speak ill of the dead, especially newly dead. I don't need ghosts wafting over the waves for me."

Marian stared at the gray roiling sea. The breeze blew dark hair around her face and she combed it back. "Yes, let's curb our tongues."

After a subdued Mass and blessing of the fleet and passing each boat through a rope circle, Wigby went fishing. And Robin Hood went with them.

He worked with Peter, who'd lost his eldest son in a storm the year before. Next eldest, too young to be married, was a squint-eyed serious-faced girl of fourteen named Madge.

Robin rowed, for he liked the feel of the waves under the wooden blades, while Peter manned the tiller and sheets for the triangular sail. Madge watched from the bow. Other boats from Wigby had put out, a dozen of them, and farther off bobbed boats from other villages and towns: Aldbrough, Patrington, Hedon, Grimsby. Peter occasionally sheared by another boat, yelled a welcome or a friendly insult, asked for news, passed on gossip. Yet no one from Wigby mentioned that two brothers were drowned and missing, that two families had been wiped out.

After a time, Madge reported this spot might do. Robin glanced over the side and gasped.

The boat floated on a sea of silver backs.

Herring jammed the water nose to tail, tight-packed as if already in the barrel. Alike as leaves on a tree, all were a foot long, mouths open and eyes like jet targets.

With no sign of elation, Peter donned an oilskin apron and unfolded the nets with an easy grace. Robin helped, so clumsy he almost pitched overside. Madge took the tiller and steered a lazy circle. In minutes Robin felt the boat slow as the nets dragged. Peter grunted to Madge, snapped at Robin, then tilted inwards a tiny corner of a net.

A silvery cascade washed the bottom of the boat. Fish boiled and roiled and flopped and flapped, some so hard they flipped over the gunwale back to their haven. In two hours of backbreaking, fingernail-ripping, clothes-soaking labor, the tiny crew made four more passes, hauling in nets until the gunwales were awash and Robin Hood was knee-deep in fish.

"S'enough," said Peter. He and Robin sat near the bow to keep the nose down and prevent the stern from foundering, while Madge turned her cheek to the wind and aimed for home.

Yet the fisherman took no ease, but honed a knife on a sea stone, handed it to Robin with a few terse instructions. Robin Hood knew better how to dress deer than clean fish, but managed to behead and gut, yet keep the fillet intact along the spine for hanging, all without losing fingers.

Always curious, Robin looked to expand his knowledge. "How many trips will you make today,

Peter?"

Hands busy, the fisherman glanced instinctively at the sky. Gulls followed them, soaring and banking, crashing into the water after fish offal. "As many as God gives us. While the herring are here, we work, for they'll be gone soon enough."

"Oh? Why so?"

But the fisherman just shrugged and wouldn't answer.

Robin sought another topic. Examining the fish he cut, he found them not all the same. "Why are they different?" He tried to hide the chattering of his teeth. Though both were just as wet, the fishermen and his daughter gave no sign of being chilled. They ate slices of raw fish to keep their body heat up.

The man flipped a butterfly fillet into a wicker basket. "They ain't. They'll all herrin'." At the stern, Madge chuckled.

Robin held up a fish in either hand, solid writhing muscles coated with scales and slime. Both were the same length, but one was slim as a snake while the other was fat-bellied. "But they ain't the same. These are —"

Clearly galled by his free help, the fisherman stopped cleaning to point with his knife. "The skinny one's a pilchard. The fat one is an allice shad. The round ones is round herrin'. The snouty ones is anchovies. That's a mayfish, comes up the rivers in May. Here." He pinched a fish by its dorsal fin. "If 't hangs straight, it's a herrin'. If 't hangs tail down, it's a pilchard. Nose down is a sprat — little and spratty, see? Shads is different. But hell, man, if they come to shore in herrin' season, they're herrin'. Like women — they all taste the same in the dark."

Robin chuckled at his ignorance and flayed with slimy hands, one fish to every five of Peter's. He kept the man talking. "Why did you say the fish would be gone soon? I thought herring season lasted a full moon."

"Not now it won't. 'Herrin' dislike a quarrel',

they say. Now that blood's been spilt, they'll vanish." He nodded grimly over side where the wind ripped whitecaps and sent spume flying. "This be all we'll see this year. It's a hungry winter we'll 've."

Robin didn't disagree, but the gray waves shone with fish deep as he could see. He failed to understand how they could disappear overnight. Shaking his head, he grabbed another fish. It squirted through numb hands and kissed him in the mouth.

While her husband toiled at sea, Marian helped on the strand. Women and girls rolled out barrels of salt dried in salt pans during the winter, broached them and crushed the white clumps with wooden mallets. Girls returned from the woods with brush hooks and saplings to repair the yards-long drying racks. Then the first boats arrived, and women toted the fillets and fish in wicker baskets, set to with sharp knives at long plank tables.

They worked and sang and joked and gossiped of wedding plans. It was common for betrothed to marry after the herring season, when hands were idle and dirty weather kept folk home. "Weddings bring stormy weather," Marian was told a dozen times. Brides chattered about plans for improving homes and husbands while the matrons shook their heads. Marian noted some needed little advice, for their bellies were swollen from wintertime assignations.

Unmarried girls took time to dig fat from under the backbone of a proper herring, a glob of gooey silver, and hurl it against a hut wall. If it stuck upright, they were teased, their husband would be upright and true, but if the fat clung crooked, so would their husbands prove false.

The only ones quiet were Lucy and Zerlina, the new widows. They grieved but worked, for no one stood idle while the herring ran.

Yet one did. As Marian returned from the privy, she noted a dark figure silhouetted against the gray sky. The woman walked the bushy cliffs and lumpy headlands north of the village, where the tide smashed to spray on rocks.

Marian stood by Sidony, grabbed a fish and a knife, set to slicing. She nodded south. "Who's that? Why doesn't she help?"

Sidony answered without looking. "That'd be Mornat. She don't associate."

"Mornat?" said Marian. "What a queer name. What does it mean?"

"S'a queer woman. The priest named her after cutting her from her dead mother. It means 'living from the dead' or somewhat. A posthumous child. So she has the second sight, and can heal with her touch."

Marian touched up a blade, sliced off the hundredth staring head of the day. Her calloused hands were pruny and blue. "Why doesn't she associate?"

"She's queer, is all. We go to her when we need potions and such. The rest of the time she's off wandering the cliffs and sea caves, or walking to Hull for her nostrums. We don't keep track of her comings and goings. She doesn't like us. She's touched. And today she'll be worse than ever."

Marian made silence her question.

"Mornat set her cap for −" she wouldn't say the name, so Marian knew it must be one of the drowned brothers − "one who's left us for a better place. When she turned thirteen, she washed her shift in south-running water, turned it wrong-side out and hung it before the fire, as girls will, you know. They say the likeness of − him who's not with us − came into her hut and turned the shift right-side out. Mornat followed him everywhere then, and let him take liberties up on the cliffs in the grass, and told everyone they were to marry in spring. But it didn't happen, for he married Lucy over there and never spoke to Mornat again."

So, thought Marian, it was the elder brother, Gunther, that Mornat had fancied. "The poor thing. It must have torn her heart from her bosom."

"If she has a heart," Sidony sniped. "Them touched with the sight don't live entirely in this world. And good enough, I say."

More boats plowed the surf and disgorged heaping baskets of fish. Men and boys took warmed watered cider and bread and chowder, then returned to the waves. Robin, his beard flecked with scales, gave Marian a quick kiss before driving his oars through the surf once more.

All day they worked. Drying racks, called flakes were hung with fillets that danced and dripped in the sea wind. More were packed in salt. When the group flagged, one woman began a song so old it was another tongue and no one knew the words, yet every woman sang along, timing the beat to the rhythm of their hands. As the sun set, old men built driftwood fires. Girls threaded fillets onto whittled sticks and propped the dripping bundles on the drying racks higher than a dog could jump. Boys lugged baskets of guts to wash out on the evening tide as gulls squawked at their feet.

When it was too dark to fish even by torch light, the men beached the boats, helped clean and thread before snatching a few hours' sleep and setting out at dawn to fetch more fish.

Robin and Marian worked together, cutting themselves often now, salt stinging the gashes. At one point in the long night, Marian asked her husband, "Well, Rob? Are you ready to eschew outlawry and take up fishing?"

Robin sliced, cursed as he shaved fine bones. "Nay, never. Not in this life or any other. You'd have to be daft to go fishing, cracked as a coal miner. It's safer riding into battle against Saracens than going head-to-head with the North Sea in a cockleshell. It's no wonder these lot are so superstitious, putting their lives in the hands of God with every scull."

Marian agreed. "I never saw such a lot for queer beliefs."

"I thought we were bad in Sherwood, what with

crossing streams with the right foot foremost and
never venturing into caves without making the
sign of the cross and making sure the light of a
full moon never falls on your face: sensible
things. But these fisherfolk. Not once today did
anyone mention two brothers had drowned for fear
of provoking their ghosts. And I was told more how
not to fish than to fish. Never point at a boat with
your finger, use your whole hand. Never call the
salmon by its name, call it the 'red fish' instead.
Never mention rats or mice while baiting hooks or
laying the nets. By Saint Dunstan, what's rats and
mice got to do with baiting?"

Marian only shook her head. Oddly, her
thoughts flickered to the ostracized Mornat, alone
and wind-blown as she walked the cliffs, like some
widow that had never known a husband.

As the eternal night dragged and breath
frosted, both outlaws grew sick of the bloody-salty-
seaweedy smell of flayed fish. The villagers were
exhausted yet worked with a will, glad the time of
plenty had finally arrived after the long dark
winter.

Three days they toiled thus, a blur of dying fish
and chilled blood and raw chapped bleeding hands,
snatching sleep and food. By late in the third day,
no one sang or laughed. Work was a soul-numbing
chore, and only future survival kept everyone
hauling in nets and flaying fish.

As the sun peeked over the horizon on the
fourth day, the women braced at their plank
tables, knives sharp and ready, not talking. Only
the sough of the constant wind and crackle of fires
was heard.

It got quieter when the boats did not return for
hour after hour. Women left tables to warm at the
fires, or found other chores neglected over the past
frenzied days.

Finally three boats came in, riding high, the
fishermen's faces long, and the women guessed.
The men splashed overside and beached the boats.
They lifted out two or three baskets of odd fish and
a few herring.

An old man ran his tongue over toothless gums, husked, "They're gone, ain't they? It's happened. The curse. Blood's been spilt and the herrin 've vanished."

More boats beached. With empty hearts and idle hands, villagers stumbled for their cottages to sleep. There was no more work, no more herring to flay and dry, nothing extra to trade.

Come the depths of winter, they'd go hungry.

"It's the witch's done it. Witches are the bane of us. Do more harm than good."

Morning, Peter's family sat around a guttering fire in the tiny cottage. They ate meager rations of chowder, already rationing, and stared at the driftwood fire, winking blue and green from burning salt.

"Look out on Lewis there," said Sidony. "One time, starvin' times, a woman was 'bout to hurl herself into the sea. But a magic cow appeared, white she was, a beauty. Told her to fetch her milking pail. Everyone in Callinish could milk her every night long's they took but one pail. Then an old witch tried to milk her into a sieve. She roared once like a lion and disappeared. No more milk after that. And they say she become the Dun Cow of Dunchurch, tearing up the countryside until Guy of Warwick killed 'er. And you know 'hat's true, because one of her ribs is in a chapel dedicated to Guy in Warwickshire.

"Nothing's good for a witch but to hang her familiar, then cut crosses in her body to let the bad blood out. There was one village — I ain't saying which one, but it's near here — had its crops blighted. A witch bred big toads and hitched 'em to little plows, sent 'em across the fields and poisoned the soil. They had to move away and never came back.

"T'was probably Mornat done in — them that's missin'."

Marian disliked arguing with a host, but could

not let this last comment pass. "How could one small woman harm two brawny seamen? I've seen the muscles on your menfolk. Any one could wrestle Little John Cumberland-style and take one bout out of three. And how could she get into their boat? You'll blame the poor woman for shooting stars next."

Sidony only looked at the fire. "There's ways o' working evil. There's ways."

Robin Hood rubbed his bow with a hunk of lard where the wind had streaked it with salt. "Is there some way to lift the blood curse? That would bring the herring back?"

Sidony and Marian both frowned in thought. Finally the fishwife said, "Might be possible. I've heard tell if you could raise the bodies and give 'em a Christian burial, lay their –" she skipped the word "ghosts" – "the herring might come back. But it's been three days now and they haven't come ashore."

Everyone knew what she meant. Lungs full of water, a drowned body sank at first. But after three days, gasses from corruption bloated the body and raised it. Yet neither brother had floated ashore, though the wind stayed in the northeast.

Marian pondered. "Perhaps we could float a loaf. But would anyone have quicksilver?"

The fishwife stared at the fire. "Aye, we might. T'would comfort the widows, too... Mornat would have quicksilver. She uses it in potions."

Without further ado, Sidony left the cottage, Marian following. They stopped at a house where Sidony borrowed a fresh loaf of dark rye bread. The goodwife guessed its intention, but said nothing. So little needed be said in this village, Marian noted, as if everyone's mind lay open.

Sidony plodded towards the farthest cottage, removed from the rest, and Marian nodded again. A wise woman, a witch, was shunned but tolerated because she was needed.

The young woman who answered the knock seemed in need of healing herself. Thin as the rail birds that piped along the shore, Mornat was tall with skin boiled red — far more red than chapped cheeks. Her mouth pouted, lips puffed out, and her breath stank like a cesspit. Taciturn and curt, Mornat declined to look in Marian's eyes. "Yes? What is it?" Her voice quavered, and she wiped away drool with a shaky hand. She salivated like a hungry dog, and Marian wondered why.

"Good Maid Mornat," Marian suppressed distaste at the sinister name, "we wondered if you might spare some quicksilver. I can pay in true silver."

Mornat's answer was a short nod to enter. She walked, Marian noted, gracelessly, straight up and down like a man.

The windowless cottage was tiny, and lacking a man's hand, drafty. The fire guttered and backblew, a sign the chimney was stacked wrong or clogged with soot. There was a table and single stool, a messy bed, jars and crocks for nostrums, and little else. Fresh seaweed lay on the hearth, a charm against house fires.

Mornat also did not question their begging quicksilver. She reached under the table and drew out a hollowed stump packed with chunky white clay. Calomel, Marian knew, fetched from Hamburg. She recalled Mornat often walked to Kingston Upon Hull down the coast. There'd be ships from the Continent there.

Mornat broke the white clay into an iron spider with a spoon, propped it in the fire to roast it. As she waited for the quicksilver to ooze from the clay, Mornat wafted her hand through the sweetish fumes and inhaled deeply. To Marian's curious glance, she supplied, "The breath of quicksilver is good for the lungs." Yet she coughed.

Marian nodded, but other thoughts flickered through her head. One Merry Man, Gilbert of the White Hand, had been a prisoner in the Holy Land and learned medicine from the Saracens. Greeks and Persians believed quicksilver touched by the god Mercury: an alchemist fathoming its secret might gain immortality. Yet Marian had doubts, for Mornat looked sick, for all she was strong and intelligent and composed. Pity welled in her breast, but she suspected any kindness would only be rebuffed.

Eventually, the witch lifted the pan away. Amidst the burned clay skittered globs of quicksilver. This fractious metal, Marian knew, over time hardened into true silver, also found in Germany.

With her Irish knife, Marian slit the top of the bread. Tipping the pan, Mornat dribbled in the quicksilver. Marian mashed the crust to seal in the metal.

Giving Mornat silver pennies, Marian said, "Our thanks. If this aids in locating the missing men —"

"T'will mean naught to me," Mornat interrupted. She stared from deep-sunk pouchy blue eyes. "Good day."

Peter and Robin dragged the dory to the surf as a crowd watched. A stout man named Vamond brought a proper anchor, the only one in the village, a four-pronged iron hook. Marian handed her husband the metal-laden loaf.

"Where shall we float it?"

Peter said, "I know."

Men helped launch the boat. Robin rowed, Vamond steered, and Peter in the bow shielded the precious loaf from spray.

Peter directed them north by east, marking a low-breasted hill. A quarter mile from the rocky shore, where the boom of surf was loud, he called, "Gunther and Yorg often fished off Turk's Head here. Thought it was lucky."

So saying, he leaned over the bow and laid the loaf on the waves. Robin shipped his oars, and all three men stood, sway-hipped, to see what the bread would do.

At first it only bobbed up and down. Peter ordered Robin to back water to reduce drag. Again they watched.

Vamond gasped. Robin felt hairs prickle along his arms.

As if towed by an underwater string, the bread moved towards shore. It bobbed up one side of a wave, crested, slid down, clearly moving towards land.

Not daring to speak, Peter signaled. Blades feathering the water, Robin rowed after the bread.

Row, pause, row, pause, row. They followed the waterlogged loaf for a furlong, close enough to shore to feel the boat tremble as green-gray waves exploded against seaweedy rocks. Robin noted dimples and cracks in the cliffs, the waves tortured them so. From the heights, gulls launched themselves at the boat, anticipating trash. Spooked already, Robin shuddered. The birds' cries were so mournful, like lost souls; the voices of the drowned, seafarers claimed...

"It's sinking!" Vamond yelped.

"It's sunk!" bawled Peter over the boom of surf. "Row up to it. Get the grapnel."

Robin fought to keep the dory on the invisible sunken mark as the fishermen tangled rope and anchor in their excitement. Staring holes in the water, Peter finally lowered the grapnel straight down, Vamond feeding out. When the line bobbed slack, he'd hit bottom. Carefully, Peter swirled the rope, snapped it to make the anchor hop. Muttering, he told of thumping rocks, empty shells, a sand bar, more rocks. Still dredging, he ordered Robin to scull closer to shore.

Finally the anchor snagged and both fishermen groaned, for the drag on the rope told what it was. Robin steadied the oars and his stomach.

The men needn't pull hard, for corruption had done its work. With a bubble and hiss and belch, a missing fisherman bobbed to the surface for the last time.

It took three to haul the cold clammy corpse aboard. Each man prayed aloud.

"Saint Peter protect us," breathed Peter. "It's Yorg. He had blonde hair. Gunther was dark."

The hair was handy, for there was little else to identify the man. The body was naked, rough seas having stripped its clothes, and bloated twice normal size. Fish and crabs had chewed round its features.

Still, Robin Hood forced himself to squat and look. He'd seen worse, he affirmed, though not while pitching in a boat that reeked of dead fish and dead men. Grimly, he examined the remains as the fishermen set sail to veer from shore.

"You shouldn't defile the body," warned Peter.

"God values probity above propriety," Robin answered vaguely. Rolling Yorg over, he found the scalp cut cleanly, a flap of skin eaten away. The skull underneath was dented. The outlaw grunted. He'd seen enough open wounds to know living bone scratched easily.

"I don't understand," Vamond muttered. "How does the bread know where a body's sunk?"

"The quicksilver steers to the blood," Peter offered, "like an iron needle floated on water points north."

"More likely," suggested Robin as he poked, "the loaf is small enough to follow the strongest current. Weighted down, it floats like a body and stops in slack water, then just sinks on its own... Unless I'm daft, this man was struck from behind... But with what?"

Immediately he knew, for the answer dug in his back: the shipped oars. He recalled both oars missing from Gunther's dory. And the bilge had been tinged red.

Peter shook his head as he took the tiller. "No surprise. They fought their lives long as only brothers can. And Gunther had a temper. So for him to cosh Yorg with an oar in a blind rage..."

Robin Hood cast about the gray roiling waves. "Where's Gunther then?"

"Where indeed?" asked Marian.

Robin shrugged. He walked the strand with Marian, glad to be off the water now he'd seen what it could do. Far behind, the village held a Mass for Yorg. The outlaws left them to it: rather than weep and pray, they wanted to talk and think.

"Perhaps," mused Robin, "Gunther did fly into a rage, killed his brother, then threw himself after? Men with tempers are often mad turn and turn about."

Marian touched her little finger to her mouth. "Could someone else have killed both?"

"Who?" asked Robin. "I couldn't kill two fishermen with a sword, they're so tough and strong..."

"He was struck from behind. A child could do that."

"... Yorg was ready to come up: one tug freed him. Gunther should have washed up by now."

"Unless he went out to sea."

"Not with this wind. It'd peel the bark off a tree." Robin had tied his hat cord under his chin. "Wait... What if Gunther's not a body?"

"Eh?"

Robin froze in his tracks. "If we don't have his body, when by all rights we should, maybe he's not – Jesus, Mary, and Joseph! The gulls!"

Marian glanced overhead, saw only tiny black-tipped terns. "What gulls?"

"Come on!" Robin snatched her hand and dragged her stumbling down the strand.

"Are you sure you're not just showing off?" Marian asked.

Robin took Peter's dory without asking permission. He and Marian manhandled it to the surf, then Robin grabbed his wife by the waist and heaved her aboard, pushed off, hopped belly-down over the gunwale. Rowing would take too long, he claimed, so he raised the sail and set the sheets as best he could. The sail luffed, flapping, but they steered in the right direction, the sharp prow slicing the waves, the bluff beam riding comfortably up and down.

"Will you please tell me what we're hunting?"

Robin told her. Afterwards, she was silent, straining to hear over the wind.

Off Turk's Head, the boat pitched as waves steepened near the rocks. Robin dumped the sail in a heap and grabbed the oars. He rowed closer to shore than last time. Marian watched waves boom and spume explode. "Rob, are you sure —"

"Hush and listen." He ceased the creaking of oars. They bobbed, the rocks coming closer, the booming louder, listening until their ears rang.

Impatient, Robin shipped oars, braced his back against the mast, cupped his hands and bellowed. "Hellooooooo!"

Listening. Slap of water under the prow. A warbling keen of disturbed gulls. The smash of surf.

Then, very faint. *"Helllllll..."*

"An echo," bleated Marian.

"No. Hush. Hello!"

Fainter. *"Helllllllpppp!"*

Robin scanned the cliffside, head wagging. "Whence came it, Marian?"

The Vixen of Sherwood marked the rocks. A shoulder of cliff jutted like an upright ax blade. "I think there."

"Methinks also. Hang on."

"Rob!" Marian scrooched her bottom in the tiny seat at the prow, clung to the gunwales with white knuckles. "What are you doing?"

"Hang on!" Craning his head around, hauling with mighty sinews, Robin rowed for a gap in the rocks no wider than the dory's ribs.

"Robbbbbb-iiiiinnnnn!"

A steepening wave curled around their stern like a giant hand and hurled them towards shore. Kept arrow-straight by the outlaw's rowing, the dory lifted high, hung just under the breaking crest of the huge wave and —

Marian screamed and covered her eyes.

— crashed down into the gap and stuck fast.

Waves clawed and sucked at the boat's strakes, but couldn't dislodge it, so gushed over the gunwales instead. Marian yelped, but her husband hoicked her from her perch, hugged her around the waist, and jumped.

They plunged breast-high. The swirling salty chill made them gasp. Robin Hood fought for footing on shifting pebbles and slime. Straining against the undertow, he broke clear, trotted onto the narrow shingle, plunked his wife down with a grin.

Wet to her bosom, Marian could only gasp and nod at his brilliance. Robin jerked a shaking thumb towards the craggy cliff. "Wh-wh-wh-which?"

Marian couldn't talk, couldn't even point, so she led the way. The bright spring wind cut like the whips of Satan's imps.

Shuffling across rocks polished smooth by the pounding tide, they clung to the cliffside and crept towards the promontory like an upthrust knife blade. At half-tide, the surf swirled around their knees, sucked at their feet, tried to trip them again and again. Timing slack water, Marian, then Robin, zipped around the corner.

There, washed by waves, was a cave mouth not waist high. Marian, in front, saw daylight wink on swirling water inside. Watching the waves, with Robin bracing her waist, Marian scooched inside the cave. After the next wave burst around his legs, Robin slid after.

Inside was a chamber big as a cottage. Daylight spilled through a grass-edged hole at the top of the cave. A dirt slide angled down to a natural rock ledge just above their heads.

On the ledge lay a fisherman.

His face was pinched with hunger and cold, his clothes sopping. A huge scab marked the back of his head, and his right leg jutted at an odd angle.

But he was alive, staring with haunted eyes.

"Gunther," said Robin, "we've come to take you home."

The fisherman began to cry.

Robin offered Marian ten fingers up to the ledge. "You know more of healing than I. Tend him. I'll see if the boat's lifted loose on the tide. We'll need it to get him home, otherwise I'll have to carry him the long way 'round."

Marian took the boot up, knelt beside Gunther. The fishermen had expended the last of his strength shouting for help. As he swooned, Marian checked for damage, tried to figure how to splint his leg for transporting.

Robin Hood crouched at the cave mouth, timed the incoming waves – higher now – crabbed through the hole, quickly grabbed the cliff and inched back. He found the boat stuck fast, half-swamped. Foam churned along the port strakes: he'd stove them beaching. He wasn't sure he could have rowed the dory out against the tide anyway. Better he walked the bluffs with the wounded man on his back while Marian ran ahead for help.

Rising tide crashed about him. Fighting for footing, Robin would have been sucked away by the undertow if not for steely fingers on the cliff face. The cave mouth was almost drowned, and he had to hold his breath and half-submerge to claw inside. Icy water almost stopped his heart.

Inside, gasping, blinded by sea water, he looked up at his wife and the fisherman. Gunther had blacked out, and Marian tussled to bind his legs together with rags.

Above them stood a third figure.

Dark-clad, wind-whipped, the woman loomed over the unsuspecting Marian, a knife held high.

"Marian!"

The Vixen of Sherwood looked down, saw her husband's expression, glanced behind –

– and jerked aside as the knife slashed down at her back.

Marian shrieked as Mornat's cold blade sheared her deerhide jerkin and wool shirt and kissed her ribs. The madwoman hurled the knife high again.

Robin had no bow to shoot, no rock to pitch, so he threw his big Irish knife.

His famous aim held true. The weapon cartwheeled, spanked flat against Mornat's breast, hard enough to rock her.

Marian reared half-erect on the narrow ledge. Unable to turn, she slammed her elbow into the woman's brisket.

Arms flailing, the murderess toppled from the ledge backwards.

Marian and Mornat screamed together, until the madwoman's head struck the rock wall.

"She slid down that chimney hole, got behind me. I didn't hear her for surf noise." Marian hissed as Robin wrapped a crude bandage around her naked ribs.

"She must have seen us from shore. She was always walking the bluffs."

"Aye, alone," said Marian. "Gunther told me a little. Mornat was always pestering him. That night, while readying their boat for the herring, she startled them in the dark. Furious, they told her to bugger off. She struck both from behind with an oar. She killed Yorg and stunned Gunther, beat him and broke his leg, then tumbled them in the boat and pushed out. Yorg she tipped overboard. Gunther she hid in this sea cave. She fed him potions to make him love her."

"The strength of the mad," Robin muttered.

It took a while, but Robin eventually boosted Marian through the chimney hole, then Gunther. Marian helped hoist, gasping with pain from her burning ribs.

Dead Mornat they left to the sea.

Grunting, Robin shifted the fisherman across his brawny shoulders. From the top of Turk's Head they saw distant Wigby like a colony of hermit crabs. They started walking through the bent yellow grass.

"T'was some poison she mucked with, is my guess. It drove her mad," Robin huffed. When his wife didn't answer, he glanced over. "Marian, you're crying."

"Yes, I'm crying," Marian snapped. "You men. Quick to blame the moon and stars for your own faults. It wasn't quicksilver killed that poor woman. She was cursed before she was born. Cut from her dead mother, christened with that horrid name — 'The living from the dead!' — so she's reminded of it every time someone speaks to her. And none would, for she was ostracized like a leper. Begged to heal all and sundry, then shunned for fear of ghosts or contamination or plain spite. Growing up without a mother, never learning a girl's graces and arts. Never to marry, never to know love. Suffering in silence while the girls chatter of wedding plans, knowing she'd never be a bride. It wasn't anything earthly killed that girl, it was lack of love!"

She sobbed now, chilled and wounded. Robin shifted his burden to catch her hand. "Don't cry, Marian. I hate to see you cry."

"Don't touch me. I need to cry. No one ever cried for that poor lonely love-starved creature, so it's time someone did, if only a stranger."

Robin clucked his tongue, saved his breath for walking. Together they trudged along the bluff.

The sea wind pushed them along.

Grinding the Ghost

"Unclean! 'Ware! 'Ware the leper!"

Robin and Marian needed no more warning. They backed down the narrow road to a trough where an ash had toppled, slid under it amidst brush. Robin drew a cross in the dirt with his right toe. "Hie then. Get yourself by and gone."

Husband and wife watched the pathetic figure straggle past. Clad in a hooded robe gray with filth, the leper hobbled on crippled feet. A tin bell atop his tall staff clanked mournfully. "Unclean! Unclean! 'Ware the leper!"

Shuffle, shuffle, the unseen feet plodded through new-fallen leaves of oak and ash and beech and elm. Robin and Marian waited until the pariah was out of sight, then took to the road again.

"There but for the grace of God," Robin breathed. "They should be cast away from decent folk altogether."

Marian tisked. "I don't abide the notion sick people have sinned, you know. It doesn't take the wrath of God to unbalance your humors."

"Only God could curse you with leprosy." Robin swung his bow as they walked. He kept an arrow crooked alongside in case they flushed game. "It's the worst fate there is. You're neither alive nor dead, wandering like a ghost yet shackled with worldly woes."

"I know that." Marian was dressed like her husband, in a tattered shirt and trousers of green — they had yet to switch to winter brown — with a

laced deerskin tunic and tall greased boots. A soft
hat with a jaunty pheasant feather spilled over
her dark hair. Both carried bows and quivers, a
knife, a satchel of provisions. "I've seen many at
the leprosarium in the caves under Nottingham
Castle. For their suffering, they should be pitied."

"I'll pity 'em. From a bowshot away."

They saved their breath for walking, and soon
breasted a rise that revealed their destination.
Long Valley Screed was a fertile pocket torn from
the tree-covered hills, almost bluffs, so sheer
shelves of yellow sandstone were exposed. Only the
east side lay open. Perched on a knoll to the north
was a small hall, more hunting lodge than manor
house, the Duke of Lancaster's. Elsewhere, cottages
and byres lay higgledy-piggledy amidst fields of
barley, rye, and wheat that shone red-gold in the
late afternoon sun.

Robin instinctively nocked his arrow.
"Something's amiss."

"Aye." With no threat of rain, everyone from
priest to crofter should have been harvesting.
Instead the rabbits and crows had the fields to
themselves.

Robin Hood pointed across the valley where a
bright stream spilled from a cleft in the hillside.
"There. At the mill."

"Woe betide the miller."

Woe indeed. The whole village of two hundred
had gathered outside the gristmill.

Marian stopped to watch the women. One –
pretty, Saxon blonde, and slim – wore a gown of red
sarcenet and taffeta that marked her from her
drab neighbors like an oriole over ouzels, though
she was dusty as any from winnowing. She wept
uncontrollably.

The men clustered at the door, peeking in. They
hushed and stared at Robin. Two greeted the tall
archer by name, though he didn't know theirs.
"Hail and met well. What transpires within?"

"Our miller's dead," said a man with salty
beard and a cast in one eye. "Fell through the
floorboards into his own works."

"It's a shilling what killed him," said another elder.

"A shilling?" asked the outlaw. "How's that?"

"Old Hosea'd pinch a farthing till it squealed. Our carpenter, Geoffrey, told him a mote a' times the floor was rotten from damp. Offered to replace his floorboards at a shilling apiece. Hosea saved himself some coin, then paid in blood." Other men muttered about Hosea's parsimony.

"Speak not ill of the dead, lest they long for company," Robin advised. "Now excuse me." He pushed past.

The gristmill was small. Centermost were two round millstones supported by posts above and below, and a hopper to feed them. Round about were a workbench of tools, a corner fireplace, a stair up and down, sacks and baskets of grain heaped high. A loft ringed the room, one side the miller's quarters, the remaining space stacked with sacks of flour. Out two small windows, shutters wide, Robin saw the great mossy mill wheel had stopped.

By the twin millstones was a squarish hole in the floor. Robin peeked through and found why the mill was silent.

Up in the loft, three dusty men moved sacks of flour to thump the walls. Two wore tabards of coarse linen, the third a knight's surcoat of lawn, all red with King Richard's three lions barred by French fleur-de-lis. Two servants, then, of the Duke of Lancaster, and the steward knight who maintained the fief in the lord's absence. They'd undoubtedly come to collect the heriot and mortuary, the death taxes.

The steward rubbed his nose, sneezed, clapped hands over his ears to keep out evil spirits. He was square-cut, clean-shaven, stern-faced. "Begone, villein. No one's to enter, by order of the duke."

"No villein I, but a free man," Robin called up. "I see your miller's dead."

Accustomed to obedience, the knight turned imperious. "Free man or no, hie your arse out yon door or I'll spank it along. We've business to attend. Who the hell are you, anyway?"

"Martin of Lincoln. Your delving has yet to turn up any silver, I'd guess."

The steward leant on the railing, brushed his breast. "You wear the green of Lincoln, I see, but then so does the devil and Robin Hood. And only that wolfshead and Welshmen carry bows taller than their heads."

"Take me for a bowyer then," Robin smiled, "late of Wales and fetching this oddity along. In my travels, I've seen something of coin and hiding spots. May I help ferret out your lord's tithe? If he lacks his share, so do you."

The steward sneezed again. He studied the outlaw, and the woman who came in after him. "Very well. If you find it, you'll receive a sixteenth. If not, I'll scourge you for intruding. Strikes you fair?"

"Let us conjoin and see what we strike. I'll begin below."

"Below? But —"

"Wait here, will you, uh, Matilda?" Marian would see the knight did nothing untoward, like rouse his followers to capture a wanted outlaw.

Robin descended the stairwell. The cellar was dank, the walls slimy stone. Slivers of light from cracks between the floorboards added to the dungeon air. Millpond water trickled through the foundation and made a gutter of mud. Stripes of flour matched the cracks overhead.

A torch of folded beech bark was stuck in the mud. Robin Hood picked it up, fanned it brighter. He flinched as something flittered overhead like an errant autumn leaf, then skittered up the stairway. A bat in the daytime: a sure sign of death.

By the light of the new-broken hole in the floorboards and the torch, Robin traced the millworks and the miller's unfortunate path.

Outside, Robin had seen, was a spring-fed millpond shored by a stone-and-mud dike. Alongside the building, nestled in a pit, was a mill wheel ten feet high. A wooden sluice channeled water that overshot the wheel and filled its deep buckets, so both the force and weight of the water turned the wheel. The mill shaft passed through the stone wall and ended in an oaken crown wheel with cogged teeth like a whale's jaw. This vertical wheel, or gear, turned a matching horizontal gear. Its post rose through the ceiling and turned a grooved millstone of granite. Atop that sat a stationary stone surmounted by a hopper.

The miller had only to lean out the window and open the sluice gate to start all these shafts and wheels spinning, and thus the millstones grinding. He filled the hopper with grain, where it settled between the millstones and was sheared to flour that trickled out the grooves onto a catchboard. The miller-mechanic swept the flour into sacks. For his services, he got a sixteenth of the flour, while the owner, the lord of the manor, got two sixteenths. Thus millers tended to be the second-richest men in the community.

This miller had valued his money over his mill.

Hosea of Long Valley Screed had been bald and near-toothless, with the paunch of a rich man. His weight had been his undoing, it seemed. A rotten floorboard had shattered and dropped him into the cellar. Half-impaled on the horizontal gear, one fat knee had jammed where the gears clashed. Under the terrible power of the mill wheel, wooden teeth had rent skin and flesh, then snapped.

Trapped, Hosea had bled to death. In agony, to judge by the lines etched in his face. He lay propped against the descending post, arms outspread. Blood had spattered gears and posts and miller. Its coppery stink compounded the fug of mud and moss.

Spooked, the outlaw wondered that the torch stayed lit: it should extinguish near a corpse. Robin crossed himself and muttered the Lord's Prayer to quiet the miller's soul.

"Rob?"

"H-here, Marian."

His wife tripped down the stairs, ducking to

admit her back quiver. "They hunt hard money.
They're not after us." Ofttimes, sheriffs or barons
or forest rangers imposed bounties on Robin's
outlaws, usually two pounds, same as for a wolf's
head. The church always rescinded the bounty, yet
rumors persisted and inflated it to ten pounds,
fifty, five hundred.

Marian assessed the scene. "The price of sloth,
poor man."

"Aye. He neglected his mill and it killed him."

"And in dying, killed the mill." Marian
wrinkled her nose, sniffed at the man's face.
"Drunk, too. That helped. Though he smells..."

"Like a brewery?"

"No. Like a vinyard. Where would a miller get
wine this time of year?"

Robin nodded upwards. "I dislike that
floorboard."

"Eh?"

He raised the torch to examine the splintery
ends of the plank framing the hole. Snapped off
clean against the joists, the boards were punky
gray along the bottom from rot, but the middles
were pale yellow. The outlaw pulled his Irish knife
and tapped. "That heart is sound as Little John's
arm. It shouldn't have broken."

"He had a heavy tread."

"No. I could rear a warhorse atop oak this
thick." Handing Marian the torch, he picked up
fragments of floorboard, moved under the square
hole for light, and fitted them together like a
puzzle.

"A small horse, perhaps," offered Marian.
"Maybe he shouldered a hundredweight of grain
while standing in the wrong spot?"

More head-shaking. The outlaw plucked
something feathery from a splintered edge.
"Fibers. A rope was wrapped around this board.
But that couldn't break even if someone yanked
hard."

"Someone down here?"

"Where else?" Robin took the torch, prowled the
cellar floor. Grit clung to his deerhide boots. The

gutter of mud and blood marred the middle, but the rest of the floor was sand stained dark by oak-leaf tannin, striped light by flour. Half-hunched, Robin searched, then grunted. Marian joined him.

Twin footprints faced a corner. Robin dabbed at a white jot in one heel print. "Bat dung. Fresh, just this morning. And the edges of the footprints are still sharp."

Marian peered around her husband's shoulder. "Why face the corner?"

"There's a woman's question," Robin jibed. He leaned over the footprints and sniffed in the corner like a hound. "He drained his bladder."

"Oh." Marian rubbed her nose. "So someone was down here."

"Someone with narrow feet and good shoes."

The outlaw crossed to the corpse. One leg was folded under the body, so Robin whispered another prayer as he wiggled the worn shoe off the leg mangled in the gears. It jiggled sickeningly. "His ankle's broken."

"A lot of him's broken, poor man."

With Marian holding the torch, Robin compared the miller's shoe against the footprints. Almost twice as wide. Marian murmured, "Fat men's feet spread to bear their weight."

As Robin replaced the shoe, the hole was eclipsed by a frowning head. The steward called down, "If you seek to rob the dead, I've already searched him."

Marian countered, "Where is your priest?"

The frown deepened. "Father Peter's so old he's abed most of the day. They'll fetch the corpse to him. I said a prayer of contrition, but Hosea had too many sins for one Hail Mary to absolve."

Floorboards creaked, shoes scuffled. Four villagers clattered down the narrow stairs toting a wide plank. It was grim work to pry Hosea's body from the gears. They roped the corpse to carry it up sideways. Robin and Marian followed, blinking in the daylight.

Still within the mill, a wise woman loosened the knots in Hosea's clothing, sprinkled salt on his

chest, and saw he was lugged out the door feet-
first, precautions to keep his spirit within his
body. Outside, women wailed in sympathy for the
new widow. Villagers pressed forward to touch the
corpse's brow, encouraging their children to
prevent nightmares. The woman in the silk robe
swooned, and had to be supported by both elbows.

The Vixen of Sherwood, nodding to herself, then
shoved through the crowd, grabbed the young
widow's left hand and clapped it on the corpse's
face.

Shocked, the girl bleated. Women stopped
sobbing to buzz at their neighbors. Men grunted.
Marian ignored them. Still clamping the girl's
hand, she watched the miller's mutilated leg. Then
she hemmed, begged pardon of the wife, and
returned to the doorstep.

"What was that all in aid of?" asked her
husband.

"Tell you later."

The steward ordered the bearers to move on.
Fuddled, sobbing, mumbling, the villagers trailed
after the bier. Hosea and his wife and neighbors
would spend the night on vigil in the chapel. The
only one remaining was the wise woman, who
washed the threshold to banish contamination.

Inside, the evening sun slanted sharp and
golden through western windows. Clouds of dust
danced in the sunbeams. The two servants idly
tapped walls. The steward folded his arms as if to
butt the intruders out the door. "Are you finished
prying then? There's nothing for you here."

He was surprised at Robin's mild inquiry. "How
are you called, good sirrah?"

The steward blinked. "Sir Luther, Martin of
Lincoln."

"Luther, you seem a smart and capable man.
We've somewhat to tell you."

Nonplussed by their casual affront to
authority, the knight waggled both hands. "I've no
time to dally with wastrels. Tell me where he kept
his money or get ye gone."

"Oh, yes, his fortune..." Robin stroked his

beard. "Where have you looked?"

"Everywhere." The knight gestured, making dust swirl. "There isn't a lot to search, but it must be here. Hosea, honest fellow, wasn't one to bury anything in the forest, not fat as butter he. And there are prying eyes throughout the valley."

Robin only nodded. Marian said, "Have you asked his wife?"

"Yes. She claims not to know. She may not. Her husband was old but no dotard. Elgiva spent money faster than the man could make it, questing after fancy gowns to lord over the parish.

"But then his fortune may not be here," he corrected with a sigh. "Our good miller hauled his share of flour to Werchesop every fortnight. Mayhaps he banked his coin with some Jew or Roman, though we've found no tally sticks, either. And traveling, he'd need worry about thieves, of which we've plenty on the roads hereabouts." He glared at Robin.

"Fear more the men of law and God who rob you. You can't call them to court." The archer scanned the main floor, crowded with baskets and sacks of grain, the loft heaped with sacks of milled flour. "Let me see..."

Handing Marian his bow, he mounted the staircase to the loft, walked to a corner where three sacks sat alone. Humming, he moved two sacks and pulled out the cornermost one. Rat-gnawed, brown flour trickled out. People below watched in wonder as Robin thumped the sack on the floor three times, then hoisted it, felt the bottom, and chuckled. He untied the top, shot in his arm to the pit, and pulled out a dusty round something he blew clean and tossed down to Luther.

It was a purse chock full of silver: pennies, shillings, half-crowns and a few crowns.

"How?.." began the knight.

Robin descended brushing his arm. "Men hide things in familiar places. A cordwainer favors a money belt, a crofter a false bottom in a chest, a tailor secret pockets. Millers hide their money in flour. It wouldn't be in the grain down here, for it's yet to be milled, so it must be above. The largest heap of sacks belong to the village, those six to his lordship, which leaves three the miller's fee. Any coin would be in the hardest-to-reach sack. Simple."

"Simple," muttered Luther. "Withal, I promised you a sixteenth part, so we needs count it."

Robin waved a dusty hand. "No need. Send to the alehouse and we'll be quits."

"What?" laughed the knight. "Better, dine with me at the hall. It's not often I entertain such a distinguished − bowyer."

"Done," Robin laughed.

Long Valley Hall was indeed an old Norman hunting lodge, a single-story stone hall with the kitchen and solar at the back. On benches at a long plank table, Robin and Marian partook of a fine harvest meal: liver from pigs and cows gone to slaughter, a plenitude of rabbits killed by scythes. Many many pots of dark foamy stout were fetched from the alehouse.

Sir Luther's wife, Lady Arelina, was cool towards the strangers until Marian whispered they too were gentry, Sir Robert Locksley and Lady Marian. (She omitted they were also nobility, the Earl and Countess of Huntingdon.) The two knights soon discovered they had both besieged Acre, and talked long of famine, pestilence, Saracen ambushes and torture, diseased prostitutes, raving madmen, mountains of rotting corpses, sun so strong it seared a man's hand to touch his own armor. It bemused the women the men laughed so often.

"This is fine stout." Robin reached for more drink and missed the pitcher. "It's got body. But what I meant to tell you, Luther, a long time ago, was... what? Oh, how curious is this mill − miller's death." He explained what they'd found poking in the cellar.

Trying to refill Robin's tankard, Luther

emptied the ale on the table. "Oops. I dislike it, Robin. Bits of rope and narrow footprints and bat dung. It seems a lot of mugger-hug – hugmug – hugger-mugger. I found a hole and a dead miller. His footprints in the – what do you call it – flour. It seems very simple, like you finding that – purse." A servant had to refill their tankards.

"It's sup-supposed to." Robin gestured and knocked his tankard into his lap. "Oh, my. Someone with narrow feet – tiny little feet – made it look that way. But I'm guessing. I'm wet, too."

Luther dropped his voice to a slurred whisper. "It's not fay folk, is it? Good. 'Course not. But who could sunder an oak board by yanking a rope? Not me. And how could they know Hosea, bless him, honest fellow, would fall in the hole? How drunk could a man be to not see a hole at his feet? Too drunk to work. If I had a hole here now, I could see it. Right there, like. And t'weren't a wide hole. Narrower than his fat belly. He would'a stuck fast. An assas-assas – a killer would needs jump on his shoulders to punch him through."

Robin waved his pot and almost clopped his wife in the jaw. Marian wrestled it away. "Right-o. I love you so, Marian. You're so beau'ful it pains to look at you. Huh? Oh, agreed, agreed. Can't prove what I didn't see, or what I did see. But if it was delib-delib – real, who profits by his death? Had he enemies?"

"Doesn't every miller?" Luther laughed. "They're all skimmers. Hosea was the worst thievin' bastard o'all, bless his soul. But whyn't they turn the mill upside down after his purse?"

"His wife – widow – interests me," said Marian suddenly. "'Dimples in the chin, devil within.'"

"May married to December," put in Arelina. "'A man who takes a young wife buys himself a peck of trouble.'"

The men gaped as if the women had just descended from Heaven. Robin fumbled with a knife to cut bread, had it taken away. He used a crust to sop ale off the wet table. "Who's miller now, with the harvest 'pon you?"

Luther waved a hand. "A young scalawag on the Poulter there. Seymour, journeyman to his father. 'E comes often, helps repair and such, carts flour home. We've good soil in this old riverbed."

"Was he around today?" asked Marian.

"Nay, not for weeks. I'd know if he were 'round. Everyone in the valley knows 'im. Speakin' of which, I better dispatch a rider t' Carberton t' fetch him." He pushed at the table to rise, snagged his heel on the chair leg, crashed back down. "Well, it's too late anyway."

Marian persisted, "Would this Seymour know he's to assume the milling?"

Luther shrugged muzzily. "I s'pose so."

"Is he young?" asked Marian.

"Aye," said Arelina. "Handsome in a callow way."

Robin laughed. "Are you thinking of marrying again, Marian? Marry, Marian marryin' again." He and Luther hooted.

"No, but I wonder how big this Seymour's feet are."

"I thought women cared about the size of a man's somethin' else," roared Luther, and they laughed until their sides ached. "Ah, Robin. I'm glad you came. You've saved me hardship, findin' that purse. T'were marvelous how you done it."

Robin roamed the room after a full pitcher. "T'wasn't me, t'was one of my men. An idiot to boot. Much the Miller's Son. He's a miller's son, son of a miller. We met him on the King's Road one day, decided to play with him. It were a slow day. Told him to produce his silver, millers always have money, or we'd string him up. But he fooled us. He said t'was buried in the flour. He dug around — quite an act for an idiot — and whipped big handfuls in our faces. Poof! Ay, it stung! Then he whacked us with a cudgel 'til our bones ached. Bunged my knee for a week. But he used his head, thick as t'was. When his father died, the bailiff turned the gristmill... over to someone else and threw Much out. We came... and fetched him... What is it, Marian?"

His wife crooked her little finger to her mouth. "What my husband would call a harebrained scheme."

Robin tried to whistle, fizzed instead. "Someone's in for it."

"Aye," said his wife, "you. Would you become a miller?"

"What? You're potted, Marian."

"No, I've a plan. Are you game?"

Luther and Arelina looked perplexed. Robin thought, shrugged. "I've been a butcher and a potter, why not a miller? Hoy, we're dry. Send for more stout."

"No!" pronounced the women.

Early the next morning, Elgiva was pitched out of her home.

"Oh, please, please, kind sir, you can't do this. You can't!"

Young and slim and pretty, the widow tried every charm to make Luther relent. She hung on his arm, wrung her hands, cajoled, pleaded, sobbed. But the steward coldly told her the gristmill was property of the duke, his to mete out. She was finished. From the loft, the two servants carried down Elgiva's chattel: a chair, two carved and painted chests of clothes, a triptych of Christ on the Cross, an effigy of Saint Audry, an iron pot and a spoon. They laid it outside the door.

Elgiva turned bitter. "You'll be sorry, Sir Luther. I'll tell Lord Lancaster what you've done at the manor court. He won't like it. Hosea, honest husband, was a good miller and I a good miller's wife. You can't cast us out — and I want my fortune."

"You'll get that once we find it," Luther lied. He pulled the half door shut and rode off with the lord's huntsman. Elgiva's curses echoed across the valley.

Meantime, the new miller scooped water from the sluice and lugged buckets to the cellar. Robin mopped the gears clean, but could not wash out the blood stains. "Proof enough he was murdered." He crossed himself.

In the village, Marian tended the outlaws' original business. Every autumn, before winter rains made roads impassable, they circumnavigated Sherwood Forest. This fief lay just within its ragged northern border. They renewed contacts in the villages and dispensed hard-won coins. Outlaws could not survive without the support of common folk, and both groups ofttimes needed to hide out, to borrow food or money, to ask favors or justice or succor. The Fox and Vixen of Sherwood toted up who was still alive, still on their side, still reliable. Marian reiterated that any "beggars" who braved the dark winter forest to fetch news to the Greenwood would receive coin, food, and protection.

Marian asked other questions, too. About millers, and young wives, and journeymen, and lepers, and wine.

Having cleaned the machinery, Robin fetched tools and whittled new teeth for the gears. By noon, he could open the sluice gate. Water rushed and splashed, the wheel buckets filled, and slowly the ponderous wheel turned. Excited as a child building a sandcastle against the tide, Robin ran downstairs as the rumbling wheel gained speed. In the dim light, he watched the gears tunk smoothly, heard the millstones grind overhead.

Alone, he crowed, "Brilliant, Master Robin, sterling. Very clever work, I must say."

Chuckling, Robin leaned out a hand, grabbed something moving, snatched away, lost his balance, and flopped on the muddy floor.

Swearing, he swiped muck off his trousers. "Pride goeth before a fall, Master Robin, and it serves you right."

In the dimness, he'd leant against the thick mill shaft that connected the waterwheel and crown wheel. "Fool, that turns too... Oh... Turns."

But the fleeting thought was erased by a new distraction. A noise.

Groaning.

Robin cocked his head. Tolling steadily, every few seconds, came a low moan. Like an dog in a trap, or a cow with an full udder.

Holding his breath, Robin tiptoed, squatted, peered at the revolving gears and rotating posts. He couldn't locate the sound. But for the first time, he noticed how the machinery seemed alive. Like a great horse or dragon, leashed and harnessed, but poised to turn on its master at the first chance.

The groaning rang on and on. Real but untouchable.

Like a ghost.

Robin Hood fled up the stairs.

Later that afternoon, as Robin filled the hopper and scraped flour into sacks – and tried to ignore the groaning – a young man knocked at the threshold.

Red-eyed Elgiva was just behind him. Handsome in a soft beardless way, the lad was proud in his neat yellow smock, sky blue hose, and round hat.

His feet, the outlaw noted, were narrower than his hands.

Seymour, journeyman miller to his father Uland in Carberton, was earnest and sincere, solicitous of Elgiva's plight. Luther had cast her out without a penny, and what might she do to gain back the knight's graces. He could help her mill. The job should rightfully have gone to him anyway, since he'd spent years repairing the gristmill, and had been Hosea's trusted friend. Was Robin capable to mill, and might he need a journeyman?

When his talk availed nothing, Elgiva loosed her tongue. "You shouldn't even be here. It's not right and it's not fair. You come out of that accursed forest, a murderin' outlaw with blood on his hands, and take work away from decent folk. You'll be in strife when Lord Lancaster comes through. He'll set dogs on you and your strumpet wife —"

Seymour jumped in. "And you'll ruin this mill with your meddling. Already you've thrown the wheel out of kilter or neglected to grease somethin'. It never did groan like that before."

Robin opened the door wider to let the sound travel. "Perhaps the mill mourns a master done wrong. Perhaps it cries for vengeance. What say you?"

The two young people shut up, turned white as ghosts. Seymour's hands shook. Elgiva backed away.

From the lodge, two horses danced down the valley. As planned, the huntsman had watched for Seymour and fetched Sir Luther. They reined in before the mill, hooves throwing mud. The knight nudged his bay palfrey sideways, swiped Seymour across the shoulder with a quirt.

"Get ye gone, wastrel. I've appointed this man miller and not you, and I'll stand no gainsaying my decision. Now hie yourself back to Carberton before I whip you out of the valley, and never come back. And you, trollop, get out of my sight."

Luther ordered the huntsman to escort Seymour home, at the end of a rope if necessary. After a hasty and tearful farewell, the boy shouldered his satchel and scampered up the road, while Hosea's widow hiked her skirts and pegged for the village.

"There," the knight sighed. "He's driven out, but Elgiva must stay till we find her money. I hope your wife knows what she's about."

"She always does," Robin smiled, "better than I."

"What you're about or she's about?"

"Either. I'm married long enough not to argue. I'm broke to the yoke."

"You and me both," Luther nodded. "Lean into the harness and avoid the goad. You've got the mill turning. Good. But what's that benighted groaning? It sounds like —"

He stopped.

"I'm glad you needs spend the night and not

me." The knight pelted away, leaving Robin to his haunted mill.

That evening, Marian returned from the village with their supper. Robin showed off his work, and she congratulated him, but added, "Why does it moan so? It sounds like a thirsty ox. Or —"

Robin raised a hand to stop her. His elation at fixing the mill had evaporated. He leaned out the window and dropped the sluice gate. Gradually the mossy wheel rolled to a halt. The silence was brittle after the unceasing groans.

They kindled a fire outside and ate supper there. "So what of your day, Marian? What have you gleaned?" Glad to change the subject, she caught him up on their outlawry business, but had little else to add. Robin was too tired to note his wife was deep in thought.

They slept outdoors.

Marian left before dawn, toting a satchel and bow, no hint of her destination. Her departure might have miffed Robin had he not done the same so often.

Robin fell to milling and found he liked it. Once he'd loaded the wooden hopper over the millstones, there was little to do except scoop flour from the catchboard. He replaced the missing floorboard with another plucked from the loft. Prowling after work, and grumbling at Hosea's laziness, he hauled sacks away from the walls, dug out rotting sprouting moldy grain and pitched it to the birds. He put down pallets and restacked the bags. He stomped so many rats and mice that he turned to the village and traded a silver ha'penny for a big brindled cat. He tested the scale and its iron weights, one against another.

He'd have loved the work if not for the infernal moan. In desperation, he fetched lard from the village and greased every moving part. Nothing diminished the groaning, though while smearing the big crown wheel he made a curious discovery.

He thought to tell Marian later.

But Marian didn't return that night, so he paid a penny for bread and meat and beer at the alehouse, then slept under a bush. Another day found the harvest in full swing, men cutting, children stacking, women winnowing. Wagons heaped high rolled to the mill door. Robin fed the hopper and stitched sacks.

Yet the villagers couldn't quite believe Robin Hood the Outlaw had turned Robin the Miller. And when they drew close enough to hear the groaning, they froze. Some prayed, some feigned deafness, but no one lingered, and eventually none would pass the door. Robin missed Marian.

At supper, the new miller got his wife back. She was puffy and dusty but bursting with news.

"Remember that leper we passed the other day? I learned in the village he hobbles through here every fortnight."

They braised pig's heart and trotters over the fire, stuffed with fresh rye bread. "So? Any beggar must. Friar Tuck had a regular circuit. And a leper cadges coins quick, because no one wants him to dally."

"No, no, no." Marian waved a greasy hand. "Remember Sir Luther said Hosea, may he rest in peace, fetched his grain to market every fortnight? The village women told me he would leave Thursday forenoons, spend Friday at the market, then return Saturday to make Mass Sunday. The leper passed through midday Thursday, then left the valley Saturday in the forenoon. Do you see? Hosea leaves, the leper arrives, the leper goes, Hosea returns."

"Every fortnight? That's curious. I guess."

"There's more. I've been from the Poulter to the Ryton. A fox crossed my path so I knew I'd have good luck. I asked of the merchants, the bailiffs, and the midwives. No one in either town ever sees this leper. Only Long Valley Screed sees him."

"Well..." Robin chewed slowly as his mind worked. "He could cut over the hills. Hard with rotten feet, though... Maybe they won't admit the

66

bugger to those towns, or threatened to kill him..."

"Mull it over," said his wife. "Oh, and tomorrow you go roving. I need you to track something."

Robin recoiled in mock horror. "Not I. My tracking days are done. I'm a miller now." Marian shoved him, but he bobbed back up like a hedgehog. "Oh. I found something. Come see."

He plucked up a firebrand and chivvied her inside, then down. By flickering light, Robin laid his wife's hand on the thick shaft that connected the mill wheel and gears. "Feel? Where's it gone? Ah, here. See? More rope fibers. What does that tell you?"

"Little, I fear." Marian shivered. "Engines are a mystery to me."

"Then understand this." He explained his idea.

Marian nodded, but still shivered. "Brilliant, Rob. Very clever. May we leave now?"

The firebrand popped a knot and extinguished. Smothered in gloom, the outlaws raced up the stairs.

"It was clever to find that rope trick. Mayhaps you can turn miller if outlawry becomes unwelcome."

"Or illegal?" joked her husband. They were back in the forest, a half-mile along the road to Carberton. Brush ticked at their elbows. "Outlawry and milling have much in common. I — hark. There's your track."

The outlaw squatted, moved a fresh oak leaf. "There's a toe print. And see that line where the brush is swept back? No deer made that — it's from a man's shinbone." Marian agreed, though she saw none of it.

Robin slid through bracken after the faint trail, halted at a forked oak. He plucked away a broken branch with withered leaves to expose a bundle in the tree's crotch.

"Ha. Show this to Will Stutly, who claims I can't track a bleeding bull through a baron's ball.

And here..."

He stooped and uncovered a staff hidden under leaves. A clank made him turn, and he yelped. Marian had pulled down the filthy gray robe. A tin bell dropped out.

"By my faith, Marian. Don't touch a leper's robes."

Marian batted the robe flat. "Fret not. If I'm right, this be all of the leper." From her satchel she drew a redware crock and soaked the robe with a whitish liquid reeking of musk: tallow. She stashed the garment back in the tree, replaced the camouflaging branch, flicked back her tresses, smiled. "Done."

Gingerly, Robin plucked an ash leaf from her hair. "What about the leper?"

A smug smile. "If I've guessed aright, there's no need for the leper anymore. But if I've plotted aright, we shall see him anyway."

"As you say, dear." Robin pushed brush aside with his bow. "I needs get back anyway. Wheat's to be winnowed this morn. And I needs rig a barrel trap to drown rats. And did I say I tested the weights? One was shinier than the others, heavier by half, what Hosea used to measure his share."

"Next you'll be curing chin-cough holding children over the hopper," laughed Marian. "You'll make a burgher yet."

"And you an obedient goodwife?"

Marian laughed again.

Three days later, Marian called through the window. "Rob! Honey! Will you fetch more wood?"

Robin topped off the hopper, then crossed to the window. Marian didn't want firewood. Any call was a signal to come watch. He chuckled, "Clever thing, my Marian."

Shuffling on crippled feet, shrouded by a hood, down the muddy road into the valley came the leper, clinking his bell and uttering his lament. "Unclean! Unclean! 'Ware the leper!"

Close by the road, Marian tended a fire under a cauldron, pretended to stir washing. As the leper came abreast, she turned her back so as not to breathe contagion.

But once past, she snatched up a firebrand, flitted up behind the leper, and set fire to his robe.

Tallow-soaked wool ignited with a ripple. The leper whirled at the heat and smell and smoke, then shrieked. He dropped his staff and ran flat out. Marian ran hard behind him.

Robin pelted out the doorway. "What the bloody living hell?.."

When the flaming leper had run a hundred feet, Marian caught up and hooked his foot with her own. The man slammed down. Kicking, she flipped him over, rolled him in the dirt and snuffed the fire.

Robin arrived just as Marian jerked back the hood. Revealed was Seymour, journeyman miller.

"A real leper can't run," Marian panted. "Their toes are the first things to rot off."

Robin stroked his beard. Seymour wept.

The Vixen of Sherwood poured herself another tot of stout and saluted the men who scooped flour into sacks.

"I saw right off he weren't a real leper. He wasn't crippled, nor did he stink of corruption. But some poor souls pose as lepers because they feel unclean, or wish to suffer penance. Or they have some rash like eczema, or Saint Anthony's fire, or scrofula, so are branded lepers. But I said nothing, for it wasn't my business.

"Until, I heard that Hosea, rest him merry, drove to market every fortnight, and during his absence, this leper passed through. Yet no other village him. Thus, someone donned a leper's disguise just for Long Valley Screed.

"Elgiva is young and pretty, but shows a venal streak. I suspected her right away. That's why I forced her hand onto the corpse to see if it bled at its murderer's touch. She passed the trial of bleeding, but only because she didn't kill with her own hand.

"She married the miller for money, then found love when Seymour came to make repairs. But everyone knew Seymour, so he couldn't visit with Hosea gone without creating talk. Thus he adopted a disguise — perfect, because people would shun him. He wore it again today, since Luther forbad him to return.

"Elgiva schemed to keep her money and position, yet gain a new husband — Seymour, next in line to be miller. One night she unbarred the door, admitted Seymour, and hid him in the cellar. Hosea, bless him, had no need to go down there. Seymour waited so long he had to splatter the corner.

"That day at dinner Elgiva gave Hosea brandy — his breath smelt of wine. T'was his favorite drink, so say the villagers, but she usually denied him. Once he was tipsy, she hied to the village to winnow, which she'd always shunned as beneath her. That left Hosea 'alone' to have his accident, thanks to Seymour."

"But how?" demanded Luther. "He's a skinny titch. He hadn't the strength to manhandle a fat tub like Hosea."

Robin bounced a sack to settle the flour. "Easy enough if you know how. If you're a miller. All he needed do — wait, I'll show you. I'd like to see myself."

The outlaw-turned-miller propped the sack on the catchboard above the new floor plank. He kneaded a corner of the sack into a ball and tied it off with twine. "That's Hosea's foot." Robin then caught up a rope and skipped down the stairs.

The only sound was the rumble and creak of the big wheel outside, the muffled tunking of gears below, the grinding of millstones. And the infernal groan.

Coming from below, Robin's shuttered voice was startling. "Here we go. Hosea, poor fool, is drunk, staggering 'round and 'round. I'm Seymour. I see his outline against the light. Quick like, I —"

Through cracks in the floor, Luther and Marian watched the outlaw's fingers work. He poked a slipknot up past the new plank, winkled it across, pulled it back down, shoved the noose up again to encircle the floorboard. Deftly, he flicked the slipknot over the balled "foot" on the flour sack. Then his hands disappeared.

Another pause, then, "Here comes the good part!"

Suddenly alive as a snake, the rope slithered around the plank, tightened, snatched the sack off the catchboard. The floorboard creaked, groaned, bent — and shattered. The sack was sucked down as if by a whirlpool.

They heard the bag tear. Flour fountained out of the hole.

The great mill wheel shuddered to a halt. Sneezing resounded below.

Marian and Luther pattered down the stairs to find Robin Hood pale brown with flour. The shorn sack was jammed in the gears. The rope was wound around the mill wheel shaft.

The dusty outlaw wiped his eyes, wheezed, "That's the link Luther and I missed. We wondered how little Seymour could break a board and drag a fat miller through the hole. But he was a miller too.

"Remember a man hides money where he's comfortable? Seymour figured how an engine can kill a man. This mill shaft pulls hard as a yoke of oxen. He had only to slip the noose over Hosea's foot and tie on here. I found rope fibers on the shaft. And Hosea's ankle was broken.

"Once Hosea crashed onto the cogs, he was stuck, probably stunned. Seymour shifted his leg between the gears, then watched his rival bleed to death. And having finished an honest day's work, he donned his disguise and fled back to Carberton, there to await word of the tragedy in Long Valley Screed."

Robin grinned. "His bad luck, though. He passed my wife, she with the eyes of a hawk." Marian smiled.

Dusty as any miller, Robin Hood led them upstairs. He closed the sluice gate, clumped back down, tugged the sack from the gears, checked no teeth were broken, clumped back up.

Luther paced around the fresh hole. "To think I'd have left it an accident, and given Seymour the mill. Now we'll hang both of them. So we'll need another miller... You, uh, wouldn't want the job?"

"Third time's the charm, eh?" laughed Robin. "No, I —"

Surprised, he stopped. He'd miss milling. It was safe, sedate, useful, satisfying. He imagined a life tending the millworks and bagging flour, meeting neighbors day in and out, working a lathe or saw in winter, growing fat and bald. No more robbing, hiding, dodging rangers and sheriffs. But... no more campfires or smoked venison, no more birdsong, no more dappled light illuminating his greenwood cathedral...

"No, I'm afraid not, but thank you for the kind offer. I'll return to what I know."

"And that is?" smiled the knight. Marian giggled.

Robin scratched his grayed beard. "What did I say I was? Ah, yes. A bowmaker."

Chuckling, he leaned out the window and jerked open the sluice gate. Slowly, slowly, the mill wheel turned. Slowly the millstones began to grind.

But no one spoke. They listened. And heard nothing.

The groaning was gone.

Shriving the Scarecrow

"Help! Murder! Oh, help!" The cry sailed across the marsh, helpless as a rat in the claws of a hawk.

"There!" Marian pointed through the slanting sunset. "There's three!"

"No, two." Robin Hood flicked a hand over his shoulder, nocked a clothyard arrow to the bow always in his left hand.

The outlaws could see for miles. Romney Marsh stretched along the gray English Channel, ditched and diked by Roman engineers, dead level. Their destination, a lonely church, jutted above the marsh like a crown on a tabletop. The village of Romney was a mile inland, tucked against trees thumb-high.

Two men ran while one stood still. The first fled for the sanctuary of the church. A smaller man pursued, waving a knife that glistened gold. The third hung crucified on a tilting cross. Elongated shadows like giant spiders streamed from the feet of all three and converged.

Robin and Marian dashed down a dike, vaulted a ditch, tore across a new-harvested field churned to mud by autumn rain. Shaggy white sheep bleated and scampered aside. Rye and barley stubble crunched under deerhide soles. Chaff stuck to their trouser legs.

But the outlaws were still half a mile off when the first man quit running for the church, staggered towards the third figure — not a man, but a ratty scarecrow. The man cowered in its pathetic shelter while the knife-wielder slashed

73

the air and ran straight on.

"You'll have to shoot," Marian panted.

Robin Hood nodded. Atop a dike, he raised his great bow, drew a tight breath with the string, curled finger and thumb under his jaw...

The knife-wielder chased his victim around the scarecrow, shoved it askew to stab...

"Rob..."

The mighty bow thrummed, the evening caught its breath, then a black shaft ripped through the scarecrow, slammed the chest of the villain behind. Killed, he bowled over into the mud.

Again Robin and Marian ran, quartering dikes, threading packed sheep. Gulls and wood pigeons and skylarks, gleaning grain from the harvest, flapped away trilling and keening.

Treading on shadows, the outlaws circled the scarecrow. The rescued man sobbed on his knees. The stricken man lay on his back, Robin's green arrow above his heart, eyes focused on Heaven.

He raised a quivering hand towards the scarecrow. "It was him. Him done it. Not me. Him."

Robin and Marian turned, confused.

The rescued man had gained his feet. "It's the — scarecrow. He thinks — the scarecrow's — killed him."

"Shrive me," whispered the dying man, "for God's mercy."

Marian bent, licked her finger, traced a cross on his forehead. "I absolve you of all sin. Rest in peace."

"It was him done it..." The arm fell.

"You've saved me," puffed the other. He was older, with a sparse salt-speckled beard and pouchy eyes. A merchant by his red robe and ermine collar. "I can — pay. Bless you both. He'd have — killed me. I can pay..."

"Keep your money," Robin snapped. "Pay me in truth. Who is he and why did he pursue?"

The merchant waved a hand. "He's Rioch. A cutthroat — reprobate. Anyone — will tell you. My coin — is good..."

"I said, keep your money."

Marian laid a hand on Robin's arm. "But why did he pursue, good sir?"

"For my money, of course." Sobbing for air, the man shook his head irritably. "I stepped outside to − see the sunset − and he jumped me. They'll tell you."

Robin looked black as he cut out the arrow with his large Irish knife. Marian frowned at the scarecrow. It was only a bag of burlap stuffed with straw, a worm-eaten purple-white turnip for a head, a tattered straw hat and rags too rotten to steal, though they had once been bright red brocade. The creature hung tilted on a rickety cross, head down as if witness to shameful secrets.

"Where the hell is everyone?" Robin squinted at the distant village. "You'd think a murder before their very eyes − there they come. But not many."

Closer now, silhouetted against dusk, they saw that west of the village stood a manor house seemingly uprooted from town. It was stone with flanking towers of wood in imitation of a castle, stables and outbuildings behind, bounded by a wooden fence. Serving women watched from the front gate while a pair of men trudged across the marsh. Romney village was twenty cottages and an alehouse but no chapel. A nearby mill, once worked by the tides, slouched brokenly: bats flitted out holes in the roof. Villagers, sharing ale and talk after a thirsty day's harvesting, gathered by sheep pens and stared, but only a man and boy plodded their way.

Marian crossed her arms as the channel wind hissed around them. Robin had wanted to show Marian this wondrous marsh, for he'd only seen it from the sea, and both wished to visit the nearby battlefield of Hastings, or Senelac as Saxons still named it. They were out for a lark before winter shut them in Sherwood Forest, but their holiday had come to an abrupt end. "Did you ever see any place so flat?"

"The deserts of Arabia. The open ocean. But not any place green." Robin wiped his bloody arrow on salt grass. "Must be the flatness gets into their minds."

Without a word, the red-robed merchant left them to the dead man and drooping scarecrow. He picked across the marsh towards the manor.

The oncoming villager wore a black robe to his ankles, a cowl edged with white, a skullcap. The priest was old and stooped, but strong in body and spirit, and plodded on doggedly. The lad trailing must be an altar boy.

The priest peered at the strangers. In tattered Lincoln green, tunics and boots of deerhide, hung with knives and quivers and satchels and blankets, they might have been king's foresters. Yet one was a woman with dark tumbling hair.

Being harvest time, beer was green, and the walk made the priest gurgle and erupt gas. He tried to be dignified, frowning at his smudged hems. "Pray forgive the blood. I've been butchering. I am Alaric DeFrier. So you've killed Rioch, eh? Just as well he's gone to God. I had to lock the poor box once he could walk, and the reeve wore out switches trying to make him farm. But it was the high road for him, with club and knife. Come, fetch him to the – church." He stifled a belch.

"Do you need help, Rob?"

"No." Testy, the archer stooped and levered the bloodless corpse to his shoulder. Free hand and bow wide for balance, he tottered across the marsh. The altar boy picked up Rioch's knife.

The church loomed large as a barn, built of brick and thick shingles, with a square tower for a steeple. Alaric explained, "A huge church for such a small village, yes. An archbishop fell into a ditch and prayed to Saint Thomas A'Becket. He was rescued, and so built this magnificent church near where he fell. It's not even on the road, and a long way to walk for morning Mass. Yet someday I fear it may stand out of sight of any living soul."

Marian asked, "Why fear for the village's future?"

Alaric opened the wooden door, but paused to wave at the endless marsh. "We can grow crops, but not well. The land holds salt and floods often. Sheep prosper but not men, and sheep little need a church. This is more a place to grow legends than food. They say Britain is divided into five parts: England, Ireland, Wales, Scotland — and Romney Marsh."

The interior was dark. The floor was uneven stone, the only furniture a wooden altar and gilt cross. Alaric lit a rush and sent the boy into the nave to fetch a mat.

Robin eased the dead Rioch down. "How is it a merchant can be pursued across field and marsh and none run to his rescue?"

The priest accepted a bowl of sea water and a rag, knelt painfully to wash the corpse. Marian helped. "Vincent is not of this fief."

The outlaw pointed out the window at the manor house. "He lives here."

A shake of the head. "Not really. He's from Rye." The seaport eight miles west.

"Surely," Robin objected, "he deserves succor from murdering villains with knives. Or does he?"

"'He is brought as a lamb to the slaughter,'" quoted the priest vaguely. "You may pass the night here if you wish. We've plenty of room."

Robin Hood took off his hat. "No, I think we'll bed in the forest. Father, can you shrive me?"

"Eh?" The priest squinted up, returned to ministering the body. "Ah, I see no need for absolution nor penance. It was clear Rioch intended murder."

"I feel guilty nonetheless." The archer gazed out the window. The marsh drew a line flat as the stone windowsill. "I've killed men before, God knows, but I don't feel right about this one."

Alaric rolled the corpse with gnarled hands. "It's tragic to lose any soul, but you are not culpable. I won't presume you were God's instrument, but... perhaps you'd best think it an accident and nothing more. You might pray for Rioch's soul. Precious few will."

Robin Hood suddenly donned his hat, thanked the priest with a silver penny, and marched out the door. Marian trailed him.

As they strode along the dikes above the alien marsh, the wife asked, "Why so glum, Rob? Withal that merchant seems not a goodly man, but the other was clearly a felon."

The outlaw shook his head. "I don't know that, Marian. I may have shot the wrong man..."

"Did you know," asked Marian, "to eat oysters on Saint James's Day means you'll never lack for money?"

"Not when I can steal it, no." Robin Hood winkled open an oyster with his knife, nicked the muscle, plopped white meat in his mouth.

Feet dangling, the two shucked oysters on a rickety pier. Rye was hilly as Romney Marsh was flat. Twin ridges like a swallow's tail projected into the sea. Each ridge was capped with sandstone and the sister towns of Rye and Winchelsea. Rye was notched into stone, girded by a city wall, and bound by three rivers: Rother, Brede, and Tillingham. All three carrying silt and sewage had choked Rye Bay into a long canal. Far out bobbed fat-bellied carracks and fishing boats, sails furled. The channel beyond darkened as the sun set.

Up at dawn, the outlaws had entered by the Postern Gate and spent the day in town. Now Marian reported, "I asked all up and down Mermaid Street. They say the locals are aloof, but I dropped coins and folks were glad to gossip about someone they hate. Yes, Vincent's a burgher, a merchant."

"Beholding only to God," Robin muttered. Independent merchants were something new in England. Outside "God's Sacred Triangle" of peasants, clergy, and noblemen, they were a whole separate class just feeling their oats.

"Vincent began as a velbrugger, a dealer in sheepskins. Then he found a demand for corn in Bruges's Grote Markt. Now, a viscount named

Spencer is the feudal lord of Romney Marsh, but he's always campaigning in France with King Richard, so he's always strapped. So Spencer sells the entire wool and corn crop to Vincent for cash and it's all exported to Holland."

"That explains why the mill falls down," Robin snuffed. "And why the priest fears the village will wither away."

"The poor peasants shear and harvest, then truck it all here to be sold to foreigners. They get silver instead of a share, but they must buy back wool and corn at higher prices, or else it's not available. And there's more. By law, the peasants keep the dikes and ditches in good heart. Vincent gains but contributes nothing, pays almost nothing in taxes. And rather than attend muster-at-arms, he pays deputies to go in his stead."

"A shield of gold." Robin shucked and nodded. "He's become virtual lord of the land, but with no oath of fealty between lord and peasant. No good will come of this mercantile class, I tell you."

"Aye. God and custom fall by the wayside, and money covers their altar."

Robin pitched oyster shells to flea-bitten cats. Gulls flew off to peck at a skinned horse floating by. "I see why the peasants didn't rush to his aid. They've love for neither Vincent nor Rioch. But he employs two hundred men, I found. He owns three of those carracks to ship his grain, and the wharves to tie to, including this one we sit on."

"No one loves him. These merchants are more a brotherhood than rivals, because they depend on each other's honesty. But Vincent cuts too fine a bargain and won't make up for errors. When his wife died a few years ago, he built that grand house at Romney and moved. Some say it's to oversee harvests, but others say he evades taxes and guild restrictions, or else it's because everyone in Rye hates him so. The only one's ever profited by him is that scarecrow, who wears his cast-off clothing to protect his crops."

"So much for the true worth of money. A wife dead, children estranged, no friends. Even his partner's dead —-"

"Aha," beamed his wife.

Robin Hood hung on her pause. "Keep talking. He didn't die in bed, did he?"

"No," Marian trumpeted, "he was stabbed. In his counting house one night. The murderer was never found, nor the money recovered. Vincent inherited his half of the three ships."

"Lucky Vincent," mused Robin, "but then, he's got seven letters in his name – Get up!"

Heavy boots clomped fast along the pier. Out of the shadows ran two men, fishermen or sailors in pitch-smeared shirts and knit caps. Each carried a gaff, an oak club topped with a shark hook. The gaffs went up as one rumbled, "You're to get out of town and stay out!"

Robin and Marian glided across the pier. Marian balanced her slim bow in one hand, drew her Irish knife with the other. Robin Hood only flexed his grip. The sailors paused as their intended victims, rather than cringe, took up fighting stances. But with roars to encourage themselves, they rushed.

Marian flashed her knife in a circle: a ruse. As the sailor's eyes flicked to the blade, the Vixen of Sherwood lunged. The tip of her bow tagged the charging brute below the Adam's apple. Gagging, he slammed to a stop. Marian tangled his legs with her bow and toppled him off the pier.

Robin Hood shouted, jabbed the bow at his opponent, snagged the fishhook instead, yanked the gaff to one side. Off-balance, unwilling to let go, the sailor lurched. Robin's knotty fist crashed alongside his head and almost snapped his neck. When he hit the pier with his face, the outlaw trod on both hands to cripple him.

Flushed, Marian peered at the water. "Mine might drown."

"A fisherman to feed the fish, eh? That closes a neat circle." Robin blew on his fist and grinned. "I like how your bosom heaves when you're excited."

Marian pointed her bow. "There's more room in the bay."

Smirking, Robin knelt on the sailor's back to yell in his ear. "Hoy, can you hear? Don't squirm or I'll slice your ear off and shout into that. You're lucky you assaulted me and not the iron maiden there. Talk. Who put you up to this? Or do I know already?"

Dizzy from the blow, a ringing skull, and daft dialogue, the sailor pretended to not understand.

"Ken this." Robin waggled his Irish knife before one eye, a silver crown before the other. "Which will you have?"

The man's eyes fixed on the coin. "It was the corn merchant, Vincent, told us to chivvy you out of town."

Straightening, Robin dropped the coin on the wharf, watched the sailor grope for it. "It'll wait. Fish out your friend first." He kicked the sailor in the belly off the pier.

Marian pouted impishly. "'Iron maiden?'"

Robin grinned. "Interesting that Vincent hires brigands for dirty deeds. Men work by habit: if he's done it once, he's done it before... Marian, did you ever hear the legend of Romney Marsh, how an offended scarecrow stalks the night for revenge?"

Marian puckered her dark brows. "Never."

"You will."

Vincent parted bed curtains of heavy silk called baldachin from Baghdad. Naked, hairy, and paunchy, he fumbled for a robe of green-blue samite. The room was dark except for chinks of light through heavy shutters.

He squinted, froze, thrust his thumbs between his first two fingers, the fig sign to ward off evil.

In a shaft of sunlight, a rat stood on two legs and wiggled its nose at him.

Vincent shouted for the cook, who was supposed to poison the rats in the galley, and the farrier to kill the beast. But as he snatched up his robe, something dropped with a soft plop. Another rat.

His shouts choked off. The solar, his

bedchamber, crawled with rats. Two dozen or more. Mostly they sniffed and scrabbled at the closed door to the stairwell, but others slunk under his bed or scurried along the windowsill.

Howling, the naked merchant yanked the door open, scattering a dozen gray creatures, and plunged through the doorway.

He slipped on something wet at the head of the stairs. Flailing, he grabbed for the bannister, but it too was slick. Sliding, he tumbled end-over-end down the stairs and crashed at the bottom.

The majordomo came running, the cook and skivvies from the kitchen, the farrier and stable boy from outside. All gasped and prayed, the boy crossing his fingers. No one helped Vincent rise.

Thrashing, swearing, bruised and battered, the merchant groped for purchase, but his hands were tacky. All of him was streaked red. With blood.

Rats spilled down the stairs and the women shrieked. Vincent bawled at the farrier to fetch a shovel —

— but again his cries choked off. The stable boy had left the front door open. Past the dying garden and low fence, Vincent saw endless marsh and fields stripped of his grain.

A quarter mile off stood the scarecrow in Vincent's cast-off rags. Not near the distant church, as two days ago, but closer by most of a mile.

As if the crucified creation had stalked towards the house.

Back in the low forest, Robin Hood pinched salt over spitted rabbits. "Almost done."

Marian returned from the edge of the woods. "I saw the farrier run into the house, thought I heard shouts. Vincent's discovered our handiwork."

"Not our handiwork," Robin smacked his lips, "the scarecrow's."

"Whoever's. I hope his household isn't dismissed right away."

"No. He'll keep them on, else he'd have to work himself. And when they are chucked out, we'll give 'em enough coin to start elsewhere." Approached last evening, the cook had admitted the female servants hated Vincent's parsimony and crude demands. Paid in silver, they'd gladly colluded. As the boys and girls of Rye had happily caught wharf rats for a ha'penny each.

"Will he know the blood is from rabbits, do you think?"

"If he tastes it." Robin was especially proud of the rabbits, which he'd bowled over with headless arrows as they nibbled grain. "But I imagine Vincent's appetite will be short this morn. Not like mine. Eat up. Rabbit flesh gives you speed, such as outlaws need."

He slid a roasted rabbit onto a slab of bark, dabbed on fresh-ground mustard seed. Marian wiped a knife on her trouser leg. "You know, we're not certain he's guilty of anything."

"He's guilty of siccing those sailors on us – on you. Assaulting the woman I love, he's bought more trouble than Satan can visit in an eternity."

Marian smiled. "So what's next, oh limb of Satan?"

Robin scanned the red-orange oaks overhead. "How do you weave those love knots girls make in springtime?"

Vincent had slept badly, but finally dozed off, when a sharp *caw!* woke him.

He didn't throw the curtains aside, but only peeked. His head throbbed, for he'd drunk a goodly portion of brandy to nod off. Now he felt sick, for the bedchamber stank of guano as if geese had paraded through.

Not geese, but crows. By cracks of daylight he saw two, four, a dozen sleek black shapes strut and flap and hop around his solar. One's caw set the others to raucous chorus.

Vincent shoved out of bed. He didn't fear crows.

But his feet scrunched in something that pricked his soles. Straw covered the floor ankle deep. He stared. It was impossible.

Shooing crows, he scuffed to the door. He'd wedged the bar with a piece of cordwood, hammering it tight, and it was still stuck. He crossed to the front window, fumbled the shutter open, shouted and flapped naked arms. The crows burst outside like a black snowstorm.

But Vincent stayed at the window, thunderstruck.

The scarecrow had traversed the marsh. It stood just at the fence, as if ready to mount into his yard.

Back in the tree line, Robin and Marian were invisible in faded green and deerhide. The King of Sherwood nodded as crows fluttered upwards.

"Do you think he's worried?" Marian asked.

"Wouldn't you be?"

"You're devious. Worse than Will Scarlett once a scheme takes hold."

"Will's my cousin. Mayhaps what he channels to mischief I turn to justice." Robin nodded again, smug. He'd given up weaving a net as taking too long. Instead he'd stolen a fisherman's net, propped it on poles, and baited the trap with barley. Having caught crows, he'd mounted a ladder to Vincent's window and winkled the shutter bar up with a knife point. He'd pitched in straw and then the crows, then hurried back to the woods.

Cradling her bow, Marian leaned against a tree. "What next?"

"Return the net, then watch Vincent. He'll be calling on help soon, or I miss my guess."

"Help from God or man?"

"Knowing him, probably both. But neither can help. That's the beauty of it."

Marian rolled her eyes. "I'm glad I'm not your enemy."

Robin grinned and kissed her. "No one could be your enemy."

Dressed in his finest robe and riding his best horse, Vincent sought the priest.

Alaric worked with others at slaughtering and salting. The priest had tucked up his black robe and donned a linen smock crusted with blood. He sliced the organs from a pig hung by the ankles. The pig was black and white and smeared with red, same as the priest.

Alaric handed his knife to a goodwife when Vincent asked to speak alone. The two moved to where the frightened squeals of corralled pigs covered their words.

"Father," Vincent looked at the ground, "I would confess."

"You should," Alaric snapped. "I expected you long before this. As has God. But to confess, you must unburden yourself of everything. Everything."

Muzzy from two nights' broken sleep, Vincent shook his head. "I don't understand. I can pay..."

"You cannot," Alaric rapped. He wiped pig's blood from a hairy ear. "You are crippled with sin, Vincent, but I see by your eyes you still would prevaricate. To celebrate reconciliation, you must tell all and leave nothing out. There are no half-measures with God."

The merchant piffed. "If you'll not shrive me, I'll go to Rye. Saint Mary the Virgin's is there —"

"Go to Rome if you wish," Alaric spat. "A pilgrimage would do you good. Or build a cathedral. No matter what bargain you strike with men, God is the judge, who sees and knows all."

"I will be shriven!" Vincent yelled, and the village heard about the shrill of pigs. "I will have my way!"

"You'll walk a lonely road. Until you confess, on your knees before the altar of God, you are barred from Mass, from Communion, from all

absolution, here and in Rye, even if your sins rot
your very core." Alaric sniffed and returned to his
butchery.

Raging, shaken and haunted, Vincent kicked
his horse towards his manor.

He went inside only a moment, then returned
outdoors with an ash shovel. Reaching across the
fence with a long shaking arm, he tipped live coals
into the scarecrow's rags and straw. Fanned by the
channel breeze, the scarecrow burned, the flames
rippling like shallow water.

"You won't get me," Vincent croaked like a
death rattle. "You won't!"

Marian returned to their camp, which was
wreathed in gold leaves above and below. "Burning
a cross brings seven years' bad luck."

Robin Hood nodded where he rested against a
rock. "He won't last that long. But he might be
visited by seven plagues, if I can think of a few
more. I'll hike to Rye. You visit the priest,
discretely, and see what Vincent had to say."

"You're having fun, aren't you?"

"I'm not having fun. This is work." But he
grinned as caught up his bow.

Vincent addressed eight hard-bitten souls in
his grand hall. Sailors, they feared neither men
nor God, only the wrath of the sea.

"There's just us here now. I've thrown the
servants out. I know they bargained with my
enemies. Now listen close or you'll not be paid.
You're to stay inside the house, one at each window
and door, and not sleep, and wake me if anything
untoward happens. Do you understand?" They did,
and hefted clubs and knives to demonstrate.

Still, Vincent was uneasy as he climbed to his
solar and double-checked the shutters and door
wedges. He didn't disrobe, but lay clothed on his

curtained bed. He hugged a brandy crock tight, and only nodded off when it was drained dry.

A crash against shutters woke him.

Clambering up, holding his pounding skull, half-suffocated in the foul room, Vincent stumbled to the shutters. They were locked tight. Yet he jumped as again something rapped from outside. Opening a crack showed nothing, for it was black night.

Lighting a candle, he found his bedchamber untrammeled. The floor was bare. Only partly relieved, he listened at the door. And heard a peculiar grunting.

Snores, he thought. Those worthless sailors had nodded off. Cursing, he used a hammer to bang the wedges out, ripped open the door. He'd pitch them out too and pay nothing —

An eye-watering reek turned his stomach sour. The grunting was loud, inhuman.

Making sure the stairs were clear, Vincent tiptoed down in bare feet. No lights showed below: the tallow lamps were extinguished. He waved his feeble candle.

Pigs, spotted black and white, had invaded his house. At the strange light, they squealed and scampered, cloven feet skidding on wooden floors. Their blundering knocked rolling objects big as a man's head. Squinting, Vincent found them purple-white turnips, dozens of them. Same as the scarecrow's head.

From the foot of the stairs, candle aloft, Vincent tentatively called his sailors. None answered. Unsure if he were awake or in the throes of nightmare, Vincent picked through his mucky house. It was only him and the pigs. How?...

The scarecrow, he thought suddenly. Where was it? If the pigs got in, so could the scarecrow. It could be in here —

He had to get out. Panicking, dropping the candle, he jerked up the bar, flung open the double doors —

— and faced the scarecrow.

Etched against the night, Vincent saw straw

jutting from rents, the blank burlap face looming, his own red rags twisting. Clutched in a crooked hand was a wicked scythe like that carried by Death himself.

"No! I burned you!" Vincent staggered back from the apparition, tripped on a turnip, fell sprawling. Scrambling up, he dashed for the back door, threw the bar aside, flung it open to —

Another scarecrow, with a pitchfork. God's pity, how many were there?

The phantom raised a rag-hung finger. A voice harsh as a crow's rasped, "Confess! It's the only thing to save you! Confess!"

With a howl like a trapped animal, the merchant whirled again. But the first scarecrow stalked into the hall, the great curved scythe bobbing at each step. "Confess!"

Stunned, staggered, Vincent covered his face and collapsed. Turnips thumped against his knees and soles as the scarecrows closed in. "Confess, Vincent! Confess and end this nightmare! Confess!"

"All right, all right," the beaten man blubbered. "I had Rioch kill my partner. I told him where, at the counting house. Gave him the key. Oh, help me, Lord!"

The taller scarecrow turned, called, "You heard?"

Alaric the priest came from the shadows of the barnyard. The village reeve and a few others followed. "Aye, we heard."

The scarecrow grabbed at his head, pulled it off. The smaller one dropped the scythe, dragged off an itchy mask. Marian's black hair was speckled with straw. "Are you smug now, Robin?"

The outlaw let go a sigh. "Not as smug as I reckoned to be. But justice is served, and the souls of two men will lie easy. That's the best we can hope for."

Come morning, Robin hefted the scarecrow

disguises and a new cross, and strode across the marsh. Marian followed with the priest. Robin talked as he replanted the cross.

"It was lucky we found these rags. I had to scour Rye to match the ones Vincent burned." He impaled the burlap sack on the upright. "You know, the only clue I had was that Vincent sicced two sailors on us in Rye. That seemed greatly vindictive when all we'd done was ask questions. Left alone, Marian and I would have probably walked clear out of his life. But the guilty see where none pursueth, or some such."

The outlaw stuffed straw into the body. "After that attack, I knew more about Vincent: that he'd hire brigands for criminal acts. (Same as he hired sailors to guard his house last night. Ha. For a handful of silver they opened the door and left, just as did Judas.) But it made sense. Vincent was a robber in his own way, cutting deals so fine he drew blood from rivals. And who else was a criminal? Rioch."

"So, some guessing." Robin speared a turnip on the cross with a sickening *chuk!* "Vincent is the richest man hereabouts, so a natural target for Rioch. What if one night Rioch came to rob Vincent, and instead was bribed to kill Vincent's partner, to stab him to death in his counting house? That would be two thieves getting cozy, both profiting. Eventually, of course, the two thieves fell out, over money, no doubt. Rioch chased Vincent with a knife, I shot Rioch. In dying, his vision failed, so he pointed not at Vincent, but at the scarecrow in Vincent's cast-off clothing, saying 'He did it.' But we misunderstood, and with Rioch died their secret bond. And any way to prove Vincent's crime unless he confessed."

Robin fussed with red rags. "So I, working through others – the scarecrow, rats, pigs, crows – much like Vincent, set out to make him confess. If he were innocent, as Marian reminded me, he'd only suffer a scare, which would make us quits for the sailor attack. But if he were guilty – and he was, so that's that." He tipped a hat rakishly and nodded.

"But why take such interest?" asked Alaric. "Why all this trouble? What was Rioch or Vincent to you?"

"Oh, nothing." Robin Hood stepped back to admire his work. "But I worried I'd shot the wrong man. I wanted to be shriven, as Rioch had been, by Marian's hand. I was absolved by Vincent's confession. That left only the scarecrow, for it had also been accused. Now it's shriven too."

"What?" The priest cocked his head as if his old ears betrayed him. "It's what?"

With a fingertip, Robin tilted the cross straight. "Remember, to offend a scarecrow offends another, who also hung on a cross to guard over us..."

Flushing Scarlett

Squinting in campfire smoke, Robin Hood sliced venison from the spit, grimaced at the flat flavor, turned as laughter sounded.

Will Scarlett and his son Tam Gamwell had finally returned from their sojourn into Nottingham. Robin's cousin, normally clad in dapper red, wore only a filthy gray rag twisted around his hips. His face was scratched and stubbly, one eye blacked, and he reeked of cows, horses, and pigs. Tam, his son, was similarly shabby, battered, and bug-bitten, but oddly clean. The Merry Men and Women laughed to see them, especially young Katie, who hooted at Tam mercilessly.

Will Scarlett limped up to his cousin, relinquished a dirty handful of silver pennies. Despite his dishevelment, he grinned. "Not bad, eh? I sold a horse and saddle. I had over a hundred crowns, but I threw it away."

Robin Hood jinked the coins in his brown hand. "Where's my salt?"

"Salt!" Scarlett slapped his forehead. "By the saints. We wuz so busy we forgot. See, Coz, it went like this..."

"Now remember. We're beggars. Stare at the ground, mumble, look vacant and stupid, like Much. We want to slip into town, quaff a dram, tickle a tart (me, not you), pick up news, and leave."

"And buy salt."

"I said that. Trust your da, son."

Days had been warm, and the spring road was ankle-deep in mud. The two outlaws had already pushed clear three carts sunk to the axles.

Robin Hood's cousins wore smocks so ragged they needed two, so where one failed to cover the other might, and nothing for shoes. Tam's cowlick stuck up through a woolen cap, and Scarlett could see through his straw brim. Father and son were girded with ratty purses and sacks, some for food, some for flint and tinder, some for pennies. They were plastered in mud and flecks of straw, for they'd slept in a cow byre, and smelt it.

Tam shook his walking stick to flick muck off the tip. "I wish we carried knives."

"That ain't beggarly. Besides, if we had fighting knives we'd be tempted to do something stupid with 'em, like fight. Running's our salvation. So's a good disguise, which is worth a good plan any day."

"I don't much like running."

"Maybe not, but it's how things work in the forest, and we're forest dwellers. Rabbits don't fight wolves, they run. Robin knows when to fly, so take a lesson from him. And running beats hanging, which is what we'll get if they catch us."

"Robin will hang us if we forget his salt."

Will pinched his son's ear, grinned. "Saints above, you get more like your mother every day."

Past the woods, fields sliced like bacon stretched away on both sides. Peasants goaded skinny oxen to break first furrows, their plows rocking like ships in a storm. The outlaws skirted a flock of waddling honking geese and approached the high gates of Nottingham. The sheriff's guards, in blue gypons painted with a white hart's head, curled their lips, but Scarlett produced ha'pennies and they got past.

Inside the gates, they got their first look at the town this new year. Houses were of beams and dingy daub. Streets were narrow, overshadowed by tilting second or even third stories. After the long winter, the streets and alleys were strewn with tumbledown thatch, gray manure, and ash heaps, all being nosed and scratched by pigs and chickens. Yet despite the dismal winter-exhausted air, people were gay for a spring day. Women and elders soaked in the sun, having dragged out indoor chores or else sprucing up with pitchforks and spades. Freighters cursed yokes of oxen and horses, farmwives delivered eggs and winter turnips, children who should have been working played tag and shrieked and threw clods. Few attended a pair of beggars.

"What do we do first, Da?"

"Don't whisper, for one. Makes folks curious. We get in and out, nothing fancy, we mind our own business, we leave. But this is queer..."

Scarlett's eyes flicked to an uncommon number of "lances": squads of fighting men led by a knight in full chain mail; a squire lugging sword and shield; men-at-arms in scales with swords and maces; peasants in quilted gambesons and kettle hats armed as archers or slingers or pikemen. The lances milled, called out to one another, crossed paths, but most converged on the marketplace.

"Hmm... Someone's raising an army," mused Scarlett. "And not a happy one. See how they march, swinging their shoulders, jaws stuck out? They've got a burr up their backsides. Wonder why..."

"Ain't we to mind our own business?" Smelling adventure, the boy wiggled like a hunting dog.

"Oh, but this is our business. If some baron's getting up an army, he'll set out to unseat some other baron by laying siege, killing peasants, and burning crops. Happens every spring, regular as dancing around the maypole. Robin'll want to know... Besides, where there's trouble folks mind things other than their purses. Shuffle on, lad, and look humble."

Nottingham's marketplace was jammed with stalls and corrals and carts, all mired in place, and surrounded by ale bars, where a householder

simply dropped a wide plank to serve beer from
their kitchen. Every bar was crammed with
knights and soldiers who banged leather jacks and
wooden noggins, talking loud and angry.

Scarlett cast about, breathed, "Christ, I'm dry
after a winter of Adam's ale. Stay close. Ears open,
mouth shut."

Careful to bump no one, Scarlett squeaked a
penny onto a bar. The alekeeper's wife sniffed but
pushed across two noggins. Slurping ale, drifting
around the crowd, the two listened. Then Tam
jumped as a soldier suddenly bellowed, "There he
is! Where's our bounty, Redmond?"

The outlaws watched a knight and three
bodyguards grimly mount the stage at the center
of the marketplace. Sir Redmond stood under a pole
from which hung a lord's shield and fluttering
banner, purple with a trio of martlets, a device
Scarlett didn't recognize. As servant of the lord,
the black-bearded knight also wore purple, but on
his breast was painted his own heraldic device, a
Saracen crescent. Redmond's face was burned dark
as a walnut noggin, and his armor was vertical
strips of steel stitched to leather, signs he was
lately returned from Byzantium or the Holy Land.

The soldiers mobbed the stage, growling,
waving gauntleted fists. "Where's our bounties?
Aye, where's our wages? We've come this far, by the
brow of the Virgin, so pay up!"

Sir Redmond let them rail awhile, then
bellowed, "Good worthies! On behalf of Lord Oliver,
who's summoned you here, I'm sad to say you won't
get your bounties or wages, for they've been
stolen!" The word was echoed like a curse by a
hundred throats. "Aye, stolen! The men fetching it
from Doncaster were murdered and villainously
robbed —"

"Uh, oh," muttered Scarlett. "Time to move on,
Tam. Tam? Oh, sufferin' Jesus."

Young Gamwell stood between two soldiers, big
and armored and armed. Heart in his mouth,
Scarlett squeaked through the crowd to hear Tam
nattering, "... ever killed anyone with those

knives? Gor! They could never stab you, eh?, not with such handsome armor. Ye must be wonderful strong."

Flattered, but distracted by the news, the soldiers shooed him idly. Yet they objected as Scarlett snaked in an arm and snagged his son's ear. "Here, now. The lad weren't doing no harm —"

"Oh, it's just he loves soldiers, sir." Will affected a gurgle. "I was one once, before the pleurisy took me." He hacked as if his lungs would burst, and the soldiers edged away.

"Tam," the father hissed, "we must go."

"Why, Da? Look what I got." Tam rubbed his ear, held low a weapon-knife with a wire-wrapped handle.

"Hide that and belt up," hissed his father, edging for the back of the swelling crowd, for all Nottingham had come to see the commotion. "That knight's blather is heading in only one direction."

"— yes, your money was stolen by that rogue, that blackguard, that rascal, Robin Hood and his Merry Men!"

"Uh oh," muttered the boy.

The two were almost free of the crowd when a soldier yelled, "Hoy! Where's me knife?" And another, "My purse!"

Sir Redmond bawled on. "— But bear with me, for together we'll take the field, mount a campaign against that red-handed Robin Hood and root him out of Sherwood Forest —"

"A fine place to be right now, all told," growled Scarlett. "Jesus, Mary and Joseph."

The outlaws halted, wedged between angry fighting men and a troop of blue-clad guards pushing in. At their head was the last person Will Scarlett wanted to see. He backpedaled and stepped on both of Tam's feet. The boy yipped, heads turned.

Nicholas, the portly Sheriff of Nottingham in a blue doublet and silver chain of office, chirped, "Hold! That's Robin Hood's cousin! The thievin' Will Scarlett!"

"Robin Hood's what?" roared a hundred voices

95

behind. At the front, guards rushed with upraised hands.

Will Scarlett couldn't back up, so went forward — boldly. With a two-handed swipe he dashed ale in guards' faces, batted noses and chins with the wooden noggins, slithered through the pack like a greased eel. Guards clutching at him only tore rags. Retreating from danger, Nicholas tripped in mud and flopped on his back. Scarlett hopped full on his stomach to vault over. Since Nicholas was at the rear, outlaw and son landed in the clear.

Momentarily. For scores of angry soldiers surged from the marketplace with a roar.

Despite his limp, the outlaw sailed around a corner into an alley, rounded another, then another. His son pelted hard behind him, feet flying. "Da. We ain't stole nothin', have we?"

"Not yet. Run anyway."

Tam called, "I thought you said a good disguise was worth a good plan, or somethin'."

Over his shoulder, Will panted, "Your mother used to talk at the wrong times, too, including when I was plantin' you. That must'a set the curse. Here, lad, get a boot up."

Tam blinked. They'd ducked and wove around pigsties and privies and clotheslines, halted in a blank-walled alley no wider than their shoulders. Tam didn't argue, took ten fingers and clambered onto the thatched roof, clung to the thick reeds. "What do I do?"

"Belt up and listen for once. Meet me in the barn behind Saint Mary's. If I'm not there by dark, slip under the wall and hie to the Greenwood. Tell Robin he was right."

The boy peeked upside-down like a cat. "Right about what?"

"He'll know. God bless."

Scarlett raced off, limping on his bad leg. The boy hunkered behind a hump in the thatch while soldiers plashed and puffed past. Then he scaled towards the peak to scout Saint Mary's Church.

Halfway to the top, he plunged through the roof.

Scarlett trotted into an alley crossing, saw soldiers at both ends. He backed into a doorway to think, jiggled the door, found it barred.

"What the hell." He knocked.

After a heart-thudding moment, the door popped open. A withered crone with ten-children hips and no teeth cackled, "Come to visit your old grandmother Gretchen, have you?"

"Huh? Oh, yes. Uh, are you offering what I need?"

"I've got what any man needs, laddy. Aged meat tastes the sweetest."

Scarlett peeked. Soldiers and city guards banged on doors. He stepped inside and barred the door. "Can't think of a better way to spend the afternoon."

Gretchen peered through a shutter crack. "Those soldiers have a grudge against you, honey?"

"Me? No. But they seek a man looks just like me. Would your house have a root cellar, mayhaps?"

"Is that what you're after, to fill my cellar with your root?" She cackled as Scarlett studied the floor. "Aye, I've a root cellar. But I don't think you'll fit, what with a fat purse and all."

Scarlett dug in his tattered clothes, pulled out one of many purses. "Hold it then for me, grandmother."

She squirreled the purse away, stepped to the back room, yanked up a trapdoor to reveal another set in the dirt under the house. Lifting that let escape a breath of rotten meat, bad cheese, dirt, and spiders. "Down there you'll be safe."

Soldiers banged on the door. "Open in the name of the sheriff."

"Safe..." Will squeezed through the first hole, stepped on something squishy in the shallow root cellar. Scrooching, he just fit under the trap door, could see the entire crawl space lit by cracks of sunlight. He reached up to pinch the strumpet's thigh. "My thanks. Mayhaps once the soldiers are gone, I can climb out of this hole and into another."

"Silly romantic," Gretchen giggled. She dropped the trapdoor on his head. "Oops. Sorry."

Through ringing in his skull, Scarlett heard the soldiers cease banging, heard the woman's singsong reply.

"Romantic, yes." He scuttled out of the cellar hole into the crawl space. "Practical too. Any trull that old knows which side the bread's buttered on. What's − oof − out − here?"

He crawled away from the alleys towards boards tacked along the house wall. His nose told him what lay on the other side. "By all the bloody Garadenes in Hell..."

Sighing, he punched out boards and squeezed through.

Swine squealed and stampeded as he crawled into the pigsty.

Curling into a ball to protect his eyes, Tam crashed onto a table covered with food and crockery. Planks collapsed. Tam bounced and just stopped himself from rolling into the blazing hearth.

The boy clambered up, brushed thatch and leeks and flour off his tatters. A goodwife in a crisp wimple stood where the table had been, flour to her elbows. Her mouth formed an O, but she stayed mute.

Tam's father had taught him, When in strife, talk hard and fast. Don't give 'em time to think.

Tam talked. "Oh, mother, how good it is to see your face. It were awful, mother, just awful." Tam tried to think of something awful. "I was... in the graveyard... at my father's grave. Tha's it. He were a bishop, ma'am, left me dead these many long years ago. Him dead, I mean. And, er, whilst I was kneeling there, between me poor old mother and me da' − No wait, he weren't a bishop then. Any road I'm a poor orphan, got no one, uh, uh... a big eagle

came down and scooped me up. Thought I was
dinner." He grabbed a chicken off the floor, saw it
was cooked, tore off a drumstick. "Like this, see?"
Tam spread his arms and swooped in a circle,
searching a way out. There was only the front door,
barred, and a ladder to the loft. "But, uh, I prayed
to the Holy Virgin to help me." He inched towards
the door. "And when I sang the *kyrie*, the buzzard,
I mean eagle —"

"Mar— Mar— Mar—" piped the goodwife, probably
trying to say "Mary."

The door suddenly leaped in the frame. "Open
up! We're hunting thieves!"

"Bloody Christ!" Tam shot up the ladder,
drumstick clenched in his teeth.

Leaping, Tam caught the rafters surrounding
the hole he'd made, nimbly swung through. As the
soldiers smashed down the door, the boy whistled
to attract their attention. To upturned faces he
crowed, "Be quicker next time if you want to catch
Tam Gamwell!"

Laughing, he ran in great leaps down the roof,
vaulted the alley, scrambled like a squirrel up the
opposite peak. Still laughing, he slid down a
thatched valley between roofs.

Smack into a water barrel.

Will Scarlett clambered erect from gluey filth,
plocked in bare feet towards the pole fence between
houses. Charging in circles, six pink-and-black
pigs squealed and sprayed muck from cloven
hooves. Scarlett hissed, "Hush or you're hams!"
and caught a clod in the teeth.

"Stand your ground, you!"

Pounding around the corner came two men-at-
arms and a leather-coated housecarl with a long-
handled Saxon ax. One man pointed a cocked
crossbow.

"A'right, a'right, you've caught me," Scarlett
grumbled. "Just let me climb out..."

He unstuck his feet, climbed atop the rail fence,

balanced as if clumsy or drunk –

– then launched himself at the crossbowman.

He struck at the weapon to deflect it, dived for the housecarl's throat at the same time. The bow snapped, *punk! twang!*, but the bolt missed. Will snagged a neckline and the two tumbled, the outlaw on top.

Scarlett levered up from the housecarl's chest, rocked backwards. A swordsman slapped with the flat of his sword to brain Will, missed and whapped the housecarl instead. Scarlett snatched off the housecarl's helmet and slung it at the swordsman's face. The man howled at a chipped tooth.

Smug, grinning, Scarlett scrambled up, stomping on the housecarl's throat for good measure, then shoved the howling swordsman backwards with a laugh.

Then he recalled. "Where's the third –"

A helmeted head slammed Will square in the breadbasket.

Bulled backwards by the running soldier, Scarlett hit the fence, which crumpled. Pigs bolted for freedom. Stumbling in filth, Will kept his feet by hauling on the man's kettle hat, for the chin strap was fastened. Tripping over poles, yanked by his chin strap, the soldier flopped face-down in the pigsty. Wheezing, Will collapsed knees-down on the man's back.

The bruised soldier and housecarl were up again. With no place to go, Scarlett scooped muck and flung it at them. "*Nyah, nyah!* Come and get me!"

The soldier stopped in shock, thinking he's roused a madman. But the housecarl pointed his ax, bawled, "Load that crossbow. Put a bolt through his lights –"

Scarlett hurled muck hard and fast, looked for a way out, found only daub walls. The housecarl yelled again –

– then collapsed as something crashed alongside his head.

Saggy, gapmouthed Gretchen held the handle of

a redware chamber pot. The housecarl, crockery crumbs in his hair, lay sprawled.

The remaining soldier yanked back his crossbow string, raised, aimed —

— and yelled as something tangled his legs.

Tam, bedraggled and streaming wet, belabored the soldier with a stolen broom. Whooping, Scarlett vaulted bodies, got whapped in the head, but shredded the soldier's gypon to rags and hurriedly bound the dazed man.

"My thanks, grandmother," panted Will. "I owe you another purse. Or his. But why change sides?"

"Oh, I'm flexible." Gretchen tossed the handle into the sty. "And any road, I've seen this lout before. He's rough on women."

Scarlett turned to his son and laughed. "Tam. You're soaking wet."

"Da," the boy hooted, "You're covered with pig shit."

Scarlett grinned, spat something off his tongue. "You get more like your mother all the time. Here, help me bundle up these soldiers. We need two of 'em, and this bloke's trappings."

Tam grabbed a foot and pulled. "What for?"

"Now that I've had a moment to think, I've thunk."

Tam's hat brim ran water into his eyes. "Robin says that's always trouble."

"He heard it from your mother. And it's no trouble. Look you, if that knight is looking for us, we've got to find him first."

"Huh?"

"Just grab that boot, will ya?.."

Black-bearded Sir Redmond directed the search from horseback, spurring from alley to street to bridge so fast his foot guard of three panted to keep up.

Now a sergeant with a tall ax came running, holding his bobbling kettle helm. "Sir Knight. A word. We've trapped the blackguards!"

"Eh?" Redmond reined in hard, his horse whinnying as the bit cut his tongue. "Where, man? Hoy, wait up!"

The sergeant waved frantically and trotted down an alley. Redmond booted his horse, but the alley twisted and narrowed until his toes scraped the walls. His three bodyguards had to walk single file behind, hands on sword pommels.

At a widening in the alley, the sergeant signaled, "Dismount, if you will, good sir. They're in that barn."

They crept towards a small barn jammed between two houses, obviously an afterthought, for doors on both sides stood open as a public right of way.

Inside, the sergeant put a finger to his lips, crossed the barn, pulled the opposite doors shut, barred them. The stalls were empty, the animals slaughtered in late winter. Left was moldy straw, wooden rakes and forks, a block and tackle for hoisting bales to the low loft. Their feet scuffed crumbled straw and made dust motes dance. The knight gaped around. "Where are the thieves?"

"Close, sir. Your plan's working," said the sergeant. Gently he shooed the confused bodyguards back out the door. One balked, refusing to leave his superior. To the other two the sergeant cooed, "Make ready to grab 'em when they come down the alley." As they turned to look, he gently barred the door behind their backs, shutting in dimness lit only by slits high above.

"God's fish and loaves," rasped Redmond. His bodyguard looked confused. "What —"

Will Scarlett doffed his helmet, raised his hands. "You've caught me, sir. Pardon the deception, but I was afraid the mob might tear me apart for stealing their payroll."

"What? Oh, yes, of course..." Thunderstruck, but thinking fast, Sir Redmond whipped out his sword. "I know not your game, cousin of Robin Hood, but you're caught and you'll hang."

Hands high, Scarlett nodded dolefully. But instead of cringing, he advanced against

Redmond's sword, pressing his leather-and-iron breast against the point so the knight backed steadily. The outlaw jabbered, "Hanging! Oh, Saint Hildegard watch over me. A ghastly fate, but a deserved one. You're too clever by far. But I pray... you'll spare... my son – TAM!"

With a squeal of blocks, the boy leapt out of the loft. A noose laid on the barn floor, under straw, unfurled like a cobra and closed around Redmond's legs, staggering him.

Will snatched a wooden pitchfork from a corner and slammed it alongside the bodyguard's head below his helm. The man dropped.

Dangling halfway to the floor, Tam grunted as his arms creaked in their sockets. Weighing far less than the knight, he failed to hoist him, so jerked like a pickerel on a hook. Tipsy, the knight bawled, shoved the noose down to his ankles, sawed awkwardly at the rope with his sword. Frantically Tam jigged, kicked at a beam, swore with his father's choicest oaths.

With the pitchfork, Scarlett knocked Redmond's sword flying. Then he bounded into the air, grabbed his son around the middle. With a bawl the knight was hoicked high, feet first, like a pig for slaughter.

Until Tam bleated, "Da! You're heavy!" and let go.

Father and son crashed into dusty straw and a fit of sneezing. The knight's mailed back slammed the floor. Desperately he fished for a knife flopping at his belt.

Sneezing, spluttering, Scarlett scrambled up, jumped, caught the rope. With Tam holding his waist, they hauled the knight high to spin in the air, lashed the rope to a post.

Bodyguards banged on the barn doors. One slipped his sword between to lift the bar. Scarlett scampered, wedged the fork behind the bar to lock the doors.

"There. That was easy," Will panted. "Now, friend, pray, let us talk."

Gently, the outlaw grabbed the knight's belt

and walked him in a circle. Inverted, red-faced and gasping, Redmond tried to swear.

Scarlett tut-tutted. "Save your breath, you thief-calling thief, you. I'll admit being a thief, as will Robin Hood and all his Merry Men and Women. But we didn't steal your bounties. I should know, after all: our band ain't murdered no one all spring.

"So you're lying. And if you're lying, you're hiding something. And what could you hide except that you stole the money. Maybe your murdered the couriers, maybe you bribed them, but you got it. You're fresh out of Byzantium, yet you failed to make your fortune, eh? Else why would you take service in a baron's household?

"So now you'd mount an expedition into Sherwood to keep everyone busy. And while this army flounders in the brush, you'd quietly disappear. Truth or falsehood, false hood?"

The knight's reply was long, profane, uninformative.

Scarlett tisked. He'd been winding the man 'round and 'round all this time. Now he let go with a sharp spin.

Upside-down, whirling, his skull ready to burst, the knight could only gasp. Scarlett thumped him so he swung to and fro besides.

"That looks like fun, Da," piped Tam.

"If you've no brains to drown, maybe. I wonder if his head will eventually burst, like a bladder in a football game." He caught the knight's arm, halted his spinning. Purple-faced, the knight drooled. "Come, brother, confession eases the soul. You stole the bounties. Say it — just to please me — and we're quits."

"All right, all right," gargled the man. He flailed his arms but could barely lift them. "But I'll see you hanged, you —"

Scarlett left him hanging, walked to a shadowed stall, tipped aside bales of straw. Underneath, speckled like newborn chicks, huddled the two soldiers Scarlett had thrashed earlier, gagged and resentful but alert. Deftly,

Scarlett drew his thin throat cutter from a sleeve to slice their gags. "You heard?"

One man spat. "Aye, we heard. The skiving skinflint. Some reckoned he was dishonest. He'd starve his own mother and sell her bones for kindling."

"So Robin Hood and his Merry Madmen didn't steal your pay, but this trustee did? Are we clear?"

Glumly, the men nodded. They reserved their anger for Redmond.

Scarlett nodded. "Then we're finished, Tam. Let's be off."

"Off?" The boy cast about. One soldier, locked out, had run around the block to bang on the other door. More soldiers joined them with loud harangues. There were no windows, only sparrow-slits under the eaves. "How are we to escape?"

"Faith, lad. Have respect for your ancestors – meself included. Remember what Allan A'Dale tells us of Archimedes?"

"He took baths?"

Scarlett addressed the swaying, barely conscious knight. "Where did you stash the money, pray? As one thief to another, I'm just curious."

"Never – you can – won't –"

Scarlett tisked. With a tail of rope, he fashioned a slipknot and draped it over the knight's head. The man's red eyes grew wide. Scarlett wrapped the hank around a post, then walked the opposite way, tugging the knight at a steep angle. As the rope tightened by inches the man's face turned black.

"New thoughts, good sir? Or shall I lash the bight to the door and then drop the bar? Brawny men, rampaging mad, will probably rip the doors off the hinges –"

"Mag–gie. Harlot. In Ironmonger's Lane. Hold–ing." He had no breath left.

Leaning against the rope, Scarlett crabbed to the doors, still jammed by the manure fork. "Stand at that side, Tam, and open 'em when I nod. Help! They're killing Sir Redmond! Mercy!"

At a nod, the bar dropped and the doors whisked open. Four soldiers charged in, swords outthrust.

Squinting in the dimness, they tried to fathom the strange scene. Scarlett cleared his throat and a man whirled. "Stand fast, you —"

Scarlett flipped both hands in the air. "I surrender!"

The rope whizzed around the post. Released, the half-suffocated Redmond swung towards his soldiers like some weird war engine. Howling, the soldiers ducked.

Scarlett grabbed the manure fork, rammed a man in the belly to bowl him into others, dashed past. Tam squirted by.

The two pelted down the alley, Scarlett still clutching the manure fork. Tam huffed, "Where're we — bound — now?"

"To see — a harlot named — Maggie."

Naked, a soldier straddled a harlot named Maggie in a squalid room with a low ceiling and walls of water-stained daub.

The door rattled and a boy stumbled into the room, peering in the gloom.

The soldier jumped clean off the bed. The jezebel finger-combed her hair.

"Oh, forgive me, sir." Tam goggled at the nude woman. "I were looking for my mother."

"Well, she isn't here, for pity's sake." The soldier's long body was riddled with scars edged in dirt. Surprise turned to anger. "You young whelp. I'll —"

He swatted at Tam's head, but the boy ducked neatly as a market cur. While the soldier cursed and flailed, Will Scarlett lunged through the door with a manure fork.

Deftly, the outlaw bracketed the soldier's throat with twin wooden tines and shoved him across the room by his Adam's apple. When the soldier's head hit the wall, Scarlett slammed the fork so the tines bit the daub and held. Gagging, the soldier clutched at the wooden haft. Scarlett ordered Tam to lean on the fork. Dubiously, the boy pressed.

"Sorry to trouble you," the outlaw smiled. "Won't be a moment."

He whirled on the harlot, who scrabbled under the mattress for a knife. Scarlett boosted her rump and dumped her on the bed. "Be easy, dear. This is business. Where's the money Redmond the Blackbeard gave you to hold?"

A shake of the head. "I don't know what —"

Ancient Gretchen creaked into the doorway. "Maggie, help the gentleman out. He's a friend of the poor."

"Oh." Bright as a squirrel, the woman hopped off the bed, bouncing in all directions. Tam's eyes bugged so he almost dropped the quivering pitchfork. Maggie plucked up a floorboard and drew out an oilskin pouch big as a pig's bladder.

Scarlett tugged the laces and tipped the pouch into his hand. Silver pennies by the dozens spilled out. The outlaw gave a handful to Gretchen, another handful to Maggie, then tugged the strings. "The rest for the poor."

"That's me," said Gretchen. She snatched the sack and drew another handful. "For my old age."

Scarlett took the sack with a grin. "You know, I like this. They accuse us of stealing the payroll so, as penance, we do. Even a bishop would bless us. Maggie, do you need bruises to prove this was beaten out of you?"

She shrugged, jiggling. "I got bruises."

"Da-a-a-a!"

With a roar, the naked soldier ripped free of the wall. Menacing as a skinned bear, he threw the fork and Tam aside, and lunged for the outlaw. Scarlett jerked Maggie into his path. The soldier grappled to hurl her aside, and Scarlett clouted him with the oilskin pouch. The sack split and silver sparkled around the room. The soldier collapsed on the bed. Scarlett swore. "Drat!"

"Din't you hit him kind of hard, Da?"

"Serves him right." All and sundry picked up coins. "He's supposed to be scouring the streets for us, ain't he?"

Gretchen wheezed, "How will you escape

Nottingham? The sheriff's men will search house to house, and Redmond's men roam the streets."

Scarlett knotted the rent pouch and stuffed it down his shirt. "Hmm. Can't go as a soldier. Hate to use a trick twice. And Tam's too tiny..."

He stooped to the floor, picked up Maggie's lousy gown. "But where there's a Will (Scarlett), there's a way."

Tam's eyes grew round. "Oh, no, Da. Not that. Please!"

A short time later, a tall woman and short girl limped and stumped down a muddy trashy street. They carried baskets as if bound to glean turnips from the fields.

"You won't tell Katie, will you, Da?" Katie was Tam's arch-nemesis in the Greenwood.

The outlaw pulled his feet high from the mud, tried to wiggle like a woman. "Well, now..."

"Oh, Da, you wouldn't."

"Shh, keep your voice down. No, we can skip this part." He pulled his bonnet straight, batted at his skirts. "How do women walk about in these, anyway? They flip up a lot easier than they hang down. No, poor Katie's too delicate, I'm afraid. She'd laugh herself into apoplexy. And talk her tongue loose telling the world. And get no sleep for heckling you. No, her health'd never stand it. Now, Polly, Tom's girl, she's sensible. We might tell her..."

"Da!"

"Oh, all right. We'll tell 'em we stole swords and cut through half a hundred men. They won't believe that either, but it's a better story. Still, I can't help think we're forgetting somethin'."

"You forgot to get Robin's — Oops."

They'd come within sight of the gate, found it crammed with the sheriff's blue guards and milling soldiers. The gates were open, though, as peasants sought a dram after a thirsty day. "What now, Da?"

"Try calling me Ma, for a start. Hmm... We could wander till dark, but they're even guarding the hidey-hole under Saint Mary's. No, we need something —"

From behind came the rhymthic jingle of horse harness, and they instinctively trudged aside. Scarlett cooed, "Ah, Saint Dismas blesses us today. Now pay attention, son..."

Blackbearded Redmond was disheveled, red-faced, blind with fury. Spurring hard, he thudded past them to the gate, yelled obscenely at the soldiers to stay alert, and wheeled his horse, it stumbling in mud.

As the knight cantered back up the road, a wife and daughter intercepted him. "Here, now, what's this? Get away, you slut."

The tall woman clutched his stirrup to gain his attention, warbled, "Oh, sir, I seen him. That thievin' rogue, Will Scarlett, a pox on his name. He's hidin' in a barn nearby, sir. He tried to feel me, sack me womanhood!"

"Bloody hell, get away!"

In a man's voice, Scarlett said, "See, son? Liars never believe anyone."

The knight's eyes bugged. He opened his mouth to yell.

Scarlett plucked a cudgel from his basket and walloped him on the knee.

Redmond howled and jerked his leg back. Will caught his boot with two hands and heaved. Redmond almost broke his neck crashing in the mud. All up and down the street, people yelled.

"Hie, Tam, let's be off!" Skirts flapping, Scarlett belly-flopped across the high Norman saddle, swung around and kicked for the stirrups. He scooped up his son in one brawny arm and slammed him across the pommel like a gutted deer as soldiers came plodding.

Will wheeled the horse and laid about with the cudgel. He clopped a soldier on the hand, smacked the horse between the ears, clipped Tam's heel, dinged a helmet. Finally the horse faced the gates, and he dug in his heels with a "Hy-ah!"

A flash of brown, they flew through the gates. Peasants scattered before the mad horseman, gawked when they saw an ill-dressed woman and scrawny daughter slung like a sack of grain. With a maniacal yell and laugh, Will tossed his bonnet to the wind. Unclear what transpired, the peasants cheered nonetheless.

Their cheers died as a trio of cavalry pounded out the gate after the felons.

Will glanced behind, saw they were gaining. Lurching, drumming, steering desperately for drier spots, Scarlett hollered, "You'd think a false knight would keep a fast horse!"

"Da-a-a-a-a!" Tam had slipped so low his bonnet trailed in the road. His hands gripped the cinch strap and his skirts drooped around his ears. A round and pink bum smiled up at Heaven.

Will clutched a skinny ankle with one hand, wrenched the reins with the other. "Just like your mother! Hiking her skirts wrong place wrong time! Hang on, I've got a plan!"

"Th-is w-a-s a pl-a-a-an!"

The horsemen drew abreast, grinning at the chase. They yelled at Scarlett to rein in.

Will laughed. Stuffing reins in his teeth, he fished in his shirt and drew out the torn pouch. He whipped it high. Silver sparkled in the sun. "Share it!"

The next time Will glanced behind, the riders had scrambled off their mounts to pick coins out of the mud. One waved at the fleeing felons.

"There you go, son," laughed Robin's cousin. He smacked the boy on the rump. "That makes an end!"

And they disappeared under the trees.

Abjuring Justice

Something splashed and thrashed, croaked and choked in the dark river.

By moonlight and the odd fire, Robin and Marian saw silver swirls in the placid Thames. Robin Hood floundered in, dredged up a gasping weedy mess. If his hands didn't betray him, it was a girl coming to womanhood.

Marian cupped an ear. "Someone's coming, Rob."

"Good. She's heavy."

"No, enemies, I think."

Cursing, Robin slung the waterlogged girl around both shoulders like a sheep, stumbled onto a muddy shore treacherous with fish heads and rotten nets.

Marian waggled her long Irish knife so it glinted by starlight. The onrushing pack seemed to be four sailors. A Mediterranean accent rasped, "Give her up! She's our charge!"

Arms full, Robin Hood backed away. "Why did she flee, then?"

"That's none of your concern."

"Fortune deems otherwise." Robin balanced the wet weeping girl on his shoulders while crabwalking away. Marian backed, knife outthrust.

The dark man cursed the sailors. "Take her!"

"Catch us first!" The outlaws whirled and ran. The rogues shouted belatedly and gave chase.

Up the beach with his retching bundle loped Robin, vaulted the old foundations of London's south wall, plocked amidst the mucky streets. He gulped hot air that stank of sea-coal smoke. Marian struggled to keep up in her red gown and chain belt with jangling keys. "Damn these skirts."

"Glad I'm an outlaw — and know how to run." Robin Hood puffed as he pounded along. "They must — feed this girl — oats and hay. Run ahead and sound the alarm."

"They'll thrash you."

"No they won't. Go."

Hiking her hem, white legs flashing, Marian sprinted fleet as a deer. Five blocks later, in Ironmonger Lane, she clattered into their alley and courtyard keening, "To arms! To arms!"

Not a minute after, Robin rounded the corner. Hard at his heels clattered the four villains. But from a tall house erupted a score of armed outlaws shouting "Sherwood!" and waving swords. The dark pursuers whirled and scampered down the alley like scalded dogs.

Robin Hood levered the mute girl to Marian, grabbed tiny Tam, Will Scarlett's son. "Get after those rascals and see where they go. Scoot."

Marian shooed people inside. The band's temporary home was a two-story hall with deep lofts and a massive fireplace. Crowded by green-clad outlaws of all ages, the Vixen of Sherwood propped the mute girl on a stool and called for more light. She was Saxon blonde, big-boned, pale from near-drowning, red-eyed from weeping. Her gray wool gown was worn thin over burgeoning curves, and bright welts marked her neck and shoulders. Oddest, the tip of her tongue protruded so she couldn't close her mouth.

"Why's her tongue stick out?" asked young Polly.

"Who whipped you?" demanded snub-nosed Katie, fourteen years' worth of indignation. "We'll cut their hearts out."

"Hush, all," Marian clucked. "Open your mouth, dear."

Mewling like a kitten, the girl complied. Her

tongue crammed her mouth so she could only croak.

Dark-tressed Marian combed the girl's straw-blonde hair, picked out eel grass, brushed away tears. "Can you understand me? Nod if so." Eagerly the girl bobbed her head.

Robin Hood shouldered alongside. "What's five and six?" Fuddled, the girl showed ten fingers, then one more. "She's not an idiot – Ow!"

Marian slapped his shoulder. "Men. Don't fret, dear. You're safe. But what was done to you? What swoll your tongue? Did someone pinch it with tongs?"

A tearful shake of the head. More grunting as the girl pointed to the rafters, where hung herbs, onions, hams, black puddings. Between shivering and weeping, Marian couldn't fathom her meaning. "Never mind, honey. Whatever it is should be right soon. The Thames is the best healer of the sick, they say. Clara, fashion a caudle, please." Hot wine thickened with eggs and ground almonds. "Grace, fetch your spare gown. She's your size. You men –"

But the plucky girl had more to convey. Tearfully she pointed to her palm, trickled imaginary money into it, pointed to her breast, held up four fingers, pointed to Polly and Katie and other girls, mimed a lock. Then her courage gave out, and she broke down sobbing.

"Ease your mind, dear." Marian enfolded her blonde head. "You're safe. You're under the protection of Robin Hood and his Merry Men. We never let a woman come to harm."

"But what did she mean?" asked Katie. "Why did she point at us?"

"I know why," growled the outlaw chief. "And someone'll come to harm before the sun's up."

A pattering at the door announced Tam. "I saw 'em. I followed 'em. I know where they went."

"Stout lad. Gird, all."

"Not the children," ordered Marian.

"The children too," Robin countermanded. Amidst squeals and the rush to grab weapons, the

outlaw chief buckled on his battered leather
baldric, slid his father's sword from the scabbard,
grimly shot it home. "Set? Then let's go."

"Doughty of her to jump off a ship when she
couldn't swim. That's English courage."
The outlaws hunkered in silver-moon shadows
at the Dowgate, an inlet on the Thames. The
chuckling river was barely a furlong across and
jammed with fish weirs and boats. Tam pointed out
a vessel at anchor: broad-bellied and beamy, both
ends turned up like a floating shoe, no lights
showing.
"A bus. Little John and I rode one from Acre to
Venice. You could sail to the ends of the earth in
one." Robin Hood scanned the black shore where
cockles and wherries were hauled up. "Fishermen
fetch their oars home, but there should be some in
those shacks. Pray to Saint Theresa and break the
doors."
Minutes later, a trio of boats with rag-wrapped
oars glided wide of sleeping swans that might
squawk. The outlaws craned like hunting dogs.
Katie hissed, "Do we kill them?"
"No, lass. Outlaws just rob folks, remember?"
Three boats bumped the bus, and the Merry Men
swarmed aboard easily as climbing trees in
Sherwood Forest. Red Tom hurled a bucket and
bowled a sailor overboard. Gilbert Whitehand
screamed another into the Thames. Waking sailors
saw a bristling hedge of steel and leaped after.
The Fox of Sherwood went hunting. Striking a
lantern alight, he pried off a wooden hatch cover
and slid down a ladder. The steamy hold was
partitioned into stalls for freight, horses, or
passengers. One stall had a makeshift door nailed
tight, and a crying like hungry kittens behind.
"We've come to rescue you!" Robin seized a
mallet. "Stand clear!"
Three lusty blows smashed the barrier, then the
outlaw was swamped by four hysterical girls.

"You're safe, you're safe." He hugged them, murmured a hundred times, "We'll keep you safe..."

"That's it. Leaves just like that."

Three days later came a morning so warm people sought the shaded side of the courtyard. The rescued Nelda was no longer mute, the swollen-tongue spell having worn off. She pointed out a flower with three pink lobes in Marian's garden. "They bade me chew leaves like that, forced them into my mouth and gagged me, then twisted the gag until I – I –"

"Don't fret, dear. It's over and done." Marian hugged the girl's shoulder, then sighed. "That plant is Wake-Robin, or Cuckoo's Pintle. It has a cousin from Africa called dumbcane because it paralyzes the tongue. You couldn't call for help."

"Who would help me?" the girl asked, downcast. "My family didn't want me. I've no one but the Virgin."

"You have us." Childless Marian couldn't reassure the girls enough. "We'll protect you all. Won't we, Rob?"

"With arm and heart and brain. With our lives, if need be." But the notion of protecting someone turned his tone grim. The outlaw band had come to London seeking Little John, captured in a free-for-all with the king's men this past spring. Robin Hood had scoured southern England for his giant friend, and clues led here, but so far the city had confounded the forest lord, who inside its walls felt out of place as a badger at sea. Privately Robin prayed the rescue of five girls was a positive omen.

The girls were all blonde, pretty, virgins, and heartsick. They'd been bought for a pittance from destitute homes by a Saxon woman named Gervase. Herded to London, then aboard ship and below decks, they'd been turned over to a dark-skinned couple who'd plied dumbcane, flogging, isolation, and starvation to break the girls' spirits. Nelda had only slipped free by an oversight, then cast herself into the Thames for death or escape.

"But you've no idea of their destination?" Robin probed again. "Did they train you to any tasks, teach any foreign commands?"

"No." Nelda cringed at the memory. "We were forbidden to speak, whipped if we spoke or cried. Whipped for anything, and for nothing."

But with rope, not leather, Robin and Marian noted, so as to leave no scars. Neither had the girls been molested.

"We were too gentle," Robin growled. "We should have sunk the lot with chains on their ankles."

"I just wonder what happens next..." So far the outlaws had hidden the girls, fitted them with new clothes, stuffed them with food. They'd watched the bus from shore, but seen little. Meanwhile Marian kept them busy, setting them now to weeding. "You've traveled, Rob. Could you tell where that dark man hails from?"

"His accent is familiar. Not a Seljuk Turk. A Coptic, mayhaps. But I want to know where this Saxon woman is, the one buying children."

Skinny Katie had towed Robin's brown warhorse Puck from the stable. While the other Merry Women had adopted gowns in the city, Katie stayed dressed as a boy to exercise the horse at Smithfield and beyond. "But why did they want these girls? No one wanted me." Katie had been found wandering lost in Sherwood Forest.

Marian and Robin exchanged glances. The Vixen supplied, "There are evil schemes afoot in the world, dear. Never you mind."

Snorting, Katie mounted and steered for the short alley that led to the street. Robin Hood donned his quiver, picked up his bow, bound to teach archery outside the city walls. Marian turned for the kitchen to oversee the cooks. The five girls weeded diligently, glad to serve. Friar Tuck's snores rippled from the tiny chapel. But people were electrified when Katie and Puck danced back in. "Someone's coming!"

Into the courtyard sauntered a man in purple sendal, with hair and beard thin and blonde, and a face a riot of white pustules. Swaggering up to Robin, with a languid hand adorned with an agate ring he offered a rolled paper and the infamous pronouncement, *"Questio quid iuris.* A certain person has sworn out a complaint."

"A summoner." The outlaw chief snatched the paper and spat on the ground. The five girls quailed along the wall like chicks under a hawk's shadow.

"Robin o' the Hood is summoned to the ecclesiastical court." For all his choleric complexion, the summoner was phlegmatic as a morning lizard. "Under pain of admonition, or excommunication."

"If they're finally excommunicating sinners, I'll needs stand in a long line." The outlaw waggled a calloused thumb towards the alley. "You've dropped your bone, so begone."

The summoner lingered, nodding towards Marian, who propped grubby hands on hips. "T'is a sin for a woman to go bareheaded, but we can pardon it for a fee."

As Robin Hood whirled, the man backpedalled. He studied Katie atop the warhorse for a moment then, cool as a cat, sashayed away.

Marian tisked. "He makes my skin crawl. They always do."

"Would Our Lady's Church could do without them, but even She has dung to shovel." Robin broke the wax seal with his thumb, frowned, handed the summons to his wife, once schooled by nuns.

Marian pouted. "It's ruddy hard to read... *Virginis* is 'girls'... Here it is. We're to bring the girls to the archdeacon's court, and answer for 'theft of property.'"

"Property? That's a hell of a thing. And if the girls were 'property', it'd be a matter for the sheriff's court, wouldn't it? Like stealing a horse."

Marian shrugged helplessly. Friar Tuck waddled up wheezing. "The church of the ecclesiastics oversees spiritual matters, but also the claims of *miserabiles personae*: widows and orphans. Their jurisdiction lies wherever the salvation of Christian souls is endangered. Then the Pope is *judex ordinarius*, supreme judge."

"Don't you spew Latin too," Robin growled. "So the bishop might what? Seize the girls to save their souls —"

He blinked at sobs. The five girls ran stumbling into the house.

"No matter," snorted Robin, "God will see it right. Will He not?"

He looked to Marian and Tuck, but both just sighed.

Living in Ironmonger Lane, Robin Hood's Merry Men attended the parish chapel of Saint Martin in the Jewry in, Friar Tuck explained, the diocese of Archdeacon Jerome, so they were summoned to Milk Street near Saint Mary Magdalene, to an old Norman keep, one of many buildings the church had bought or been given. The curtain walls had been carted off and the moat filled in, but orange Roman bricks still marked their outlines.

Twenty-five tanned, scarred, scowling, knotty-armed outlaws in Lincoln green, men and women young and old, guarded the clutch of frightened girls. They wore only weapon-knives, for swords and bows were disallowed within the city walls. Still, a gang of drunken Frisian sailors circled them rather than cut through.

Ominously, it was Lammas Day, a haunted time. Nearby houses had crosses of rowan wood tied with red and blue thread over doors and windows to keep evil spirits at bay. The hot air reeked of latrines, roses, butchers' offal, willow trees, manure, incense, dust; and binged and bonged and clanged with the unceasing carol of bells of a thousand kinds.

Robin Hood peered at the keep's facade and huffed. "You can't all come in, so stay or go as you like. Here, shake my hand, all. Clasping is a sign of the cross, and we need the protection."

Bony Katie hugged big Nelda. "God's love. Robin and Marian will protect you." Crossing their breasts, the outlaw chiefs and Tuck shooed the five girls up wide stone stairs.

The main hall was partitioned with wood, and noise echoed off the ceiling. A clerk read their summons and ordered them against a wall. Friar Tuck kept clearing his throat and pulling his fat fingers so they cracked. Marian frowned in thought, occasionally asked Tuck questions he couldn't answer. Robin glared at every clerk that swished by in long robes, but most studied scraps of parchment or hardwood slates. The five girls huddled behind the adults, quiet as sparrows.

Once Robin groused, "My left ear itches."

"Someone speaks ill of you," Marian replied. "Bite your little finger to get back at them."

"Why so many clerks? They're thicker than bees in a hive."

"God's church has two arms," wheezed Tuck. "Church Triumphant for the spiritual, Church Militant for the corporeal."

"Two arms to rake in tithes twice as fast." Robin's sarcasm was dampened as a man with a noose around his neck was led downstairs and outside. His appeal to Mother Church had failed, so he was trundled off in a cart to be hanged.

"Let us pray the archdeacon's not in attendance, for he's said to be more corrupt than Satan's own summoner." The fat friar, who'd killed men and devils with sword and prayer, was terrified of facing his superiors. "We're lucky it's an ecclesiastical court, actually, for their sentences are usually lighter than the sheriff's court. Or the court of the king's bench, not that the king sits, for the citizens won't let him. A shame we're not under the Archbishop of Canterbury rather than the Bishop of London. He's said to favor pilgrims..."

"A pox on them all," Robin groused. "I'll never fathom the webs this city spins to entangle a man.

And all their vassals: watchmen, city guards, sheriffs, pardoners, summoners, wardens. Just the other day some fool 'alderman' demanded we keep full water barrels in case of fire. Said he works for the 'mayor', whoever the hell that is."

"And if this archdeacon is corrupt," sighed Marian, "his underlings will be ten times so. Hello."

A young tonsured man in a too-long black robe stumbled up, looked fuddled at the frowning outlaws and cowering charges. "Uh, I am Sedgewick. I'm to be your advocate for the trial."

"What's an 'advocate'?" snapped Robin.

"A promoter of justice. I'm to interpret what the court says and help you say the right things."

"All we needs do is speak truth."

Marian nudged her husband. "Thank you, Sedgewick. You're kind to help us."

"It's not me, milady." He was young, barely bearded. "It's the church insists you be fairly treated."

"It's these girls need fair treatment," Robin countered, and earned another nudge. Sedgewick shook his tonsured head absently, asked a few questions, excused himself to chase papers.

They'd been summoned to appear at the hour of Tierce, but the bells tolled Sext and they missed dinner before they were shepherded to the second floor. Friar Tuck cleared his throat as if a noose were tightening. The outlaws handed over their long knives, and Robin felt more naked than ever. Belatedly, Sedgewick tripped up and almost brained himself on the door frame.

The ecclesiastical court had formerly been the master's bedchamber, a large room paneled with wood. Outlaws and girls were escorted to the center and promptly ignored. Despite open windows along one side that overlooked the street, it was hot.

"Christ," muttered Robin. "Who are all these folk?"

Prodded, Sedgewick identified. In the corner was a deep chair raised knee-high. The occupant wore a black robe, a three-peaked hat, and a signet

ring big as a guinea coin. Radiating from his
throne were chairs for canons, doctors of law and
theology, monkish assessors and auditors. Most
were bareheaded and tonsured, or wore small red
hats that covered their ears. At the rear of the
room was a table for scribes chalky and inky. In a
corner lounged the pimple-faced summoner.

"Where's the jury?" asked Robin.

"There isn't one."

"Isn't one? Henry decreed a man must be judged
by a jury of his peers."

"In the king's court. This is the bishop's."

Robin knew less every minute. He nodded at the
dour man in the high seat. "Is he the archdeacon?"

"No, that's his agent, the judge *delegate
officialis*. Brun D'Ager. He has a degree in the
Decretum Gratiani from Oxford."

"What's that?" asked Marian.

"Canonical law."

"A lawyer runs a church court?" harped Robin.
Marian shushed him. There was some new
beginning. Officers of the court lobbed legal catch-
phrases in plodding Latin and lyrical French.
Sedgewick answered questions from the court, so
Friar Tuck and Marian struggled to translate.
Robin ignored Tuck, whose Latin was rote-learned
and garbled, yet Marian stuttered too.

"They have to prove the, uh, competence of the
court. *Domocilium*, that's our house... in the
diocese, so we're in the right court... *Res mixtae* is,
uh, matters civil and churchly, um, mixed
together, complicating things. *Jus praeventionis.
Jus, jus*... Um, either court has authority, or both
do, so they do... They go so fast."

"I thought you spoke Latin," objected Robin.

"To sing hymns. To read the holy word. This is
as far from holy words as one can get. Don't shout
at me."

Friar Tuck prayed from the High Mass.
*"Miserere mei, Deus, secundam magnam
misercordiam tuam.* Have mercy on me, O God, in
Your Goodness."

Robin Hood glared him into silence, then

snapped his head around. Amidst the doggerel he'd caught the word "Huntingdon." He hissed at Marian, "How did they learn my title?" Robin hated to have his noble birth touted.

The Countess of Huntingdon shivered as if surrounded by wolves. "I don't know. They must have spies." Behind them, the girls whimpered as a quartet was escorted in. Robin and Marian got their first real look at the girls' persecutors.

Foremost strode a man in black robes, a proctor, a hired lawyer. Then a woman Saxon-blonde and blocky, clad in rich blue and a wimple wilted by heat. A dark man with a black beard and a gray smock belted with rope. A woman wrapped head to foot in brown, only her dark eyes showing.

"Those two are Saracens, Muslim infidels," breathed Robin Hood. "They must be servants, or slaves, else they couldn't move through the city. What's this Saxon woman playing at?"

Sedgewick hissed, "She bought the girls you stole."

Robin glared at the advocate. "Freed. Christians shouldn't to be held slaves. Whose side are you on?"

"God's." But Robin Hood sniffed in dismissal. The man was dozy as a stunned rabbit.

The plaintiffs were Gervase; Phineas, an Egyptian name; and Drisana. Their proctor began to recite from notes on a slate. Robin and Marian listened thunderstruck.

Gervase, the proctor explained, bought unwanted girls, poor girls whose parents could never afford a dowry. She saw them installed in a nunnery so their lives might be dedicated to God. As proof, he exhibited five chips of wood marked with black Xs: receipts from illiterate fathers or uncles releasing their daughters to Gervase's care. A flowery document from an abbess in Lisbon stated the girls would be received as novices. A statement by the local sheriff asserted Robert Locksley, Earl of Huntingdon, likewise known as Robin Hood, had invaded the Saint Stephen, terrorized and assaulted her crew, and stolen away the five girls. The ship's manifest listed five names that matched the five receipts so...

"Deny God!" exploded Robin. He jabbed Sedgewick in the back, rocking him. "For Christ's sake, stop this farce."

"It's balderdash," Marian put in. "How can she transact business? The weaker sex are prone to sin and need to be watched." She didn't believe that, but knew these men did. "Where's her husband?"

Blandly, the villains' proctor explained in English, "Phineas, here, is her husband-to-be."

"What?"

"She's been passed unto Phineas's care by her father, the marriage contract sealed. Though in this case, with her father and uncles dead, and no close male kin, a priest acted in *loco parentis*."

"But he's an infidel. A Christian woman can't marry —"

"Marry, no. Be betrothed, yes. In the meantime, he studies and prays to convert to Christianity, and shall, when God judges him worthy."

"But if she's betrothed to him —" stammered Marian.

The proctor nodded. "Under common law, all her possessions pass to her betrothed."

"God's fish and teeth," burst Robin. "That includes the girls. You can't surrender Christian girls into the hands of a Saracen satyr!"

"True," came the bland reply. "It isn't mete. So the girls pass into the care of this woman, Drisana. Phineas's wife."

"Wife? He can't have two wives."

The proctor waved that away. "Before he converts to our faith, he'll put Drisana aside. Once baptized, he'll acquire juridic personality, then marry Gervase."

"When Christ comes back." Robin choked on his anger. "Meanwhile, five girls are crammed aboard a ship like cattle. What about that?"

Fumbling, Sedgewick phrased a question in Latin, then turned miserably. "The ship is protected under the 'law merchant' that guarantees the goods of foreigners aren't unfairly seized."

"Goods? Damn their forked tongues and infernal babble. Anyone can see what they're up to."

Marian caught his brawny arm to shush him, but he bellowed at the hushed court. "By the brow of the Virgin, what a scheme. Satan couldn't spin a web this tight. See how it signifies? It's −" His thoughts roiled like water through a weir. "You can't sell Christian slaves to infidels. Everyone knows that. Yet when Gervase buys a girl, she becomes the property of this heathen. She's not 'sold' but − I don't know what to call it."

"Assumed, mayhaps," put in Sedgewick. Robin had forgotten he was there.

"Aye, assumed. Then they sail to Lisbon, of all places. It's in a state of siege. It's not two leagues from the Dominion of the Almohads. These girls might be delivered to this nunnery, but I'll bet a hatful of crowns they're marched right out the back gate into Moslem territory and sold. Why else are they all blonde virgins? You've twisted law and custom to profit in white slavery. How many girls have you already sent down that dark road?"

Another infuriating shrug from the proctor. "Even were it true, the girls act as missionaries to convert the heathen. There's no danger to their souls' salvation."

"Which is why they chose an ecclesiastical court," gasped Marian.

Behind, the girls wept and wailed, and Marian was hard-put to hug them all. The canons and monks buzzed. Judge Brun sat as if carved from stone, obviously bribed, and now his accented English smoked the air. "Gervase acts within the law to bring poor girls to God. It is the judgment of this court the five girls be returned forthwith. Robin o' the Hood must not interfere again. Gervase and Phineas are free to bring damages against this interloper in the sheriff's court for disrupting their business."

"Business," blurted Robin Hood. "Selling the bodies of Christian girls into the hareems of bloody-handed devil-worshippers for lust? They fed the girls dumbcane, starved them, flogged them raw. Nelda here threw herself into the Thames to drown rather than be defiled —"

Lofty as God, the judge ignored this outburst, the muttering and whimpering, and barked in Latin to a clerk. Robin Hood clenched impotent hands, then gaped in shock. Through the open door to the corridor he saw his Merry Men shuffle and growl at the oily summoner, who cooed as if to chickens. Robin Hood made to march that way, but his wife snagged his arm.

"Marian..."

"Don't." Half plea, half command. "For love of Heaven, we can't brawl in God's court. They'll excommunicate the lot of us."

"We have to —"

"We can't fight them here, Rob. We — oh, no!"

From the midst of the foresters, the summoner towed a gangly girl in drab boy's clothes. Katie.

The court recorder caroled Latin. Marian and Friar Tuck struggled to grasp the intent. Dragged alongside Robin Hood, Katie chirped upon hearing her name amidst the gabble.

Sedgewick trembled at a question from the judge, then asked Robin and Marian, "Uh, do you admit to willful control of this girl, who is abominable in the sight of God, disapproved and forbidden by all law, that she be attired, dressed, and armed in the habit and state of a man?"

Dumbfounded, the outlaws could only stare. Then Robin erupted, "Wait, wait. I don't know how they do things here, but in a sheriff's court you finish one matter before starting another."

The judge gobbled, and Sedgewick shook harder. "The other matter is finished. Answer the question. And have you any documents to show ownership of this girl?"

"Documents? We found her hiding in the forest after her family was butchered." Robin's brain was boiling. His hands itched to strangle that smarmy summoner.

Marian breathed, "Dear God, they can't —" Katie

began to sob, and the Vixen of Sherwood hugged her into the circle of weeping girls.

Sedgewick listened to the judge, echoed, "*Quod non est in actis, non est in mundo.* 'Anything not written is nonexistent.' Uh, the judge would ask..."

"I'll be damned —" Robin sputtered, "We came to win five girls. I'll be damned to lose six."

"Hush, Rob," hissed Marian. "Hush. We can't win here. We'll try something else, but later. Just do as they say."

More Latin, more legal jargon, men snapping back and forth like curs over a bone, until finally the judge cut the charade short. "It is our decision that, since the girl has no clear owners, she be remanded to the care of this Robin Hood as before. But that she be attired in woman's clothing and so presented to an officer of the court before another day has passed. And for their ungodly actions, Robin o' the Hood and Lady Marian must recite seven penitential psalms once a week for three years; pay a fine of six shillings, eight pence; and fast every Friday."

Quills scribbled. Summoners blocked Robin and Marian while the five girls were hauled away shrieking. Blinded by tears, Marian called to Nelda, "Trust in God! We'll rescue you! I promise!"

The judge barked Latin. At the prompting of Sedgewick, Robin and Marian were forced to kneel and read the abjuration of their crimes, then sign it. The outlaw's hand shook with fury as he scrawled "Robyn Hode" in his schoolboy script.

Turning, he bulled through his Merry Men. Marian half-carried Katie, who wept with relief. A white-faced Sedgewick slunk away. Friar Tuck sighed with the weight of the world and rubbed his empty stomach.

Outside, in the heat of the day and a barrage of questions, Robin Hood clenched his fists. "I'll kill someone, that's what I'll do. I just don't know who..."

"Well, if we can't kill someone, what can we do?" Robin demanded of his wife. "Even standing on the shore, I could peg an arrow through that filthy blackamoor Phineas."

"Stop, Rob. It's no good."

The two again walked the steamy strand of the Thames. The river flared red in the late summer sunset. Robin walked when he was angry, and he'd walked miles today.

"We must pray for guidance and we must think," chided Marian. "We did the right and honorable thing, which was board the ship and free the girls. Now a court's undone all that, and would again, so we needs find another way. A legal way."

"Legal? We're outlaws."

"Trapped in a city with walls all around. We're no more free than the fish in that weir. Bashing our heads against bars won't help!"

"It was bribes did us in. That judge wasn't surprised by those twists and turns: he anticipated 'em. And that shaveling – What was he, an advocate? – was a bumbler, probably the worst in London, probably hand-picked by the judge. And that two-faced Phineas, planning to convert to Christianity. I'll be stooped and gray before he's baptized. And that Saxon woman, Gervase, buying girls like geese and spitting in God's eye. Hell can't be too hot –"

"Yes, yes. Old fish stinks. Now think. If those slavers can mishmash law and custom to their ends, then so can we. Before their ship sails."

Robin planted his foot on the gunwale of a beached wherry. "You're smart, Marian, you know that? I'm glad I married you."

"I'm glad too," she laughed, "else I'd be a spinster. Most men don't like smart women. Now stop gassing and start thinking."

"Will Stutly says that when we play chess. Think now... If they hide behind bishops and knights and pawns, how to breech their castle?.."

Two nights later, Robin Hood perched on a keg on a wharf near Dowgate under twin torches on poles. But he couldn't sit still, and kept hopping up, pacing, sitting, hopping up again. With him were only the older Merry Men such as Friar Tuck, Old Bess, and Will Stutly.

The outlaw craned at the darkness beyond the torches. "The night air is so cool. Hard to believe it carries fever. I wonder who'll return first? Hoy, there's Tom and David."

From a dark street, two foresters braced a thin figure who tripped on his black robe. Jolly Robin beamed. "Welcome, Sedgewick. Good of you to join us on such short notice and such a late hour."

"Join you?" The young lawyer burned with indignation. "Your men broke down my door! They dragged me out of bed, bade me don my robe or go naked! They forced me —"

Robin cooed, "Howsoever, we're glad you came. And think yourself lucky: some I'm summoned in the past couldn't dress first. Prop him on that rail, lads. We'll need him. Who comes now?"

Two more Merry Men and a grinning Tam Gamwell, who was small enough to scale a wall, pry open a shutter, and unbar a door. Their charge, judge Brun D'Ager, was ruffled but uncowed. "Beware, outlaw. You dice with death. I'm a duly delegated authority of Our Mother Church. Threaten me at your peril —"

"No threats, good judge," Robin replied. "Only a desire burning deep as yours to see justice done and souls saved. Pray, sit."

Black Bart's heavy hand mashed the judge alongside Sedgewick. Robin drummed his fingers on his wide belt and hummed *Summer is A'Coming In*. Others waited in silence. Finally, from the darkness came a scuffle and scamper like mice, then a bout of swearing cut short. "Ah, the last of our guests."

Five English virgins were shepherded by Marian. Prodded by swords trudged the child-buyer Gervase, the exotic Drisana, and lastly the

Egyptian Phineas, hands bound behind.

Judge Brun objected, "You have no right to accost these people. Your case was duly tried before God and myself and found wanting. Now —"

Torch light glistened on Robin's upraised palm. "Duly delegated by myself and Our Lady, I've convened court to review new evidence. And as witnesses we need members of the Church Militant. You and Sedgewick. True, this isn't an ecclesiastical court, more like a piepowder court." A panel of merchants that settled disputes in the marketplace. "But may suffice. Bear witness."

A smirk belied his pomposity. "Friends, we all know Phineas, a Muslim, has studied to convert to Christianity when God feels he's ready. In our chapel, Friar Tuck and I prayed for a sign and, thank the Virgin, we think Phineas is ready. Hallelujah! Tuck, if you please?"

Grinning, Friar Tuck smoothed his wispy curls, cleared his throat, and gestured grandly. Two foresters hoisted a squawling Phineas and dropped him into the Thames.

People gasped or tittered or cried out as the man floundered, but he'd plashed in waist-deep water and quickly gained his feet. Tuck waded in, robes and all. The friar keened the baptismal in a high singsong, added, "Lord, we ask that you receive unto your bosom this sinning infidel. I baptize this child in Thy name —" Hammy hands grabbing, he plunged Phineas's head beneath the black water. Bubbles exploded as Tuck prayed. The gasping man was submerged three times, then hauled up the bank before Robin Hood.

"I give you," the half-drowned man collapsed to his knees spluttering, "our newest convert, Phineas."

"Excellent." Robin backstepped to avoid the spray. "Finally a Christian: because we know even a forced conversion is a conversion, as many a former and unhappy Jew can attest. Is that not true, good judge?"

The judge only glared out of baggy red eyes. Sedgewick supplied, "T'is true. And 'by their silence they give their consent.'"

"So he's acquired – what was it?"

"Juridic personality."

"Thank you again, bold advocate. Oh, my my... Look how circumstances shift now that Phineas is a Christian. For one thing, he can only have one wife."

"One wife," blurted the judge, interested despite himself.

"Aye. One's plenty, as any husband knows. And Phineas already has a wife, there." He pointed to the dark woman in her concealing robe. "T'was said in court that Phineas planned to put Drisana aside before he converted, but he's gotten mixed up. Can't be married to one and betrothed to another, so..."

He pointed at the blonde woman, whose eyes glowed with hatred. "Phineas's betrothal to Gervase becomes invalid. She is released from the promise of marriage, but of course owns nothing, for Phineas assumed her property. Too bad. And since a woman isn't allowed to roam loose, can't be – help me here, advocate."

Sedgewick piped, "'Abominable in the sight of God, disapproved and forbidden by all law.'"

"Lovely. So, since she has no living male relatives (as attested in God's court), she must be remanded to the care of a cleric. Friar Tuck, would you step forward, please? Are you willing to take willful control of Gervase? Perhaps install her in a nunnery? To have her head shaved, forego all loving save that of Jesus, pray on her knees the livelong day –"

"She's gone, Rob," said Marian. Gervase had bolted into the night shadows.

"Oh, well," the outlaw clucked. "I've no doubt she'll find some new occupation. Rat catcher, perhaps. Uh, where were we? Oh, yes, the conversion of Phineas. Now, you churchmen, isn't it customary for a new convert to give the greater part of his wealth to Mother Church, in gratitude for receiving his soul unto her bosom? To divest himself of worldly possessions that he might begin his second life free and untrammeled as a spring lamb?"

Friar Tuck nodded, jowls jiggling. The judge said nothing. Sedgewick grinned. "That's been known to happen in a transport of ecstasy."

"I thought as much," Robin chuckled. "Now recall – But soft, what light illumes the night?"

Phineas spoke for the first time, his voice a shrill clack. "My ship! My ship!"

Faces were painted orange by a fireball drifting on the river. Crackling flames outlined the black hull of the Saint Stephen. Tarred ropes sparkled. The pool of yellow light rippled as it drifted towards the sea twenty miles distant.

"A pity," pronounced Robin. "But t'was always unlucky to sail on a Friday. And since there's no proof of wrongdoing, the destruction can only be an act of God. Let's see... Phineas controls these five girls. So – You look perplexed, good Sedgewick."

The lawyer shook his head. "You fly with dizzying speed, good sir, but I follow."

"Well and good. We'll – Hark." From the darkness on the riverbank came a low whistle. Robin Hood put his hands together. "The trill of an angel. How opportune, for never more did we need guidance. Let us all pray. Our Lady, Infinite Mistress Divine, send us wisdom –"

The outlaws bowed their heads, the judge and Phineas made to bow theirs. No one saw a figure limp from the dark, shove something against Robin's back, and limp away.

"– Thy infinite grace. Amen." Robin opened his eyes to discover an ironbound box in his hands. "Behold, a gift from the Virgin."

"That's my strongbox, you thief!" Phineas spat in impotent fury. "You dog, you heap of stinking camel dung! Mine!"

Robin Hood rotated the box. Metal chinked. "Nay. T'is a plain box, with nothing to suggest it's yours. Didn't we learn just the other day that 'Anything not written is nonexistent?' But I'll grant a boon. If, Brother Phineas, in your ecstasy, you see fit to give ownership of these five girls to our Mother Church, not in Spain but here on the Thames (Friar Tuck is handy), I will bestow on you this coffer, to hie you along your new and righteous path."

"Yes, all right." The dark man lunged for the strongbox. "Take the damned wenches. Just return —"

Robin whipped the box aside. "Tut, tut. Sign there, please."

"*Scripta manet*," echoed Sedgewick. "'What is written endures.'"

From the folds of his vast cassock, Friar Tuck plucked a paper and lead pencil. Marian cut the Egyptian's bonds, for unbeknownst, other foresters had melted away. Scowling, Phineas scratched his name, grabbed the strongbox, and dashed off into the dark. Forgotten, Drisana galloped after. The freed girls raced to embrace Marian, Robin, other foresters, each other.

Robin sailed on smiling. "And so, five Christian girls are wrenched from dire slavery and returned to the bosom of the church. Let us raise our voices and sing Hosannah, Hosannah, Hosannah!"

His shouts drowned out a scuffle up the dark street. Momentarily, Will Scarlett limped up and, with a grin, offered Robin a suspiciously familiar strongbox.

"Behold what good deeds hath wrought. Our Lady again showers us with wealth." Robin Hood beamed at the dazed crowd. "(Bear with me, we've almost arrived.) In celebration of our fine luck, I propose that, this money having descended from the Virgin, it be divided amongst these virgins, for their dowries against marriage, or entrance into a convent, or guild fee to learn a trade, or howsoever they wish. Have I your permission, good Tuck?"

"Bless you, my son," intoned the fat friar. Marian and others laughed merrily.

Stepping to his barrel throne, Robin Hood bashed open the box. Silver sovereigns, guineas, crowns, half-crowns, and even gold spilled in a heap. The girls squealed with delight. Grabbing a double handful, Robin waved the rest away.

"Blessed be." Robin waggled fists full of money. "Good judge Brun, may we, in all fairness, see you stamp approval on our transactions?"

The tired judge watched the fists as if weighing them. "You'll brook no argument from me." Robin shook the man's hand, careful not to drop any coins.

Robin turned with the other fist still clenched. "And you, good Sedgewick, we thank for your efforts. Mayhaps associating with outlaws will make you a better lawyer. Saint Germain ended a bishop."

Sedgewick laughed. "I can honestly say I've learned a few things." They shook on that.

The King of Sherwood dusted his hands, squinted at a rising sun. "A good night's work and a new day dawning. Perhaps t'will bring news of Little John." He wrapped his arms around Marian, kissed her on the nose.

"'Make a chore a game and enjoy it,' my husband says."

"A veritable Solomon, he must be. Remind me never to engage him in chess." Robin peered across Marian's head where Will Scarlett and Gilbert Whitehand shuffled up. "Ho, Will. What's become of Brother Phineas and Drisana?"

Looping an arm around his son's shoulders, Scarlett sank onto the keg and scratched idly. "Clumsy bloke smacked his head on something in the dark. We helped him up, but both of 'em tumbled right out of our hands and landed in a bus. They must have rolled under a tarp, for we couldn't find 'em. The crew will, I suppose, once they reach the Germanies. But the poor buggers might be tooken for infidels and end up slaves."

"I want to find that scummy summoner." Unhampered in her boy's clothes, Katie took a practice hop. "I'll kick him where it counts."

"You've my blessing to try, but I suspect he's a eunuch," chortled Robin. "Oh, I've said it before, and I'll say it again. Thank God we're outlaws and not honest men."

Tilting the Tournament

"So this knight — he doesn't have a name in the story — was traveling to a tournament to settle a debt of honor. But he came to a crossroads and found a shrine to the Virgin Mary. So he stopped to pay homage, because he was so pious, but he lingered until dusk, see? He mounted and rode hell-for-leather, but it was too late. The tourney was over. But everyone acclaimed him champion because the Holy Virgin herself had descended from Heaven in disguise and jousted in his stead. D'ya see, Rob? You'll win if your heart is pure. D'ya see?"

"I see." Robin hadn't heard a word. A helmet wrapped his ears in straw padding and leather, his warhorse jigged under him with tackle jingling, and the shouting never stopped.

Robin Hood was one of two hundred knights in two long lines undulating down the tourney field like shattered rainbows. A roaring crowd pressed a rope fence, seemingly all of London, who'd enjoyed the Opening Parade and now chanted for the Grand Charge to begin. All along the lines horses stamped and their masters fidgeted while marshals in blue-and-gold tabards inspected lances, running both hands over blunt tips to assure all were wood with no iron, true "lances of peace". Tournaments were for practicing war, not waging it, even though three hundred knights battling for two days had yielded eleven deaths, so far. Robin was soaked in sweat, his gauntlets squelching, his helmet steamy. The horse staled, a rank salt smell, and its rider wished he might also.

As Marian chattered, Robin Hood studied other knights, since any might become an opponent or partner. He waited between a red-clad knight on a black horse and a gold-clad knight on a white. No faces showed, for all wore the newfangled "bucket helms" introduced in the last crusade. Farther down the line a red knight with a white eagle claw painted on his gypon and pennon fought a blonde horse that bucked and crowhopped. He pounded the horse's head to subdue it, and Robin hoped the man would be dumped and trampled. A pair of priests sprinkled holy water and Latin blessings, defying Pope Celestine's ban on tournaments.

Hidden inside his helmet, Robin Hood grinned like a wolf. Despite the danger and madness of jousting, these bold lines on a bright summer's day were a glorious spectacle for God and Man. And he was ready. He wore a new green helm bisected by a Maltese Cross, a gypon fresh-painted with his family's hunting horn and wheat sheaf crest, his father's sword and a new-forged dagger, and he carried an ash lance painted green with three red rings same as his famous arrows. Even his mount, a high-stepping roan destrier, was decked out, not with a horse cloth, but with green ribbons braided into her tackle and tail. Sex notwithstanding, the children had named her Puck, and she panted to run.

Around the field marshals signaled all knights were safely armed, then scampered for cover. The crowd roared approval. Robin Hood dragged up his helmet. Dark-haired Marian hung at his stirrup, dark eyes brimming with tears. She sniffed, "What I meant was, I love you. Please be careful."

Smiling, Robin bent and kissed her. "Don't fret, leman. I can't be hurt, for my heart is pure. Or yours is, anyway." Allan A'Dale's son acted as squire and held the warhorse's bridle. "Allan, remember. Keep off the field, no matter what happens to me. You could get killed out there. Understand? Then go." Marian and the boy retreated under the ropes.

High on a canopied balcony sat the Lord Mayor of London, the Archbishop of Canterbury, and King Richard's Chief Justice, since the king campaigned in France, who waved to begin. The tournament's king-of-arms raised his staff. A kettledrum rolled. Two hundred knights lowered lances. Robin Hood couched the butt in his armpit, settled his shield on his left arm, scrooched his bottom in the saddle.

For a moment all was calm. Pennons snapped. Horses' ears twitched.

A trumpet blared.

"Go, girl! Hey, yup!" Swept up in a giant wave, Robin Hood and Puck walked, quick-walked, cantered, then galloped. Neck in neck, knee to knee charged the line until the ground rolled by dizzyingly and eight hundred hooves drummed like thunder. The opposing line of knights grew tall and thick as a thorn hedge, until details leaped out: a horse's brown eyes rimmed white, brass tacks on a bridle, a black helmet with black eye holes. Robin's vision suddenly filled with a white gypon and red lion and matching shield. Keep the tip up, keep your shield close, keep your knees together, keep your arse down... The painted lion loomed large as a real one, a wooden tip reached for Robin, who aimed dead —

Robin's lance swept past brown ears and slammed his opponent's shield just left of center. The blunt tip skittered and snagged the iron rim, smashing the lion shield and oncoming lance wide. All in a second. Something belted Robin's shoulder, a horse's rump banged his knee, then Puck burst clear of the line where the crowd hollered in the distance. As trained, the horse dropped to a canter, then quick walk, then slow walk. Robin drifted up his lance but found it curiously light. Waving it before his eye holes showed only two feet jutted above his gauntlet. He laughed, "A chaste lance tells a craven hand." Puffing, Robin tossed the stump and wheeled his horse to see what was left of the Grand Charge.

Chaos. Horses milled and spun. A few knights were dismount, a few on their backs. Riders calmed frightened beasts and Robin remembered to praise his. Two knights had their tackle tangled. One knight dangled from a stirrup by a pulped ankle. A grudger had drawn sword and slashed at a foe while men-at-arms interposed halberds. Squires dodged flashing hooves to aid their masters, but one boy was kicked and fell hard. Marshals and London city guards pushed the crowd back. Sweepers cleared splinters and manure. Judges tallied grievances and heralds shouted incoherent results. A new widow wailed. The band thumped and wheedled while a dance troupe capered before the balcony. Priests scurried to drape monks' cassocks onto dying men, for a knight killed in tournament was denied a church burial – unless he first took the cloth.

Robin couldn't see the white knight he'd struck, didn't know if he'd unseated the man. He did note the red knight who'd abused his mount suffered a common problem: his bucket helm of mild steel had been bashed so hard he couldn't pull it off, so his squire led him by the hand to find an armorer. The archer muttered, "Serves you right, you vicious lout."

One scene set Robin's curiosity buzzing. Judges clustered around a body stretched on the field while more officials ran up, then more. Kneeing Puck to the sidelines, the outlaw dismounted and tossed Young Allan his reins and helmet. Raking back sweaty curls, he strode towards the commotion with his scabbard banging his calves. Marian slipped under the ropes and trotted to catch up. "Are you hurt?"

"Eh? Oh, no." He grinned and she smiled in relief.

The downed knight lay on his side because a long red lance jutted from his breast. His yellow gypon was bloody from neck to belt. A priest administered last rites while marshals pointed and argued. Robin Hood shouldered close and swore in surprise.

138

Catching the shaft in two hands, he pressed a shoe against the dead man's breast and yanked the lance free. It was painted red with a white spiral and bore a bloodied pennon. Robin Hood wiped off gore with his gypon's hem. "I'll be damned."

The lance was shod with an iron spike long as a man's hand and tapered like a dart, with the tail firmly socketed in a shaft sawn square.

"Deuced queer. And look." Marian plucked something from the dead man's breast. A red splinter big as a man's finger had pierced the cloth gypon but been stopped by leather-studded armor. Robin Hood tried to match the splinter to the lance, but there were no chips or gouges. Unsure what it meant, but reluctant to discard it, Robin Hood slipped the splinter down his mail shirt.

He thumbed the iron spike with a frown. "I've never seen such a thing. A Norman war lance is like a long arrowhead with a collar outside the wood so it don't fetch up when it strikes. And how did the marshals miss this?" Unfurling the bloody pennon showed an eagle claw, white on a red field. "Whose device?"

"Here now." The lance was snatched away by a chunky pockmarked official. King's colors edged with ermine marked him as the Tower of London's master-at-arms, today overseeing the tournament as king-of-arms. "Who the hell are you?"

Normally Robin declined to use his titles, but now seemed expedient. "Earl of Huntingdon, Sir Robert Locksley, elsewise Robin Hood of Sherwood Forest." Earls ranked highest on the social ladder below royalty, but it was the latter name, heard in ballads, that made knights and officials murmur. "I ask again. Whose lance?"

A junior marshal consulted the list of contenders where a heraldic crest was sketched beside each name. "Sir Redvers of Kersey. Is he here?"

"God's love," barked a burly knight. Everyone turned. His black coat displayed an eagle claw before a red chevron. "His helm was stove in so he couldn't doff it. He was led off the field."

"Show me," said Robin.

"Hold hard. I'm in charge," snarled the king-of-arms. Feeling Marian's gentle hand on his elbow, Robin Hood nodded and begged pardon. The official's anger no doubt stemmed from guilt, since his marshals had inspected all the lances. "Show me, by your leave."

Robin and Marian squeezed into the party that entered the "knights' village" north of the tourney field. Tents of all shapes and sizes were plain or brightly painted in house colors. The black knight conducted to a conical marquee with roof and seams striped red. Painted and plain lances, neatly tied in a bundle, and a banner pole leaned against a weapons rack. Three picketed blonde horses cropped hay.

The guide threw back the tent flaps to reveal piles of horse tackle, travel chests and sacks, armor and clothes. On an erratic bedroll lay a man, lopsided as a discarded doll or a drunkard. His red gypon was bunched around his neck, exposing chain mail and baldric and sword. The black knight froze. "Jesus wept."

Robin and Marian crowded after the king-of-arms and marshals and judges. Marian, who knew healing, pushed past, dropped to one knee, pried up the knight's eyelid, touched his eyeball and saw it flinch. Tilting his head wet her hands with blood. "Someone's like to have crushed his skull."

"His helmet was knocked in." The burly knight pointed. The battered red helm lay near the knight's hand.

The king-of-arms picked up the helmet, inspected it, tossed it down. "Bah. Let me see his other lances."

Marshals pushed back the throng at the tent flaps. Outside, officials untied the bundle of lances. Robin Hood trailed and craned his neck but kept mum. Three lances were plain wood for practice, two were painted red and white for jousting, but all were blunt without spikes or crows feet. The king-of-arms threw the bloodied lance among them and stamped back into the tent. Momentarily alone, Robin Hood tucked the death lance out of sight under the tent wall, though he couldn't have said why.

Inside, amidst hurly-burly, Robin Hood picked up the fallen red helm and found it crumpled along one side. He showed the black knight. "This doesn't seem crimped tight enough to trap a man's head. And did Sir Redvers pluck it off and then black out? Or did an armorer pull it off? Or did his squire — Where is his squire?"

"Yes, where is that dastard?" The black knight's shaggy blonde hair and beard were damp as Robin's own from jousting. "I'm Quincy, steward for Sir Redvers's manse in Sudbury. My father was vassal to his father."

Marian wet a rag from a water bottle and mopped Redvers's face and scalp wound. "T'was a savage blow. He mayn't wake ever, poor soul."

Sir Redvers's servants had been found, and the king-of-arms stepped outside to harangue them. Marian asked Quincy, "Would Sir Redvers flee the field because he killed a man?"

"Never. He's a mickle courteous knight."

Robin Hood frowned. "Did Sir Redvers know the knight in yellow? Would he wish him dead?"

"I've no idea. I never saw him before. Who was he?"

A junior marshal reported, "Sir Peter of Bath."

"Clear across the kingdom from East Anglia."

"So he cou'n't have known him," said Quincy.

"They may've crossed swords *en meleé*," Robin objected. "We've had two days of hard fighting. And feuding."

"But could Sir Redvers pick him out in the charge?" Marian arranged the felled man comfortably and drew a blanket over his breast. "We saw you all crammed into line cheek by jowl. You don't choose opponents aforehand, do you?"

"Nay," said Sir Quincy. "It's chary enough to charge straight ahead."

"He's right." Swept up in an irresistible mass, Robin had simply attacked a random opponent as the lines closed. "It'd be the devil's dilemma to vie for a special man."

"Mayhaps he was killed accidentally," mused Marian.

"No one can find his infernal squire." The king-of-arms returned, angrier than ever. "And t'was no accident Redvers plied that iron-tipped lance. That was deliberate."

"No, I meant — any dead man would do. No." Marian persisted, "Any man dead would do."

"Bells have tongues too, and hollow heads. Stifle your prattle, woman."

"Venerate the Virgin, sir, and those cast in Her mold," Robin grated. "How mean you, Marian?"

"I mean," Marian's brown eyes burned luminous in the tent's red-yellow glow, "if you can't strike with certainty, perhaps any victim will do. Killing an innocent man would be a ghastly game, but t'would mark Sir Redvers as a murderer."

"Poppycock," snorted the king-of-arms. "Sir Redvers killed Sir Peter plain as plain. Wielding that war lance'll cost his spurs, if not his life."

"How is it," drawled Robin Hood, "he did wield an iron-tipped lance? Your marshals inspected all our tips before the charge. No knight left or entered the field, nor accepted a lance over the ropes or from a squire. So how'd the ironshod lance gain the field?"

"Damned if I know. Satan must've sent it into his hand. Or some alchemist transformed it with witchery. We've seen that before."

Marian rolled her eyes. "'Beware the door with too many keys.' What is it, Rob?"

The outlaw chief only shook his head, and stood rooted, thinking. Marian wiped her hands on a blanket and waited patiently.

Curses sounded at the flaps, and into the tent bulled a knotty dark man in a blue gypon with a yellow trefoil of arrowheads. He carried a three-lobed sword and matching dagger high in front as if eager to draw steel, and his spurs were gilt. A grizzled man-at-arms attended him. The blue knight stepped straight to Sir Redvers and felt the pulse in his neck. The king-of-arms asked who he was.

"Sir Stillwell, Viscount of Foriers."

"Of Kersey," added Sir Quincy. "Cousin to Sir Redvers."

"Cousin?" Robin Hood echoed.

Sir Stillwell spun on his heel and lifted his bearded chin. "Is that some business of yours?"

"Not a whit. I beg pardon." Yet Robin asked Sir Quincy, "If Sir Redvers is derogant, stripped of his knighthood, even beheaded or hanged, who profits?"

"Eh?" Sir Redvers's vassal looked puzzled, as did others.

Robin Hood pointed. "Sir Redvers wears a king's ransom in ring mail, and gilt spurs, and a sword from Milan. He's got servants aplenty and three bonny horses. His fief must be extensive."

"Oh, aye. He's got a big keep and three manors, hunting lodges and granaries and orchards and what all."

"And heirs? Who inherits?"

"His sons are just babes." The burly knight made a face. "The castle 'd descend t' —"

"Curb your tongue, Sir Quincy, lest I jerk it from your jaw. I'll not have my name bandied by a homager." Sir Stillwell shook a fist, then swung it toward Robin. "And you, sir, ask impertinent questions."

"Milord Earl, you'd best call me, Viscount. And my questions beggar for answers."

"Fie. You besmirch me and my cousin." Stillwell snatched a gauntlet from his belt. "Will you apologize?"

"Will you apologize, milord."

"I challenge thee." Sir Stillwell flung the glove at Robin's face. "To combat. To the death."

England's quickest archer snatched the glove from the air and lobbed it back. "Unknot thyself, pray. New blood won't wash out an old stain."

"Your blood will expunge the stain on my honor."

Robin Hood swallowed his temper, refusing to play along, then shot blind. "I don't recall your crest illumined the parade or Grand Charge."

The blue knight was too furious to speak, or feigned so. His man-at-arms growled, "My lord the viscount hurt his leg in a joust yestereve, so couldn't ride this morn."

"Yet he'd joust now?" Robin asked innocently. "I take advantage."

"And how is it, good sirrah," Marian pouted in thought, "all these knights look newly baptized, so wrung with sweat are they from jousting, and so do you?"

Stillwell unconsciously raked back matted hair. Then sneered to Robin Hood, "Muzzle your bitch."

The archer's hand flashed. His sword sizzled from its scabbard to slit the tent's roof, admitting a long whisper of sunlight. Sir Stillwell jumped back on two good legs. Robin Hood growled, "Arm thyself, vagabond."

"Bide, Rob." Marian's strong hand pressed down his arm. To Stillwell she pronounced, "We'll meet you in the lists."

Stillwell stormed off with his servant in tow. The scowling king-of-arms had the bout tallied on the afternoon roster, ordered a junior to watch over the benumbed Redvers, then departed, as did others.

Robin Hood sheathed his sword and stroked his beard with a shaking hand. "Clever, that Stillwell, to spy a way to avoid questions."

"You've already one duel to surmount," sighed Marian. "S'why we partook of this folly in the first place."

"Sing hey for the morrow. Today I'll bounce Stillwell on the turf and see if he cracks. But how is 't I always suffer these disaccords?"

Marian tapped his armored breast. "Ask how a lodestone attracts iron."

Robin Hood shared a pavilion tent with two partnered brothers from Cumbria. Most of his gear was either new-made or bought or lent, for he truly did give to the poor. Marian and Young Allan helped him shuck his gypon and the Damascan mail borrowed from Gilbert of the White Hand, which constricted Robin like snakeskin. Donning a tattered shirt, the outlaw breathed freely for the first time since dawn.

Then stooped, for the red splinter had fallen from his shirt. Robin frowned. "Where does this damned thing belong?"

Marian patted a blanket beside her. "Eat." Ale and bread and cheese made a light dinner, then the couple rested at the tent's mouth, for it was hot with Midsummer just a fortnight past. Marian napped, but Robin was too wrought up to rest. "I'll visit the jakes. 'Haps 'pon my return we can close the flaps and tilt in the blankets."

Marian smiled with her eyes closed. "First we needs inspect your lance, see it be blunt or sharp." Chuckling, Robin tousled her hair and passed outside.

He checked that Young Allan guarded and tended Puck, found the boy dampening the horse's legs with water, drying them with grass, then currying out the chaff. Satisfied, the Knight of Sherwood threaded a maze seeking the "necessaries".

The knights' village gradually merged into the fair that had sprung up in this tree-ringed vale north of London. Jumbled together were wooden stages showing miracle plays, animal pens, a mock castle and ship, archery ranges, gambling dens, football games, cockfights, water wagons, rings for Cumberland wrestling, open-air chapels, pig roasts, traveling shrines, heaps of manure and vegetables and hides and ashes, a bearded lady, fantailed peacocks, dancing bears and monkeys, drunken pirates, scolding friars, near-naked women, screaming children, barking dogs, caroling hawkers, capering jugglers and acrobats. And ale bars at every hand. If any man in the crowd were sober, Robin Hood didn't meet him.

Distracted, the outlaw failed to immediately recognize the grizzled man who stepped from behind a hay rick. The man's stance and face were grim —

— and belonged to Sir Stillwell's man-at-arms. Robin whirled, his speed taking the aggressor by surprise.

Then Robin was surprised as something smashed against his head.

"A bout of honor to the death! Between the Earl of Huntingdon, Sir Robert Locksley in green, and the Viscount of Foriers, Sir Stillwell, in the blue!"

The herald boomed Norman French to London's high-borns through a leather megaphone while another herald echoed Saxon English to the masses at the ropes. People booed Sir Stillwell and cheered Robin Hood, having picked favorites in two days of pageantry.

Signaled, Sir Stillwell rammed heels into his blue-draped white warhorse. The two exploded through the roped-off southern entrance, thundered onto the tourney field, and reined back hard to chop grass and dust. The crowd jeered, then fell silent and waited. Stillwell had the field to himself, and he smiled inside his hawk-faced helm.

Marshals checked rolls and dispatched pages. The crowd murmured and catcalled. The king-of-arms signaled the herald to announce the next bout when a cheer arose at the north entrance.

"God's wounds!" Sir Stillwell gaped as onto the field rode a knight in green bucket helm and gypon who carried a kite shield and sword and lance. The roan warhorse stepped lively so ribbons fluttered while Young Allan trotted alongside with spare lances. "It can't be. It can't be!"

No inspection was made, no rules given. The knights were only admonished to use "no magic, nor charm, nor potion for this contest, so God might favor the righteous and decide the outcome." As would iron-speared lances and razor-sharp swords. Yet Sir Stillwell trotted his horse to the field's far end in a daze. "How? How?"

A drum warned to prepare. *Bom-bom!* The two knights squared off across seventy yards of scarred turf. The blue-clad Sir Stillwell craned on his white horse like a raven crouched on a chapel, trying desperately to grasp what he saw. It was impossible, but there sat Sherwood's knight, though slumped in the saddle with his upright lance wobbling.

A second warning. *Bom-bom, bom-bom!* The crowd roared like a rainstorm as the knights lowered lances. Stillwell swore in perplexity. He watched Robin Hood brush his helmet back to better see. The clumsy bucket was loose —

In a flash, Stillwell understood why his opponent looked so small and ill-equipped. Horrified, he croaked aloud, "Wait! Stop —"

Came the charge. *Bombombombom bombombombom...*

Trained to war, Sir Stillwell's horse launched into a gallop. Stillwell gulped and hung on and lifted his lance tip by instinct. Wind sailed through the eye holes of his helmet, his body thrummed to the drumming hooves, yet he cursed steadily, damned by honor to finish this farce. He steered straight for the four nails on Robin Hood's shield, aiming to skewer the painted hunting horn. Yet the green knight bounced in the saddle so wildly his shield and lance bobbed. Mocking me, Stillwell thought. Fueled by fury, he crouched, raised his lance tip —

A double crash resounded as Stillwell's lance smashed Robin's green shield so it slammed the green helm and gypon and bowled the Knight of Sherwood from the saddle.

Stillwell dropped his cracked lance and wheeled his warhorse. Flat on his back, the green knight kicked feebly as a crippled turtle. Yet still the blue knight cursed. Vaulting from the saddle, yanking his sword, Stillwell marched to loom over his helpless opponent. "Damn your meddling! You've sullied my honor before all England!"

Panting, Stillwell lowered his sword point to his enemy's eye hole. Instantly the outlaw fell still, ripe for the death blow. Yet Stillwell flicked his wrist and flipped off the green helmet.

To reveal Marian.

"Body of Christ." Stillwell's voice rang hollow in his own helmet, so he doffed it to clunk in the dust, a signal the joust was over. "I knew it. You've ruined me."

Marian's dark eyes blazed as she struggled to her feet, dizzy but game. Blood ran from her nose and cheek where the helmet had bashed her. Raven hair entangled her sweaty face. Leaving her husband's shield lying, she drew his sword with two hands in clumsy gauntlets.

"So you knew t'was I." Marian spat blood and snot. "How did you know?"

"You tawdry jade — What?" Stillwell watched her heft the long blade. All around, the crowd had fallen   silent.

"How did you know t'was I?" Marian hoisted the sword like a darksome angel. "How?"

"Uh, I didn't." Sir Stillwell was flummoxed. Nothing in a knight's training had prepared him to trounce a woman. Honor and horror held him hamstrung.

"I'll tell you." Despite sagging armor and clothes and a scabbard that dragged in the dust, Marian advanced while the big bony knight retreated. "You knew Robin couldn't appear because you kidnapped him."

"I — didn't." Stillwell stumbled back from her basilisk   glare.

"You did! Where is he?"

"I —" Stillwell's mouth worked, helpless even to speak.

Marian of Sherwood swung. Stillwell flung up his shield, and the sharp blade skinned paint and wood from his heraldic trefoil. Another blow struck sparks from the iron rim with a nerve-paring screech. Marian lunged to stab his belly, was parried by the shield. She swung high and left and chipped more iron. All the while she shouted, "Where's my husband? Where is he? Where?"

Backpedaling, Stillwell caught his heel and crashed on his back. Two-handed, Marian slung the sword towards heaven to chop down –

– and Robin Hood hit her in a flying tackle.

As the dust settled, the husband clambered up, holding onto his wife for support. Despite his weakness, Robin Hood laughed to see Marian like a child playing dress-up. After him staggered the red Sir Redvers, pale and propped by two servants. Officials ran from all over while the crowd cheered louder than ever. The king-of-arms guffawed, "Mother of God, what a woman!"

"Oh, Robin!" Anger evaporated, Marian hugged Robin until he grunted. "I feared you'd been killed!"

"No, just bunged." Robin Hood rubbed his sore head. "Thanks be to a thick skull. I woke up tied under a pile of blankets and kicked my way out of a tent. But you shouldn't have posed as me, Marian. You could've been killed."

"No, I couldn't, silly." Marian hugged him again. "Love was my shield."

"She should have been killed." Sir Stillwell snapped. "Posing as a man to spoil our sport."

"But she's not the only poser, is she?" Robin's face hardened. "You posed as Sir Redvers in the Grand Charge."

"I? You're cracked."

"I'm cracked because you crowned me, same as you sapped Sir Redvers early this morn." Robin massaged his sore pate. "You donned his red gypon and joined the charge, but just barely, for his blonde horse bucked at a strange rider. After the clash, you pretended your helm was jammed on, then slipped into Redvers's tent and switched gypons back. That's why his garment was bunched around his neck. It's why you were all a-sweat, belying your blither about a game leg."

"Why should I pose as Sir Redvers? It's balderdash."

"You posed as him to kill a man with an illegal lance and thus poison his name."

"And how might I, or anyone, bring a war lance onto the field?" the knight sneered.

"With this." Robin Hood fished in his shirt and held up the long red splinter. "I wondered where it fit, since the murder lance bore no nicks. But I didn't search wide enough."

"You're mad!"

"See if Sir Quincy agrees." Robin pointed outside the rope barrier. Everyone turned. "He's been sifting the rubbish swept up after the Grand Charge."

Trotting as fast as armor allowed came Sir Quincy with the iron-tipped red-spiraled lance and a clenched fist. Drawing near, he proffered red and white splinters speckled with horse manure. "S'all we could glean."

"It's enough. My gracious thanks." Robin Hood fanned the splinters across his palm, then closed his fist around the lance's gory spike. Together the splinters almost covered it. "A lance of peace concealed a lance of war."

Marshals gaped and the crowd strained as Robin explained, "Some joiner or crofter carved a thin wooden cup to cover the fatal spike, then painted the lance in Sir Redvers's colors so cleverly the marshals never saw the joint. Who'd notice inspecting a hundred shafts? In the mad charge the hollow head shattered on a man's breast and gored him with iron. So was an innocent man killed and Sir Redvers condemned. Thus would Redvers's lands forfeit to his next of kin — to you, Stillwell."

"Fairy tales. There's nothing you can prove."

"A witness will vouch. Sir Redvers's squire escorted you off the field, Stillwell, aiding your disguise. Then the dastard disappeared. No doubt he hides. What did you promise him? His own fief once Sir Redvers's lands descend to you?"

"I won't abide —"

"Will you abide that my wife turned the tables? As you posed as Sir Redvers, so she posed as me, and upset your plot. Marian's more clever than you with one eye shut."

Enraged, the blue knight stooped to snatch up his sword, but the king-of-arms stamped on it. "Never again sword, Stillwell, and neither spurs. More likely a rope." Marshals caught the knight's elbows and hustled him away.

"Oh, Rob." Marian snuffled blood on her husband's shirt. "I so feared you were dead and dumped in some ditch."

"Oh, my pet. My honeybee. My shy little desert rose." Robin Hood kissed his wife's tousled hair. "Why did you meet Stillwell in the lists? Why not just run to the marshals?"

"I wanted to thrash him same as you would." Marian piffed. "Imagine his shame conceding to a woman. And my heart was pure, so I couldn't lose."

The wise husband didn't contradict, only chuckled. "And since an image of the Virgin jousted in my stead, neither could I."

Mandrake and Murder

Squaring the Circle

The song rolled on and on, crooned by children's voices. "... Where hast thou been since I saw thee? On Ilk-la Moor Bah T'at!.."

Muddy to his shoulders, Robin Hood growled, "For Christ's sake, Will, pick up a spade and pitch in."

Will Scarlett yawned. "Beg pardon, Coz. I'd love to, but all the spades are in use."

"You can have mine," the outlaw chief groused. "How anyone can ply a wooden spade the livelong day is beyond me. I'd sooner dig ditches for corpses at Acre again."

"... I've been a'court-in' Mar-i-lyn! I've been a'court-in' Mar-i-lyn..."

"You might see if Kerwin'll lend his," said a peasant. A glint in his eye matched his grin.

"Who? And don't call me master. I'm no man's master."

"Sorry, uh, Robin. Kerwin's our smith." The villager pointed to a shed that trickled a plume of smoke. "He's got a spade with a steel edge."

Robin Hood studied his shovel. Made of ash, it was sturdy, but the end dull as a turnip masher. "I might do that. But why isn't this Kerwin helping us?"

The village headman had a cast in one eye, so Robin never knew where to look when he spoke. "Kerwin has good days and bad. It's only Gwen there, his wife, keeps him civil."

Marian spat mud off her lip. "Keeping a man civil is an occupation for a lifetime."

153

"Very well. I'll test Kerwin's mettle, and his metal spade." Climbing out of the trench, Robin Hood handed his wooden spade to Will Scarlett, who wedged it under his rump for a seat. Little John's boot nudged the handle and Scarlett tumbled into the trench with a squawk. Marian laughed, until Robin swatted her seat and tumbled her after.

Robin squelched across the marsh, past yellow cowslips and lavender lady's smock, and plodded up the hill. He nodded to glum Gilbert of the White Hand, who stood watch. A withered right hand forbade the Crusader from plying any tool but his Milanese sword.

Walking backwards up the hill, Robin surveyed their progress. The village of Thirbycliff clung to a wooded slope above a valley where the rivers Rother and Doe Lea mingled. Sluggish creeks sliced the valley bottom into a torturous bog. Descending the forest one day, Robin had ventured that a drainage ditch cut between the rivers, would dry out fifty acres for tillage. Fens were being so drained all over the East Midlands. The villagers had been keen, and Lord Leonide, whose fief it was, agreed to pay for their labor. Now in autumn, with crops in, time slack, and insects on the wane, the villagers and the Merry Men dug. Sixty-odd people made muck fly, but it was man-killing work with wooden spades.

"... There wilt thou catch thy death of cold..." Endlessly, the children sang a new "circle song" that chased its tail. Mounting the slope, Robin Hood heard the thud of the blacksmith's hammer like an erratic countermelody. Pungent charcoal smoke tweaked his nostrils. "Hello, the smith!"

Inside the dark hut, the artisan struggled to round a red-hot harness ring on his black anvil. Robin boomed, "Ho, Wayland. May I borrow this marvelous spade I hear of? T'is said —"

"No, you mayn't."

In the gloom of the windowless shed, Robin saw Kerwin was thin, knotty-armed, and sour-faced. His tongs slipped, and the ring bounced and scorched dirt. The man slammed down his hammer. "I've been telling folk all morning. No."

Robin Hood frowned, crossed his arms, and leaned on the door frame, which leaned too. "I should think the most important man in the village, with all his skills —"

"Be damned to your false flattery. You ain't getting my spade. Be off."

Robin Hood stayed put. "Might I ask why? It seems a selfish thing, with all your neighbors pitching in, and you owning the best tool for the job. All stand to benefit from the assart." The improvement of land for cultivation.

"Belike they'll die in their beds, or get wandered off."

"Eh?"

The man's eyes glowed like the coals in his forge. "You shouldn't meddle with that marsh. I've seen rings left by the good people's dancin'." He meant fairies. "And white hares. And will o' the wisps to lure a man into a sough. Trespassin' in their kingdom'll mean bad times f' all."

"Bosh. There's plenty of fen for feys and men. (Oh, that rhymes.) Come, lend me your spade —"

"No."

"I'll pay —"

"No!"

Far out, the children sang in round, stitching the sky with skeins of song. "... Then we will come and bu-ry thee..."

Robin Hood wanted to throttle the cranky smith, but choked his temper. As his eyes adjusted to the dimness, he spotted a short shaft leaning in a corner. Both men jumped, but the quick outlaw snatched the shovel handle.

Kerwin blocked the door. "You'd take it, like a thief?"

"Like a man in need, not a dog in a manger. I'll return it when we're done. Step aside."

"If I don't, what? You'll kill me?"

Robin Hood snorted. "I've no doubt you'll meet a bad end, but not by my hand. You've the right to be surly, and friendless. Good day."

The smith grabbed the archer's arm, but an iron grip was no match for a hundred-pound draw. Shaking him off, the King of Sherwood passed into daylight.

"... Then worms will come and eat thee up..."

"You took Kerwin's spade away," marveled the headman. "Not many 've done that. He can't be left smiling."

"He's lucky to be left with teeth." Then Robin laughed at his own sour notes. "Move aside. I can dig to the Wash with this tool."

He checked the edge to make sure it was tight. A strip of steel had been riveted along the wooden bottom for a cutting edge, albeit red with rust. "You'd think he'd polish the apple of his eye." Pressing aside sedge and tansy, Robin Hood kicked down. The shovel sank with a sigh of pleasure from both of them. And the iron, Robin noted, would keep fairies at bay.

"... Then ducks will come and eat up worms..."

Merry Men and Thirbycliffers dug and dug along a line of stretched yarn. Robin led, slicing a trench one blade wide that everyone else enlarged. Then someone yelped. People crowded, cried, and muttered prayers for the dead.

From the bottom of the trench jutted a brown hand.

Kneeling with long Irish knives, Robin and Marian scraped crusted muck while villagers craned to see. Three feet down lay a youngish man, painfully thin. Airless mud had preserved the corpse, dyeing his skin and hair and shirt brown as the peat.

"What are these stitches?" Marian fingered feathery curves along the clammy shirt's hem.

"Palm leaves," said Robin, "a sign he's been to Jerusalem. He must have followed Richard – Hoy!"

A weight like a sack of flour flopped across Robin Hood's back. Blonde hair swept past his ear. Gwen, the blacksmith's wife, had fainted.

"It's Lester!" cried a woman. "Lester. He marched off to the King's Crusade and we never heard from him. We thought he died." Wails sounded as Gwen was laid on clean grass.

"Look here." With her knife point, Marian moved the dead man's slimy hair. His temple had been punched in, a neat square hole.

Robin Hood mused, "This poor bugger walked all the way from Jerusalem only to die in the last mile..."

"That explains the lights over the moor. T'was his ghost walking abroad," rasped the headman. "It were seven, no eight, year ago a friar come and sermoned us about fighting the heathen. T'would be a boon to God, he said. Lester's eyes got shining bright. He stole his father's sword — he were a derogant knight — and marched off. That's the last we ever saw o' him."

"Gwen waited and waited," added his wife, "then married Kerwin. He'd wanted to wed her since forever."

"I wonder what broke his head?" mused Robin. "Wait. Where's his sword?"

"Ain't it there?"

"No." Marian scraped dirt to uncover a black streak of leather, then punctured it. "Scabbard, but no sword."

"Maybe he lost it in battle," opined the elder, "or sold it get home."

"Why keep the scabbard, then?" Marian looked at her husband. "Rob? What's the matter?"

The outlaw chief stared at his muddy spade. Slowly, laying it on his knee, he scraped off muck with his knife. "Gil, look."

The exposed metal was not plain hammered steel. Rather, rippling lines thin as wheat stalks showed how the edge had been folded and refolded dozens of times by a master armorer. Gilbert the Crusader grunted. "Damascan."

"That's what I thought." Brushing gunk off his trousers, Robin Hood tramped the marsh and marched up the hill.

Kerwin waited outside his smithy. Streaks of soot down his nose resembled black tears. He spoke without prompting.

"Aye, I killed Lester. I met him on the road one

day when I was making for Staveley. He was
returnin' from the Holy Land, strutting like
Chanticleer, either him or the devil in disguise.
Claimed he'd come back to marry Gwen. I said he
couldn't have 'er. He drew his sword. I hit him with
m' hammer."

"Then buried him in the bog by night," said
Robin, "in soft soil."

"Aye. I hoped in digging your damned ditch
you'd miss his carcass, but no such luck. I never
had any."

Down on the fen, Marian shooed the villagers to
dig farther along while elders pried dead Lester
from the peat. Marian raised her voice to start the
children singing again.

"... Then we will come and eat up ducks..."

Stroking his beard, Robin Hood watched awhile,
then grunted. "No witnesses, he had a sword, and
you only a hammer. Sounds like self-defense and
n'more."

"No more." Kerwin stared with hollow eyes
while his wife Gwen sobbed and sobbed over the
brown-stained corpse. "All I ever wanted was her,
and now she's gone back t' him."

"... Then we will all have et thee up..."

"We never would have guessed," continued
Robin, "but you were too good a smith. You
couldn't waste that exquisite sword of Damascan
steel. You forged a piece onto the end of your
spade."

"Aye. And the cursed spade found him."

"... On Ilk-la Moor Baaaah T'atttt!"

Fathoming Fortune

"Dast you call me a liar? I'll flay your hide to bones, you sneering swine. Where's the royal forester? Summon him at once."

The shouting came from the long wooden hall not far from the village center. A brown palfrey cropped guelder roses. Petitioners queued at the door peered within. Beholding Robin Hood, they immediately beseeched him with a dozen requests and complaints. Fending with both hands, the outlaw pushed past into the Forester's Hall.

The counting house, or "office", was awash in scrolls, parchments, codexes, and books heaped on tables, squashed in a press, stuffed in wicker baskets on the floor, and even hung on the walls in burlap sacks. Every scrap, Robin knew, had to be sorted, read, answered, or recorded, but fortunately not by him, who considered the place a glimpse of Hell.

Two officials quailed before an angry knight. Tall and rawboned, he wore a gray gypon painted with two popeyed hawks' heads and a baldric and sword. A heavy quirt twitched in his hand like a horse's tail.

"I'm the king's keeper," said Robin. "Berate me if you must. What's your grievance?"

The knight sneered at Robin's tattered shirt and puckered hose, which contrasted so oddly with his silver hunting horn and Irish fighting knife. "You're never the king's keeper. You look like a beggar."

"I am royal forester, appointed by King Richard

159

for — many reasons confounded. Consider it a penance, and I've ta'en a vow of poverty. Call me Sir Robert, or Robin Hood. Who, pray, are you?"

"Sir Laird, steward to Lord Percival at Mount Royal."

"And where's that?"

"Where's — Up the hill, by the beard of Christ." The knight flailed his quirt in the air. "Viscount Percival is liege lord to all this valley, and I manage his estates. How can the royal forester not know that?"

"I stand in the wrong forest. Sherwood is my home." Robin wished he were there. This was the New Forest in England's far south. "Your grievance?"

"Your dastardly clerks would jew me out of a pound."

"All this shouting for a pound? I'd pay it myself to buy peace." Robin turned to his bailiff, the forest's true administrator. "Sloan, what transpires?"

"Sir Robert, we seek to collect all the outstanding fines levied by the last court before convening the next." Sloan was built like a bear, grizzled and scruffy in a forester's green shirt embroidered with a bow-and-arrow badge. A cast in one eye always regarded the ceiling, so Robin never knew where to look. "Sir Laird's fine is delinquent. We sent a note as a reminder, but — disagree on the amount."

"This's not what was levied." The knight flung a scrap of parchment, which Robin snatched from the air.

The sheep's skin had been scraped so often it was translucent, then chalked white, then inked in smudgy Latin. The scrawls meant little to Robin, who passed it to his bailiff. "What charge does this fine reconcile?"

"The verdict was 'waste without warrant,'" snapped Sir Laird. "A rascally family in a far hamlet felled king's trees without permission, then let their damned cow eat coppices. The blighters were fined for purpresture, but so was milord viscount. And me. The forest court claimed I should have kept better eye on the tenants."

Considering a steward's job was to oversee both land and serfs, Robin thought the accusation just, but kept mum. "And your fine was — what?"

"One pound, two shillings." The quirt jiggled in the air. "I was standing right there when it was pronounced. One and two is enough a small fortune, let alone two and two as your clerks claim."

Silently Robin agreed, since a steward might only receive five pounds a year in hard money. Helplessly he turned to his bailiff. "Sloan?"

"The attachment roll stands, milord. Show them, Courtland." The clerk was a dark and vacuous man in a forester's shirt with no adornment. Courtland unrolled an illuminated scroll calligraphed in Latin. With practiced ease he fingered Sir Laird's name and fine. "Two pounds, two shillings is set down —"

"Call me a liar?" Red-faced, Sir Laird flung back his quirt and slashed the air. The blunt whip smacked Courtland's ear and cheek, and knocked him spinning. Tumbling, his head whacked a door frame with a *clonk!*

Furious himself, Robin hammered Sir Laird's arm and stole the quirt. The knight drew steel. His sword sizzled in a vicious arc that barely missed Robin's belly. Backing, the knight's eyes jigged in their sockets with fear: he'd gone too far. Fending Robin back with his blade, he crabbed through the door and scuttling crowd, flung himself in the saddle, and drummed away in a cloud of dust.

"Curse the lout. With a bow I'd split his spine." Hurling away the quirt, Robin knelt by the sprawled clerk and felt his head. "No blood. Nasty, but just a bump, I think. Can you sit?"

"I — can." Dizzy, Courtland sagged, rubbing his head and wincing. The handsome clerk fancied himself a ladies' man, Robin guessed, for he sported a bronze ring inscribed *Pensez de moy*, "Think of me," and a slim leather belt whose bronze tips were enscrolled with lovebirds and flowers.

"Rest. And don't fret," Robin joked, "you've still got your looks."

Sloan had stepped to the door. "That bully. Temper like a bee-stung bull. He'll return to Mount Royal. Shall we send a pair of foresters to arrest him?"

"Tomorrow or after? That's too late." Robin weighed his forces. Foresters patrolled their bailiwicks by day, or days, so were unavailable. He lacked his Merry Men, only Marian, while the knight might boast a dozen retainers up at the manor. "We'll sic the sheriff on him. Who is it here?"

"No one worth mentioning." Sloan sought solace in straightening piles of parchment. "I shan't excuse Sir Laird, but neither can I fault his ire. We're all of us plagued by documents *soi-disant.*"

"English, please," said Robin. "It may sound like a dogfight, but t'is a useful tongue."

"Spurious documents, milord, counterfeits. Regard." Sloan took two scraps from a basket and held them side by side. They looked alike to Robin, who said so. "Exactly. That's our problem. We keep finding duplicate deeds with different names."

"So?" Robin Hood scratched his elbow. "I thought that's what scribes did: copy deeds and tot up sums. Besides, what matters? A man knows his own property, don't he?"

Sloan aimed a basilisk eye. "Generally, milord, but where the properties don't agree we can't levy the correct taxes and rents. You saw Sir Laird's reaction."

Robin Hood looked blank. All he knew of money was what he robbed from saddlebags and purses. "Perhaps I should —"

"Speaking of rents." A parchment came to Sloan's hand. "Here's another gone unpaid. The Cistercians along the river rent from us a *sylva de centum porcis*, 'a hundred-pig wood', but their woodward refuses to pay cheminage because the last swainmote —"

Robin raised his hands in surrender. "Sign my name and I'll swear to 't. Meantime, I'll whip up our sheriff. Where does he reside?"

"Good Sheriff Garrett 'works' beyond the hammer pond these days." Sloan rolled a cast eye. "But you'd get more busyness from my wife's cat."

Robin Hood only cared about getting outdoors, but first he had to brave the gantlet of petitioners. "Milord, my pigs — Never mind her pigs. My neighbor's laid claim to my woodfent — Sir Forester, I can't afford meat, so I were given a flitch of venison —"

"Talk to the bailiff." Robin avoided eye contact. "He manages the forest, not I. Talk to the bailiff —"

Striding, he broke free and fairly skipped along the village common towards the millpond, scattering chickens before him. Lyndhurst was named after the lime trees that adorned the hills stacked about. The village lay in a narrow bottom split into three fingers, and was comprised of a dozen cottages, a church and tithe barn, and scanty fields. Yet Robin looked to the forest. The lime trees made him homesick, for his beloved Greenwood was shadowed by a mountainous lime, half a hundred leagues north.

The lower end of the vale dipped to a millpond shored by an earthen dam and wooden spillway. Beyond it, a second pond was being constructed within new embankments and a taller spillway. The millpond was fairly clean, but the second pond, evil and oily, was dark as peat. A dirty stream trickled from it into bosky woods hemmed by hills.

And it reeked. An eye-smarting fishy fug made Robin's nose run. He hadn't smelled anything this vile since the trenches before Acre, where heaped corpses had rotted in desert sun. As Robin watched, a miller in a flour-dusty apron tipped a barrow into the lower pond, discharging pig offal and manure, dregs of beer yeast, spoiled grain, rotten cabbage, and a dead cat. The putrid offering touched off a boiling explosion of green heads and needle teeth that made Robin blink. That unlucky cat, he supposed, would be a skeleton before it hit bottom.

Perhaps two acres, the pond was unfinished. Dark water lapped at the heels of men and boys who toiled to enlarge it. They plied grub axe, mattock, slasher, and weedhook to fell trees and root up undergrowth. Nothing, Robin noted, was wasted. Trees became posts, branches became treenails and bavins, and leaves were dragged away for cattle browse. Saplings were trimmed into spars for roofs and fences and beanpoles, or split into wands for baskets. Topsoil was grubbed into baskets and sold for gardens, and rocks, clay, and sand were tamped into the dikes. Only thorn bushes were burned.

One man sat idle on a stool under a willow tree. Full-bellied, he dressed like a pauper in an undyed shirt, holed hose, and cracked shoes, and his only action was to pick up twigs and crumble them to bits. Occasionally he called for a lopper or feller to work harder, but otherwise rested. Robin could guess his identity.

"You're Garrett, the sheriff? I'm Sir Robert, the king's new forester." The fat man rose and slowly doffed his hat, but said nothing, so Robin added, "A knight assaulted one of my clerks. Sir Laird, steward for yonder manor."

"Has he now?" Groaning to vaunt a bad back, the sheriff creaked onto his stool. "Beggin' your pardon, milord. 'At's shameful."

Tools clashed and leaves rustled. Robin asked, "Will you arrest the villain? A sheriff's job is to preserve the peace and pursue justice."

"Oh, I know 't, sir." The man took no offense. Fat fingers punished a twig: snap, crack, snap. "But Sir Laird, he's a different sort."

"What sort?"

"Oh, you know." A stick waved vaguely. "No point tryin' to arrest him."

"No point?" Robin wanted to kick the sheriff's shins. "Call a hue and cry. Walk up the hill and accost him. Clap him in shackles."

"That's not how it's done, milord." Fat lips pursed. "You're new here'bouts, or you'd know."

Marveling at the man's lassitude, Robin asked, "How long have you been reeve of this shire?"

"Ah, since forever." The man smiled as if complimented. "My father were sheriff, so naturally I took it on. T'was my b'holden duty."

Robin wondered the word "duty" didn't stick in his throat. He turned to go, but then realized what he'd seen. "Sheriff, these men hag royal forest."

"Aye." Garrett nodded, sober as a cow. "I've a charter signed by Sir Dunton, forester b'fore the last. He 'lowed it because I'm improving the king's land in a dozen ways."

Catching a whiff, Robin snorted. "The stink don't improve the air."

"Ah, 't smells like money. Like raisin' pigs: 'The fouler the food, the sweeter the meat.'" Garrett smiled at his small jest. "The village gets shet of its garbage and gets back spars and firewood, men are workin', we're rootin' out vermin like foxes and badgers, and we'll have more meat for pies than we can eat."

"And you make a profit sitting a stool," noted Robin.

"Oh, a shillin' or two, 'haps. I done the hardest part thinkin' 't'up. Come to me in a dream while I were nappin' under this tree."

"Truly a gift from God. Good day, sheriff."

Shaking his head, Robin stalked off. He wanted to march up the hill and seize Sir Laird by the scruff of the neck, but couldn't do it alone unless he worked by stealth. If at all. The knight might go unpunished.

Deep in thought, he rounded the bend for the Foresters' Hall. Immediately he saw the queue of petitioners, who saw him, and the outlaw sagged at the knees. He'd rather mount a gallows than juggle complaints and palimpsests. Seeking sanctuary, he noted the sun slanted long through western trees. The day was old enough. Feeling guilty, he nonetheless diverted for home.

The New Forest was actually ancient, and home to ghosts uncountable. Under these trees blue-painted Picts and druids had burned alive Roman soldiers in wicker cages. Witches had sacrificed victims to the sun with bronze knifes. The Wild Huntsman and his phantom hounds sometimes rode in moonlight to sweep unwary souls to Hell. In a shadowed glade King Rufus the Red had been killed by an errant arrow, a death foretold by a naked spirit riding a black goat. Even the trees were queer, Robin knew. In glades and hollows never walked by men reigned prickly hollies, paired like animals male and female; the man-hating elm with its silent widowmakers; and the malicious yew that poisoned the ground. When night clothed the New Forest, villagers barred their doors, carved crosses in the wood, and hung garlic at every window.

Robin Hood had use of the Keeper's Lodge a quarter-mile removed from the village. A large house built on crucks like wooden wishbones, it was clad in boards and shingles with a chimney at either end. The name "Foxarbre" was carved into the lintel, which the Fox of Sherwood had taken for a good omen, until he saw a red fox skin nailed to the door. Vines in chalk circled the door frames front and back: unbroken lines to bar the devil from entering.

The lodge had come with a steward, a chamberlain, three maids, a cook and two sculleries, a hired hand and his boys, cattle, swine, fowl, three horses, two dogs, a ginger cat and, in spring, a stork who nested on a chimney pot. More than the new master Robin had muttered, "Half of Dorset hangs at my elbow."

As Robin sat down to supper in the spartan dining hall, Ralph the chamberlain poured him a foaming flagon of ale. Marian sipped wine, a taste developed among French nuns. A maid brought cabbage soup ripe with pepper, pandemain bread, cold sliced tongue, goat cheese, and blood pudding.

"And how was your day, other than short?" Defying custom, Marian sat catty-corner at

Robin's elbow, not at the table's far end. Further defying custom, she dressed like a man, though called her shirt a smock and her jerkin a bodice. Wood crackling in the fireplace made purple highlights ripple on her raven hair.

"A knight half-killed my clerk, then threatened me with steel. That was the best part of the day." Robin told about Sir Laird's quirt, Sloan's counterfeits, and the sheriff's indolence.

"Poor Courtland, caught in the backwash. He's not the first to be struck by lightning intended for Robin Hood," Marian teased. "If the sheriff won't act, you can always ambush Laird and thrash him. That's an easy fix. It's those counterfeit deeds seem the greatest danger to the forest."

"Not you too." Robin dunked his bread in melted butter. "I don't trust letters a'tall. Credit ledgers and bills of exchange smack of Jews and usury. A man's word and his neighbors' should suffice to identify his property. I lent Sir Richard at Lea money to pay back his mortgage, and it returned twicefold, and never a scrap of parchment passed between us."

"Piffle," returned Marian. "You, of all people, should know the pen is mightier than the sword. A stroke of a quill let the Sheriff of Nottingham steal your family's estate."

Robin Hood stopped eating. "True, but I was away on crusade and he reckoned I'd be killed. And he's a thief, so a liar. It's not the same."

"It is. Don't you accuse King Richard of selling tracts of this very forest for hard cash, then selling the same tract twice and thrice? Don't underestimate men of letters. An eagle can lose a brood to a rat that gnaws its eggs."

"I could stand to eat some eggs. And I ate rats at Acre and was glad to get 'em."

"Did you say Grace aforehand? Don't be crude. And don't change the subject. You could grasp letters and accounts if you wished 't."

"I've no wish to be a clerk." Robin shook his head. "The dons at Oxford would set the 'lered against the lewed', the learned against the unlearned. I'll remain a lamb of Christ and inherit the earth."

Marian laid her hand on her husband's. "A ram of Christ, perhaps. Stubborn and hardheaded."

"Careful," Robin warned, "I might smear ink on your smock."

"You spurn my caress?" Mock-pouting, Marian cranked Robin's little finger until, yowling, he and chair crashed on the floor.

Tilting her head, batting her eyes, Marian simpered, "No dessert? It's pears in ginger."

"Courtland's gone?" The sun had barely risen and already Robin Hood was besieged by his bailiff.

"Disappeared. Just when I need him most." Sloan absentmindedly sifted parchments. The other two clerks, a husband and wife, kept their heads down. "When he didn't arrive, I sent a boy to his cottage. He went out by night and never came back. He's not anywhere in the village."

Which left an entire forest, thought Robin, though he doubted a callow clerk would venture into the woods. He mulled possibilities. "Not in the village... Wandered off? Could his head wound have addled him? Unlikely... Waylaid? By whom? Any strangers would be noteworthy... I wonder if he ran afoul of Sir Laird?"

"Sir Laird?" Sloan's cocked eyes pondered the ceiling and door at the same time. "Because he thinks Courtland cheated him? He may've met him on the road."

"Laird and I have unfinished business," stated Robin. "Now's the time to brace him. And this time I'll drag along our sterling sheriff. He's not much, but all we have."

"Courtland was much. Two good hands." Sighing, Sloan turned to his work, parchments heaped like autumn leaves.

Dew still wet the path as Robin trekked down the vale to Sheriff Garrett's new pond. The *tok, tok,*

tok of a mallet told him someone worked already.

Past the first spillway, he saw Garrett wobbling in a flat-bottomed boat while hammering tall stakes into the pond's bottom. The stakes formed a narrow X. The portly sheriff looked up, almost upset the boat, and only saved himself by clutching tight to one stake.

"Good morrow, Sir Sheriff." Robin Hood climbed the dike above the stinking pond. "I catch you working. Perhaps pigs will fly before noon."

Garrett wiggled the two stakes to ensure they were seated, then poled his boat clumsily to Robin's bank. The outlaw's craggy hand brought the fat man to safety across stumps not yet drowned.

"You labor too hard, Hercules," Robin teased. "Callus those soft hands and folks will think you honest."

"I'm honest enough. It's my brain's callused." Garrett wore a deep belt pouch, and from it plucked a kerchief to mop his sweating face. The outlaw wondered if he carried his money in there, close to his heart. "And I needs drive the stakes myself to see 't done right."

"I nod to that notion," replied Robin. "Many's my plan has foundered for handing it to another. What do the stakes?"

"Oh." Puffing, Garrett gestured vaguely. "They mark the pond's center. I can sight the notch and judge how fast the water rises, so know how high to stack the spillway."

"Clever." Robin nodded absently. "And as you've spied since dawn, have you seen Courtland?"

"Courtland?" The sheriff wiped his face again, then folded his kerchief. "You mean, who clerks for you? No, I've not seen him. He's nothing to me."

Robin would have thought the last comment odd, but profit mattered to Garrett, not people. "He's gone missing in the night. Nowhere in the village, and I doubt he'd brave the forest. So I wonder if he's not ta'en by Sir Laird of Mount Royal. The knave's snappish and bloody-minded.

He may've come back to finish cracking Courtland's pate. I suggest we ask Sir Laird his whereabouts last night."

"Eh? Sir Laird?" The sheriff peered as if Robin babbled nonsense, then seemed to understand. "Oh, aye. A'course. I'll walk up the hill and talk to 'im. We can't have knights accosting our clerks and gettin' away with 't."

"Good." Robin was surprised by the sheriff's easy obedience, but then he excelled at inspiring others to duty. "I'll go with you lest he draw steel."

"What?" The fat sheriff blinked. "Oh, no, m'lord, you needn't do that. I'll go alone. Here, you take sumpin' home to your cook. I know Lucy. She can bake a rare fine crust."

Before Robin could object, the sheriff grabbed a long-handled net and basket from his low boat. Waddling down the embankment to the spillway, where the water sank deep, he dipped the net. Green coils boiled, and the net came out bulging. Garrett dumped the writhing load in the basket, then held it to Robin Hood with a grunt.

In the basket roiled a dozen eels. Dark shimmering green, a cubit long, the creatures had beady black eyes, fanning gills, needle teeth, and a rippling fin running half-round their bodies. As the eels thrashed and squirmed, slime oozed through the basket's weave. The topmost creatures would have spiraled and pitched out but for the sheriff's deft jiggling of the basket.

"They'll settle soonest. Make sure Lucy bakes 'em all at once. Water snakes gotta be fresh."

"I shall, good sheriff, and my thanks." The basket quivered in Robin's hand, and he leaned back lest slime spatter him. "I'll have a boy fetch it home. You'll need a good right arm to tame Sir Laird. I've handled criminals, having associated with such, same as our Lord Jesus."

"Jesus? Jesus." Garrett tugged off his battered round hat and smoothed his sparse curls. "Very well, m'lord. I'll just fetch my stick..."

The walk up the hill, hardly a "mount", was refreshing to Robin Hood but taxing to the sheriff. They found neither manse nor keep, just an outsized hunting lodge built of stone and beams with a stable, kennel, and mews. Dogs barked at the arrivals, and Robin bid a stablehand fetch Sir Laird.

The rawboned knight buckled on his baldric and sword as he bustled from the hall, no time even for helmet or hat. "What's this? I didn't summon either of you."

"Sir Laird." The sheriff waggled his walking stick as if berating a child. "We've come to arrest you for murdering Courtland, the forestry clerk."

Robin Hood stifled a groan. He'd have concealed their mission and vied for an unguarded confession. But Garrett was the law.

"What?" Sir Laird goggled like the popeyed hawks on his gray gypon. Behind, dog handlers and stablehands pricked their ears. "Murder? The boy barely grazed the door post. He was sitting up when I left, dazed and n'more. Now begone b'fore I loose the dogs on you."

The fighting man faced a fat sheriff and a vagabond with a weapon-knife, so he slapped a hand to his sword and exposed a foot of keen steel to send them packing —

In an eye blink, Robin Hood slammed his left hand against the knight's protruding elbow. Laird's own arm banged his face, stunning and blinding him. Robin's right hand caught the knight's pommel, whisked the blade from the scabbard, and flung it backhanded down the road. Stooping, Robin caught a boot and wrenched skyward. Hoisted heels over head, Laird's skull slammed dirt so hard he lost a patch of hair. A deerhide boot stamped on his stomach.

"That's grazing the ground," growled Robin. He leveled a finger at the knight's retainers, who stayed put. "Twice you've drawn steel, Sir Laird. Was it thrice during the night?"

"Night?" Breathless, the knight wheezed from

the ground. "I was abed by night! Ask my squire!"

"Who?" Robin barked. An older man with weak eyes answered, then recited in detail the knight's hours, all spent at home.

"Then 'xplain this." Sheriff Garrett had wandered away, Robin realized, but now returned. In his fat palm lay three objects: a worn ring inscribed Pensez de moy and two bronze tips snipped from a leather belt. "I found these in saddlebags in the stable. Where did you hide Courtland's carcass, Sir Laird? Down a well or under a manure pile? Or did you leave him in the woods for the wolves?"

"You're mad!" The knight puffed under Robin's foot on his gut. "Those things were never in my saddlebags! Someone's put them there!"

"Arise yerself, m'lord." The sheriff tilted his walking stick at a jaunty angle. "We'll walk to the village."

Dazed and dazzled, with Robin Hood clutching his elbow, Sir Laird stumbled down the hillside into captivity.

"So Sir Laird's hauled off in chains to the prison in Southampton, 'attached by the body', as our bailiff put it. Swears he's innocent. He even apologized for striking Courtland, though Courtland's not around to hear it. Still, I mislike it."

Seated at the long trestle table with Marian, Robin washed his hands in water laced with rose petals, then accepted a tall fresh-brewed ale. He sipped small to keep a clear head, and spooned oxtail soup. "Mostly I wonder, why should Sir Laird kill Courtland? To hold a grudge —"

"You're the one holds the grudge." Marian pointed her spoon. "Sir Laird abused his authority, true, but you condemn him as the Antichrist."

"The man's a brute, Marian. He's quick to draw steel."

"'Quickest hot is quickest cold.' Did any of Sir

Laird's huntsman see him go and come? Ahorse, for a knight never walks? Did dogs bark by night? Did his squire tell how he spent the night?"

"Yes, but you can't believe him. And the sheriff found Courtland's jewelry in Laird's saddlebags —"

"You're not thinking, Rob. Sir Laird didn't fly through the air. Was he seen in the village? Were hoof beats heard? No one in Lyndhurst owns a horse but you and he. Did Courtland's landlady see —"

"Is that eel pie?" Robin beamed as a maid bore a steaming pastry to the table. Reverently Ralph cut Robin a thick slice. Robin dug in, sucking flakes from his fingers and smacking his lips, while Lucy the cook simpered in the doorway. Chopped in thumbwidths, with green skins peeled off, the eel meat proved soft as white bread and fragrant as the ocean. "Here I maligned Sheriff Garrett as a miser."

"Must be the moon." Stoically Marian ate her pie rather than waste it. "He's gone queer too. Working hard, giving away eels, arresting a criminal like a real sheriff. Why does he do your bidding and then bribe you?"

"Garrett's nothing to ponder." Robin signaled for another slice of gooey pie. "It's Courtland who's wandered off or been killed. As you say, if no one saw Sir Laird or Courtland... 'Haps the boy was spirited off."

"Oh, nimble wit. Blame the devil for the trespasses of men." Marian rolled her dark eyes, then conceded, "There's a thought. Courtland wasn't dragged from his home, so he must've gone willingly. What could send him haring about at night?"

"Love? Catting? I doubt he poaches." Mouth full, Robin shrugged. "If he were affrighted for his life, figuring Sir Laird knew where he slept —"

Fast as a mink, Marian whisked Robin's plate from under his nose. "Stop stuffing and think. And forget Sir Laird. What else could've set Courtland wandering?"

"In the office? Nothing." Robin reached for his

plate, but denied, drained his mug. "Nothing goes on ever. The clerks scrape parchments and ink them anew, then do it again. Which is foolish, since even Sloan can't fathom false from true."

"False from true? Oh, yes, the counterfeits." Marian froze, trencher hanging in the air. "You said Sir Laird protested that his fine was too high, yet the higher tally was writ down. Did Courtland hear Sloan complain of these false documents?"

"Eh?" Robin squinted. "Uh, aye. Yes. He sat nursing his head, said he was dizzy."

"Aha." Marian returned Robin's trencher with a clatter. "Finish your pie. We needs take a walk."

Courtland rented the loft of a cottage owned by a freeholding widow. After some hesitation, the landlady allowed Robin, as Courtland's master, to search his room, though she looked askance at Marian in a man's attire. The two outlaws climbed the short ladder and hunched under roof beams and thatch smoked by soot. Kneeling, they looked around by the light of a rush lamp.

A rope bed with rumpled blankets. A chamber pot underneath. A three-legged stool. Clothes hanging on pegs. A spare pair of scuffed shoes. Two stacked chests, the upper one locked.

Smudges marred the small chest's lid. Marian rubbed a black streak and tasted her finger. "Vitriol. You dissolve it in oak-apple water to make ink. Break it."

Robin Hood twisted the lock to tear the hasp from the wood. Marian opened the lid. "Aha. More scripts."

"Grand." Robin yawned, for the hour was late and the loft warm. "Sloan will be glad to get more."

"As am I." Squinting in the wan rush light, Marian shuffled scraps of all sizes. "Look."

Robin pretended to look, even gave an intelligent grunt. "In'eresting."

"Noooo." Marian caught his nose. "Some problems you can't solve with a bow, says my husband. Look. What's this top sheet signify?"

Reluctant but obedient, Robin studied a parchment so old its edges crumbled. "I see... scratchy Latin."

"Blessed Saint Hildegard," gasped Marian. "The same legal passage is inscribed three times – here, here, and here – but in three different hands."

Robin Hood looked blank.

"Oh, Rob, you're so honest it's painful. Why would a man practice to vary his handwriting?"

"To copy – no. To match –" Feeling slow as Much the Miller's Son, Robin pieced it together. "Courtland's our forger."

"Yes. It explains how false scripts infest the forestry office. Courtland forged deeds and sold them to unscrupulous landowners so they could lay claim to neighbors' land, or the king's property in the forest, and reap its profits."

"Sold the forgeries for money, you mean." Robin rooted through scraps and stripped quills to feel the bottom of the chest. He found only a few half-crowns and silver pennies. "Where's his fortune?"

"He must've buried it out back." Marian waved a hand. "Everyone does that. Otherwise invites robbery. And some wealth he wore: remember his fancy ring and belt tips? D'ya see? Sloan complained about finding forgeries while Courtland lay listening. The guilty fled where none pursued."

"Jesus shall judge the quick and the dead," said Robin absently. "So he fled here, thence into the night. Why? And where?"

"That I don't know," Marian conceded with a huff. "But I'm sure the answer is here. Sit. Let me read."

Robin lolled, half-dozing. Marian read parchments, her finger and pouty lips moving. "The rogue forged whate'er profited. No surprise, I suppose. He had access to every document in the forest. The fox guarding the chickens... See how these 're scraped thin? I'll bet he changed the amounts of some fines, skimmed the excess, then changed the numbers back. So Sir Laird was right:

his fine was too high... Oh, my, real paper: that's expensive. A letter of introduction... Perhaps Courtland was too bold. A fraudulent deed bonds forger and buyer in secrecy, but who can trust a thief? This is a fair bill... Oh, my, a royal charter – Uhh!"

Marian startled as Robin's hard hand clamped her wrist like a bear trap. "I know where Courtland sleeps."

Past midnight, the outlaws slid down a hill and left the woods. The vale of Lyndhurst was a black bowl striped silver by the moon. The lower pond glittered, its surface dimpled as eels nipped at water beetles.

Marian ascended a dike to keep watch. Ankle-deep, broadax in hand, Robin waded the putrid stream to reach the spillway. It was tall as he could reach with the ax. Pairs of stout posts supported crosswise logs and saplings chinked with moss and grass. Only a little polluted water spilled over or trickled through the barrier. On the nether side brimmed thousands of gallons.

For the nonce.

Marian laid on the bank and watched the vale, but only a few curious cows grazed by moonlight. She whistled like a quail's *Wet my lips!* One call for Go ahead.

Bracing his feet on slimy rocks, Robin Hood slung the ax far back and swung low. The steel tooth bit a dark post. Swinging high, the archer knocked loose a kerf of white wood that floated away in the black stream. Quickly he chopped away half the post, then crabbed around and attacked the other. Soon only three fingers of wood held up the posts – and a wall of water.

Robin paused to hone the ax with a whetstone from his belt pouch. Pale moonlight was shadowed by earthen walls, so he held the blade close to his nose. He hissed, "Anyone?"

"No," buzzed Marian, "but it's loud."

"Can't be helped. And t'will be noisier anon."

Pocketing the whetstone, Robin aimed for the two white vees. He chopped alternate sides, shifting his feet on the treacherous stream bed, ears alert. Under one blow, the high wall of logs and saplings groaned. Water spurted from cracks, stinking of cows and eels and garbage. Robin clamped his mouth shut and sucked wind through his nose.

He smacked loose another chip and felt a tremor through the ax handle. Crouching and squinting in darkness, he debated whether to strike again or to clamber up the bank and push.

"Someone comes!" chirped Marian.

From the darkness charged more darkness, a ragged shape like a haystack toppling. It dashed around the curved dike opposite from Marian. A straight line above its head gleamed like silver in moonlight.

For an instant Robin Hood panicked, fearing a ghost, then he realized who the blocky attacker must be and what it carried. Silver flashed an arc as Robin canted the ax haft over his head in both hands.

A sword chunked on the ax's ash handle. Robin didn't wait for the next blow, but slung ax and sword aside, and punched. The blow connected with something soft that elicited a grunt, so Robin punched again. The ragged assailant curled around Robin's fist and collapsed, sword and attack forgotten. Grabbing folds of cloth, the outlaw yanked hard. The attacker plashed into the stream bed at Robin's feet.

Wood snapped. Marian yelped.

A cataract sprayed Robin Hood. A spinning eel struck his cheek. Whirling, the outlaw jumped for the bank, slipped and skidded back. Marian snagged his slimy hand and hauled.

A severed post let go. Logs and saplings burst free. Their twisting weight snapped the other post. Water and eels sucked at Robin's ankles and knees, then he scrambled like a demented squirrel and flopped atop the dike.

A wall of black water crashed in the stream bed and gushed towards the black forest beyond.

The ragged attacker was washed away.

By sunrise, the pond had gurgled to extinction.

Robin Hood stripped and scrubbed his body and clothes in the cow pond, but Marian still hung back from his evil reek. The villagers of Lyndhurst filtered onto the earthen dikes to see the newly revealed bottom of the eel pond. Then someone shouted from the woods.

Robin and Marian squished not far into the forest. Fat Sheriff Garrett lay befouled, openmouthed, and staring, with his ratty tunic twisted around his broad belly. His white face was scratched where Robin had slammed him to the rocky stream bed.

"He's drowned," marveled a man. "Why would he cut down his own spillway?"

"Perhaps something on the bottom needed airing," replied Robin vaguely.

People stared as the erstwhile royal forester and his wife climbed the dike. Marian made a face. "Oog."

The stench in the summer morn was stiff as a stone wall. Manure, rotted leaves, animal guts, soured grain, putrid vegetables, and the fishy slime of the eels made a stink so high and hard it was almost visible. The pond bottom was a mire of tree stumps and roots, black leaves and muck. Hundreds of eels flip-flopped in scummy puddles.

Marian covered her nose and mouth with her sleeve. Robin Hood calmly surveyed the bottom. "Ripe as a seven-day pheasant. But wait'll the sun rots these eels. That'll reek — Ho, ho. There he is."

To Marian's horror and the villagers' amusement, Robin slid down the bank and walked out onto the foul pond bottom. His deerhide boots sank to the ankles in black gunk, but held. He turned. "Marian, will you come?"

"I'll wait —" Marian pulled her sleeve from her

face and gulped. "I'll wait here."

The archer waved lazily, then duckwalked over stumps and roots to the middle, where the sheriff's two tall stakes crossed. Eels pitched and squirmed against his boots.

"Good morrow, Courtland."

Robin Hood addressed a corpse. The twin stakes pegged it through the ribs to the pond's bottom. Eels had gnawed it, and slime coated it from head to toe, but the body wore a green forester's tunic and a slim leather belt missing its bronze tips.

"Waste of a fine hand, lad. Sloan won't be pleased having to do your work too." Robin wiggled and pulled at the stakes, but they were sunk too deep to dislodge, so he retraced his erratic path to the embankment. People stepped back. Marian's face was white as bone.

"You were right, Marian. The answer was hid in those letters," chuckled the husband. "I can stir things up and muddy the waters, but you see clear to the bottom. You found the practice sheet for a royal charter. Sheriff Garrett bought a forged charter from Courtland to build this eel pond on king's land. Garrett profited twice: first selling the felled wood, then growing eels for near naught. But as you said, 'Two can keep a secret if one is dead.' When Sloan complained about false deeds, Courtland feared the game was up. He must've run to the sheriff and demanded money to flee: he could threaten to expose the sheriff's false charter. But thieves fall out. Garrett the miser killed Courtland rather than surrender a penny.

"And imagine," Robin laughed, "I watched Sheriff Garrett hammer down the body. Garrett dumped the clerk in the deepest part of the pond, but had to stake him lest the gasses float the corpse in three days. I thought the sheriff was blown from exertion, but he was sweating-blood scared I'd caught him in the act. He even gave me eels to go away. But did I notice he was rattled? No. I was hot to punish Sir Laird, and Garrett was glad to help. He pretended to find Courtland's jewelry in Laird's saddlebags, when he had 'em in his wallet 'cause he robbed the corpse. I thank the Virgin you stepped in, Marian. You saw the invisible and put me to shame."

Robin peered at the broken spillway. "I wonder where that ax went? If I cut those stakes, we can lay these jolly bedfellows in a Christian grave. Gad. Another few days, and those eels 'd've eaten Courtland hoof, hide, and hair."

"Rob," Marian gulped, "we ate of these eels."

"Oh, aye, but I've et worse. Grasshoppers and rats and horse lights at Acre, washed down with ditch water so scummy and buggy you had to strain with your teeth. Eels that 've drilled a dead man are nothing. 'The fouler the food, the sweeter the meat.'" Robin dusted his hands on his seat. "Yes, I'll say again, Marian, you've a sound head."

Marian didn't hear. She'd staggered down the ditch to retch.

Robin Hood glanced after, then shrugged. "A weak stomach, maybe, but a sound head."

Plucking a Mandrake

The hunter's ears pricked to the gabble of ducks and bate of wings. From under an old blanket stuck full of sweet flag and canary grass he watched the flock jitter across the sunset: teals, mallards, pintails, and fat graylag geese.

All afternoon Robin Hood had lain sopping wet amid tussocks of reeking marsh under his blind. With the caution of a hungry man, he nocked a bird arrow with steel spines like a hedgehog's. As he'd guessed, the weary ducks dropped towards this pond, for it was sheltered from the north wind, removed from foxes and badgers, and warmed by the southern sun. Slowly, Robin shrugged the itchy blanket from his shoulders, came to one knee, drew as he rose —

— and jumped at a cry of "Yah yah yah!"

Ducks exploded off the water, groping for sky, colliding and dodging and quacking. With his eye on the graylags, the outlaw loosed. Steel tines ripped the female's breast and she tumbled. Within seconds he dropped five more birds, but he'd hoped for twice that.

Cursing, Robin pushed through reeds. What bastardy fool blackguard had rousted his birds with that idiot croak?

He stopped. Dying ducks and feathers dotted the pond. Amidst them sloshed a bedraggled stick-man in a filthy smock and matted hair and beard. He seized a dying duck, stretched the neck and bit to sucked heart's blood.

Shocked, angered, and disgusted, Robin

shouted, "Drop that, varlet! T'is mine!"

The man crouched, cringing, his mouth smeared with blood and feathers, eyes vacant. Robin saw a rude cross stitched to his smock: a cure for madness. The fool swatted water at Robin, hooting, "Yah, yah!" Clutching the duck, he floundered out of the pond and scuttled up the wooded slope toward the village.

Swearing, teeth chattering, Robin slogged through icy water to retrieve his ducks. Piercing the webbing on a string, he trudged up a twisted path between trees. He'd lay a few stripes on that madman. Even a dog knew better than to steal a man's game.

But shooting ducks was foolish, he decided: gigging hooks or drowning nets would gather more sooner. He needed many ducks. With Easter past and May Day looming, winter apples and rye and salt pork and herring were all eaten, and famine stalked the land. Food was so scarce in the Greenwood he'd dispersed his band until fatter times. Not that that was why he hunted so far from home.

Muttering, dodging branches, stumbling over roots as dusk fell, absorbed, Robin bumped into a pair of dangling feet. In horror, he snatched a handful of grass to scrub his face, then crossed himself repeatedly.

The dead man hung from an elm. Shrunken to a skeleton, neck stretched like an sausage, skin curdled a moldy gray, his lips were cracked and his eyes picked out by crows and sparrows. The sockets glared at Robin in accusation.

Snatching his bow and birds, Robin Hood dashed up the trail towards the village.

Skegby Moor was ponds and fingers and rills and marsh and tall grass and brambles. Above the moor on low mounds rambled the village of Skegby, thirty cottages linked by muddy tracks and bridges of fallen trees. A fief of Tevershalt, a manor in the north, Skegby was old, squirreled away like a motte-and-bailey castle in the dark days of raids by blue-painted demons. The occupants spoke in canted words and archaic idioms and had gaped at Robin and Marian as if they were elephants from Egypt.

Yet the wattle-and-daub cottages were neat, the gardens and patchwork fields tended. The air was ripe from privies and pigs, yeast from the alehouse, coal smoke from the smithy, and incense from the chapel. On the outskirts stood the cottage of a wise woman, or witch. Robin Hood stopped running at her door.

The cottage was buried under vines and rosebushes, lapped on all sides by a garden like a spring tide. Bees bumbled at a hive, two brown goats rooted through chaff, and chickens scratched for weevils. Indoors was just as crowded. Robin ducked hanging herbs. The only furniture was a plank table crowded with pestles and bowls and pots, a pair of stools, and a pallet that unrolled for a bed. A white cat licked its paws by the hearth.

Fitful rush light surrounded Marian's dark head like a halo. She was dressed like Robin in winter-brown shirt and trousers and greased deerhide boots. The witch was barrel-round in a faded red gown and kirtle. A headscarf made her chapped cheeks rounder. Her name was Rocana, an old name Robin had never heard before.

"What's wrong, Rob?" asked Marian. "Why do you pant so?"

"Dead man." The outlaw gulped air. "On the path at the bottom of the hill. Hanged. Walked right into him."

"Aye, a sad place to hang a man." Rocana's eyes crinkled in sympathy. At the fireplace, she turned turnips buried in dock leaves and ashes. "But that elm is traditional. I'm sorry, I should have warned you. Ducks and a goose. Lovely."

Robin shucked his sopping clothes and hung them near the fire, then cleared a spot on the table for the ducks. Fingering a diamond on a hen mallard's wing, Marian recited, "'Touch blue and your wish will come true.'"

They lopped off heads and winkled out innards while Robin got his breath back. "What was he hanged for? Who is he – or was he?"

"Ingram. Our local rake. Fathered half the bastards in the parish. A poacher of sheep. The hills are full of deer and the moor of ducks and eels, but Ingram wanted mutton. And I'd cook it for him," Rocana hooted. "But that half-Irish beast, Fedelm, the bailiff, finally caught him. He always danced the Jack in the Green, too. Don't know who'll do 't this year."

"It's almost May Day, isn't it?" said Robin. The first of May meant festivity, when a man donned the Jack in the Green, a cone of wicker and leaves for the forest spirit, the mythical tree man. Escorted by Green Men in face paint and leaves, and Morris dancers with sticks, and cloggers with swords, the Jack would caper while people danced after it, till the Jack was felled with swords to die and rise again, to show spring had arrived. It was Robin's favorite holiday, and he was suddenly homesick for the Greenwood.

Marian asked, "How long must he hang there?"

"Till he's ripe and falls. Like a pheasant."

"We'll have to tell our cousin, Will Scarlett. He's gallows fodder too."

Robin carried guts to the back door to pitch them on the midden. A snuffling at the stoop jarred him. "What the hell?"

On hands and knees, the madman from the pond lapped from a wooden bowl.

"That's just Serle," called Rocana. "He drinks the milk we put out for the wee folk. They don't seem to mind."

Robin stepped around the madman, pitched the guts, and wiped his hands on mint leaves. Serle scuttled off. The outlaw huffed. Every village had an idiot: even he had Much the Miller's Son. Returning to pluck ducks, he asked, "What was Serle's offense, that God punished him so?"

Rocana seared duck breasts in a kettle, then added water from a red clay ewer. "I'll stew 'em to

184

go farther. Serle abused his family. After a pot of ale he'd see in his poor wife and children all the demons of Hell. He pickled his brain. Now he's one with the beasts, and may God bless us all, I say."

"Beasts," Robin groused. "Better we lived like beasts. They follow God's will without questioning. Or meddling."

Marian sniffed. "Rocana says we needs stay a few days more."

"As you wish, honey," sighed Robin. "T'will let me lay in more ducks. If we can keep – Serle? – clear of the marshes."

"We can." The witch plucked herbs from the sheaves overhead and crumbled them in the stew. "I have a special way with him."

Long after dark, the cat lifted her head. Robin, an outlaw since boyhood, felt for his knife and checked the back exit. Something scratched at the door like a small dog.

Rocana admitted a young woman in faded brown. Her belly was swollen and her gown damp at the breasts. She carried a big baby, almost a toddler. She gasped at the witch's company and, timid as a deer, had to be coaxed inside. She sagged on a stool and relinquished her toddler to Marian, confessed that her child had stopped kicking, and was that right? While Rocana asked questions and ground herbs and seeds in a pestle, Marian cooed and kissed the baby's blonde head, inhaling its milky fragrance. Robin sat by the fire and fletched an arrow with a gray goose quill.

"Such a beautiful child." Marian touched the woman's swollen belly. "And another on the way. You're lucky."

The young woman smiled vacantly and touched her stomach. "This one's father is an angel."

"What?" Marian bobbled the infant.

The simple woman was sincere. "His father's an angel that comes in the night. He's tall and dark. This child will be doubly blessed."

"Yes..." Marian stroked the ash-blonde head. "I see..."

The cat picked up her head and scooted behind a sheaf of woodruff. Robin Hood laid his arrow on the hearth.

The door rattled and banged as a priest barged in. "Willa! You're not to come here! I've forbidden it!"

The young woman upset her stool, but Marian caught her. The priest offered no help. His dark cassock bore buttons from throat to hem and was girdled by a rosary with a wooden cross that banged his knee. His high brow, eagle's nose, and sharp cheekbones recalled a talking skull.

"And you, interloper," he snarled at Marian, "you'll not talk to this women either."

Robin Hood rose. "How is that your business?"

"Everything that transpires in this village is my business."

The outlaw stifled a rising temper. Robin took clerics as he found them. Friar Tuck was poor as dirt, dedicated, and honest. The greedy Bishop of Hereford had been forced to dance in the Greenwood at arrow-point. Robin kept his voice level. "Not today."

Snorting, the priest grabbed Willa's arm. Robin Hood seized his, and the priest gasped. "Father, pray contain your zeal. The women discuss women's affairs. Men are not needed."

The priest could not wriggle free. "It's a sin to manhandle a cleric."

Up close, Robin was distracted, for the glitter in the priest's deep eyes was somehow familiar. He brushed the thought aside. "It's man's nature to sin. I but do my part." Robin pitched the priest out the door. The man just missed rapping his head on the lintel. Robin shut the door.

Rocana swept her mix into a clay cup, then instructed Willa how to brew a tea. It took three tries. Marian surrendered the baby and Willa slipped into the night, tears of fear in her eyes. Fletching again, Robin asked, "Does the priest visit often?"

Smiling, crinkly, Rocana tidied her work table. "Alwyn's forbidden the women to come for my curings. They come anyway."

Robin licked a split feather. "What does he dislike?"

"Competition. We wrestle like boars for the same wallow. He's got his Latin and holy water and incense, I my Gaelic and magic water and herbs." She banged vessels as she worked. "We villagers are partial to harelips and webbed fingers, living on rabbits and ducks as we do, but you won't see Alwyn wield a needle or a knife. Yet he rails that I defy God's will with blasphemous magic. So when Young Gerald slashed his palm with a knife, Alwyn could only pray. I drew the blood poisoning with a sage and apple poultice and saved his arm and his life, thus defying God's will."

The wise woman sighed. The cat rubbed against her hairy leg. "But it happens all over. Witches bein' driven out by churchmen. There're more of them, and better organized, with their bishops and councils and diets and edicts, while we're a handful of old women who pass on secrets from mother to daughter. And men are hungry as wolves. You know 't, don't you, Marian? Men rule this world and women endure it."

Neither the Fox nor the Vixen of Sherwood denied it. Marian asked, "Why does Willa think her husband is an angel?"

"I let her think that. Her true husband is Serle, who's been mad more than a year. Better she's visited by an angel."

Robin Hood cleared his throat. "Rocana, if this village ever drove you out, you'd find a home in Sherwood."

The witch cocked her head like a girl. "Would I? That's very kind. But," she peered around at leaves and vines and flowers, "you can't grow a garden in the forest. And I'm rooted here the same way. Whate'er others may think, I'm part of this village."

For days, the women worked on Marian's "problem". Married more than a year, she had yet to conceive. Word was Rocana had cures. "Don't fret, dear. We can fix 't. A good marriage is a prolific marriage."

The witch suggested many things. "Like cured like", so Robin set braided snares around clover patches, and Marian ate rabbit until she swore her ears grew. She drank tea of mugwort picked in May. For lovemaking, husband and wife slept outdoors under a rose arbor and the moon, yet with faces covered lest the moonshine drive them mad. Around their bed of blankets they scratched a six-pointed Seal of Solomon. Before and after making love, they prayed to Saint Anne. Rocana joked she had no pearls, or she'd grind one into Marian's food. And they eschewed green as unlucky for lovers.

Robin Hood chafed at probing questions. Did they have relations twice a week? Did he shed enough seed to fill the hollow of her palm? What of their families? Marian listed brothers and sisters while Robin had none, living or dead. Yes, it had taken his mother years to conceive, but how could that matter?

By day, unneeded, Robin hunted alone. Yet Marian was hopeful. One night, dreaming at the sky, she piped, "Look, Rob, a falling star. The soul of a child coming to be born. Maybe ours."

One night, Rocana woke Marian from their pallet, bid her dress, and gave her a knife and basket. The witch carried a frayed rope. Marian pressed her husband's shoulder to keep him abed. "Rob, stay and watch here, please?" Pleading and apologizing at the same time. Her husband neither nodded nor shook his head.

A full moon etched the world with silver light. The earth seemed blown of milky glass lit from below. The two women bustled to the dark garden, where the witch slipped the rope around the neck of a brown goat. Then the three hobbled off into the dark.

Catching up his bow and quiver, Robin followed the witch's creaking knees and wheezing. He couldn't hear Marian. They trod the path down the hill. Robin guessed their destination and muttered charms of protection, but wondered what they planned.

Like a lost scarecrow, the dead poacher Ingram hung from the elm. Under his dangling feet, Marian dug as Rocana instructed. Pressing alongside an oak, Robin watched and listened.

"I didn't think it grew in England," said the young woman. She grubbed in the soil some time. "I don't find it."

"Oh, dear. My memory's not what it used to be... No, it don't grow in England. I planted it here before they hanged him. Ah, got it? Careful. Just uncover it, don't disturb it." Rocana nickered to the goat and fumbled with the rope. "My rheumatism hates this spring damp. Slip the bight under a stub of it."

Robin hissed. Were they both mad?

"Stay. Stay. Move up the slope, dear. Stay." Leaving the goat under the hanged man, the women backed past Robin's post without seeing him. A hundred feet up the slope the witch warned, "Cover your ears."

Robin Hood clamped both hands to his head. Dark against dark in silver-splintered light, the goat tugged, then plodded up the slope towards its mistress. Gingerly, Robin uncovered his ears. He heard the witch reward the goat with a treat. She untied the rope and stuffed their prize into her basket.

"*Yah yah yah!*" The raucous blat split the night.

"*There they are!*" boomed a voice. Golden torch light banished the silver moonlight.

Rocana muttered in Gaelic. Marian trilled, "Shall we run?"

"No, child. Stay put."

Through the trees came the priest, Alwyn, and

three villagers, alike as stalks of wheat. They carried torches. Leading the pack like a dog shambled Serle, the madman. The priest's cassock and rosary flapped about his knees. Catching Serle's arm, he called, "Rocana. You dare defile the dead? You'll bring down the wrath of God with your doubly damned blasphemy."

"I've touched not the dead, Alwyn." The witch waved a crooked hand. "The lord's tree still bears fruit."

The priest ordered a torch held near the grotesque body. "If you don't trifle with the dead — and we may've interrupted your grisly work — what do at this witching hour?"

"It's none of your business," the witch snapped, "but we harvest by moonlight. Oak buds and cuckoo's pintle and such oddments."

Hidden in the dark, Robin Hood grunted. Those innocent plants were not what the goat plucked from the ground.

Unsatisfied, Alwyn refused to leave the women alone with the corpse. "Seize her! Drag her to the chapel. We'll see if she's innocent or not. Go on, grab her!"

Robin Hood startled everyone when he slipped to Rocana and planted his feet. The villagers balked, but the witch muttered, "No, let us go. We'll get this over with, once and for all."

Nonplussed, Robin didn't move. Marian tugged him away. "Watch and wait, darling. We'll make sure she suffers no harm."

The three men caught Rocana's elbows, gently, reluctantly, and avoided the basket on her arm. They escorted her up the slope after Alwyn.

Robin waggled his useless bow and squeezed his wife's hand. "I'm sorry I broke faith, honey, and spied. It's hard, but —"

His wife sniffled in the darkness. "We need help for me to conceive, Rob."

"Not that. I won't let you do it."

"Hush. We'll discuss it later."

Torch light ringed the village chapel and common like fairy fire. Barefoot villagers streamed from their cottages, rubbing their eyes. Alwyn waved a bible as he exhorted the crowd in a high singsong. The three men held Rocana, who waited, resigned and hardly terrified. Beside her stood the pregnant and confused Willa, wife of Serle. Beyond the crowd, in a disused byre, Robin saw the Jack, an eight-foot cone woven of wicker and thatched with prickly holly leaves for the dance on May Day.

Alwyn ranted against sin and the villagers attended. A few men hollered agreement, some women vexed, but most just listened. This was neither sermon nor trial by ordeal, but entertainment, another round in an ancient village feud. Robin Hood had seen grimmer football matches.

"... Too long, witch, has this village tolerated your heathen interfering ways. Like the Witch of Endor, you've urged our women to wickedness. You've dealt out potions and salves that keep wives from conceiving even when visited by their husbands. You've dazzled the minds of good women, and made them like drunks so men might ravish them in the fields. You've caused father to lie with daughter, brother with sister, and son with mother. You've stolen the bowels and members of babies to conjure flying potions..."

Rocana clucked her tongue. "Stop this rubbish, Alwyn. Everyone knows my healings, and everyone's profited by them..."

"Why not mount her on a horse again? Perry, fetch your cob," a man joked. "Touch her brow with an iron knife," jibed another. "Float her in the pond," a woman shrilled. Even the jests were ancient.

The priest ranted, fulfilling his duty if not moving his audience. Robin Hood wondered if he were drunk. Or partly mad. Madness ran deep in this isolated hamlet... Suddenly Robin gawked, realizing why the priest seemed familiar. "Marian, Alwyn is Serle's brother!"

"Yes, yes, Rob. Listen."

Robin Hood pouted. "Why do women always

know these things first?"

"It demands in Exodus, 'suffer not a witch to live'. Yet this village harbors a viper at our bosoms." The priest raised a bible as if he'd squash a fly, then thumped Rocana's brow. "Be condemned. Feel the fire of the holy word. Know the burning pits of Hell beckon."

Rocana pushed at the book with feeble hands. "Get that thing off me." As she struggled, her basket upended. A knife and a dirty root thumped at the priest's feet. Alwyn pounced on the root, holding it up to catch the light. It resembled a triply forked carrot crusted with dirt.

Silence fell hard on peoples' ears. Alwyn's eyes grew feverish in the torch light. "This you harvested under the gallows tree? You've done worse than defile the dead. You use them for purposes too foul to bespeak. You'll burn for this."

Rocana bleated. The villagers murmured as the game took and ugly and unfamiliar turn. The priest wrung Rocana's shoulder. "There is no pit deep enough. No damnation strong enough —"

"Stop." Rocana writhed in the priest's grip. "Unhand me, you rake. Must you paw every woman in this village —"

Quickly, Alwyn slapped her, then raised his hand again.

Quicker, Robin Hood's bow snagged the priest's wrist. "I'll break your arm, you black-bearded bastard. Don't you dare strike a woman." Marian tugged her Irish knife loose in its sheath.

Maddened by his own ranting, Alwyn pointed at Marian. "You outlaw interloper. You'll suffer torments unimaginable when your wife conceives a demon's child."

Growling, Robin Hood gripped the man's throat. The priest struggled as he waved the root in the air. Everyone saw it, and knew it.

Mandrake was the most ancient and mysterious of herbs. Its manlike shape let it breathe beneath the ground, where it stored up power for fertility and prophecy. Dangerous and jealous, a mandrake hugged the earth and hated to leave, so if carelessly plucked it screamed, loud and harsh to drive men mad. To harvest it, a witch tied the root to a dog or a goat, then whistled the animal from out of earshot to yank it from the ground.

"See you this?" rapped the priest. "A mandragon. A denial of God. She buried it under a dying man to soak up his seed that spilt upon strangling. And she'll compel your wife to purge your seed and insert this instead. Thus do Christian women birth devils —"

"Oh, no! Oh, no, no, no!" A soul-wrenching cry cut through even Alwyn's bellowing.

The deluded Willa pushed at her swollen belly with clumsy hands. "No, no! She said t'would make the child strong, t'would ward off the madness. Oh, get it away. Help me, Mother Mary. Get the devil child out of me!"

Villagers surged back as if from a mad dog. Rocana reached, but Willa lurched around the firelit circle, grasping at people, pleading. "Get it away, please, sweet Christ, get it away!"

No one could help, she saw. Her hand snatched at a man's belt for a knife. The blade flashed yellow in the torch light.

"Stop her!" screamed Marian, and shoved at the crowd. Robin tangled with a man backing up. Rocana swiped at the young mother's hands.

All too late. Willa drove the blade into her low-slung belly. Transported by passion, unmindful of pain, she stabbed until blood and water gushed red and white and splashed in the dirt. She stabbed until she stumbled and fell. People screamed and howled and prayed as if the world ended.

Rocana flopped on her knees, clutched the dying woman's head, and wept. Willa's bloody hand floated toward Heaven.

Robin Hood hoicked Alwyn in the air by his cassock. "You —"

A man howled in the darkness. A woman screamed. "The Jack! It lives! It's Ingram come back! God have mercy!"

People shouted, screamed, pushed, ran. Robin fought to see and remember. What about the Jack?

And who was Ingram? Then he saw.

Jerking and jigging, the Jack in the Green, a living dancing tree, thrashed and shivered as it dashed amidst the shrieking villagers. The cone's shiny leaves shimmered in the wild light as torch bearers ran hither and thither. Only Rocana kept her place, cradling the dying woman's head.

Alwyn squirmed from Robin's grasp. He fumbled his cross high to banish the evil apparition, then his nerve broke and he ran.

The crowd melted like a breaking sea wave. Despite fear and superstition boiling in his brain, Robin noticed bare feet stamped the turf under the green cone.

Sensing that the outlaws stood fast, the Jack rushed.

Shoving Marian aside, Robin snaked an arrow from his quiver, pulled to his cheek, and loosed.

The arrow slapped into the Jack, parting leaves at the height of a man's breast.

The spirit kept coming.

Superstition conquered reason. Robin hollered, "Run, Marian!" His wife had already bolted for sanctuary. Robin loped after. Marian dove into the chapel like a quail into a hedge. Robin grabbed the door and slammed it shut. In black stillness, their rasping breath was loud.

Visions whirled in Marian's mind: ghosts and fire and blood and wonder. But one picture stood out starker than the rest. "Robin — you missed!"

"What? No! I never miss."

"He didn't go down."

"I never miss."

It was hours before the outlaws dared peek. The moon was down, the common deserted, even the dead woman gone. The night was still, as if God had called home every man, woman, and child.

Close together and casting every whichway, Robin and Marian crept down the path to Rocana's cottage. They had only starlight to see by, but walked fast because they argued. They'd fought ever coming to Skegby Moor, Robin reflected. What prompted all the anger in this village?

Robin's bow sliced the air as he whispered, "It's necromancy. I'll not have it, not mandrake. It goes against God's plan. It's criminal to put that — root up your — insides —"

"Women have used mandrake for centuries. It's in the Bible. Jacob's wife Rachel was barren until she asked Leah to borrow her mandrakes —"

"But plucking it under a corpse by the full moon."

Marian hissed, "This is our only hope. Maybe the old ways —"

"You want the seed of a dead man? A living ghost? So you birth an imp or a changeling?"

"That's a man's help for you. Forbid everything and offer nothing in its place."

"It's dangerous. You could go mad from the mandrake's scream. That priest was right about one thing. God's wrath has descended on us. You saw that poor woman kill herself —"

"That fool priest killed Willa, surely as if he plunged in the knife himself. Him and his wild accusations."

"It wasn't the father, it was the witch. She duped that poor woman and the devil seized her. Retribution comes from crossing God's ways."

"Oh, hush. You sound like these other ignorant sots. Men know more about breeding dogs than women."

"That witch causes harm. She has a goat for a familiar —"

"A goat can't be a familiar."

"Satan takes the form of a goat. Cloven hooves, a beard —"

"Satan's form is a man."

"Oho. So it's men who — Whoa!"

Robin Hood spilled headlong over an obstacle across the path: a round springy mass of rustling leaves. Robin felt pricks along his arms and legs. "What the — These are holly —"

"It's the Jack!" Marian breathed. Now they

could make out the shape, a long interwoven with leaves.

Robin huddled close to Marian. "Christ, look where it lies!"

Here the path split, one fork leading to Rocana's cottage, the other down the hill toward the marsh, passing under the gallows elm.

"Oh, Mother Mary..." squeaked Marian.

Both were reluctant to touch the fallen icon, but Robin's curiosity goaded. In the dark, he fumbled inside the wicker frame. "Nothing. Neither body nor blood. Nor arrow."

"It'd go through a ghost."

"A ghost couldn't lift this frame."

"A dead man, then."

"Then the arrow would stick him. Let's not talk of such things..." Robin sucked wind. "I'm going down the hill."

"I'll go with you."

"No, see if Rocana's returned. She might need guarding."

"Be careful."

"Oh, yes."

Crossing his breast, holding his bow foremost, Robin Hood wafted like a ghost down the path. In dead quiet, no night birds sang, no owls hooted. Robin crossed fingers on both hands.

Straining, he recognized the widened spot under the elm tree. The noose still dangled in place. Ingram was gone.

With a knife, the outlaw cut the rope's shank and tugged it down. The hangman's noose of thirteen turns was yanked almost closed. Robin Hood shuddered.

Noose in hand, he dashed up the slope.

The door of the witch's cottage hung open. A rush lamp flickered on the work table, and he was grateful for the light and life. But something made him stumble at the threshold, a bad sign, and he snapped his fingers to dispel ill luck.

The place stank, he realized, rank and cold and brassy.

The work table was bare. Pottery shards and

herbs littered the floor. Ashes were scattered like snow. The stools were knocked over. The back door hung at an angle. Marian sat on the hearth, tears on her cheeks. Hard by the fireplace lay the squat shape of Rocana. Deep blue fingerprints marred her throat.

Wordlessly the outlaw held up the noose. By rush light they saw the tiny noose was foul with grime and sloughed skin.

"So it's true," Marian breathed. "Ingram came back —"

"Hist. Don't say his name. You'll call him hither."

Marian rose to shrink against her husband's chest. "The hanged man, then, the poacher. He got down off one tree and climbed into another. He donned the Jack to dance again. To take revenge on the village. The dead taunting the living. Oh, sweet Lord."

Reaching under Robin's arms, Marian made the sign of the cross at the doors. "So much death in this village. It's in the air, like contagion. Maybe we should leave."

"Yes. With the dawn."

Yet they stayed, for with the sun came work to be done.

Father Alwyn refused to administer last rites for Rocana, or to hold a vigil, or to bury her in the chapel graveyard. Pagans could rot, he said, as offal for dogs. And he had Willa's funeral to minister. So Robin and Marian sank Rocana in the garden she'd loved, and entwined a wooden cross with yellow cowslips.

Warned off by the priest, most villagers stayed away. The few women who came crossed themselves as they talked. They'd all seen the abandoned Jack. They guessed dead Ingram murdered Rocana because she'd berated him for fathering bastards. And the dead resented the living. Ingram killed Rocana the same as he'd died, by strangling. At every Mass, Alwyn preached that "one sinner had fetched away another". No one, they reported, ventured out after dark.

Each night, as Robin barred the doors, he cut a fresh cross in the wood.

Ducks winged in, and Robin needed meat, so for days the archer netted and hooked and shot birds, then dressed them, smoked their breasts over a low fire, and packed them. The birds' numbers dwindled as the flocks nested in summer grounds farther north.

In spare moments, Robin returned to the common, to sight, pace, and crawl with his nose to the ground. Finally he discovered his arrow buried in dirt lengthwise. It lay yards from where he'd shot it. When he plucked it free, he learned why. It lacked a red hen feather.

Back at the cottage, he showed Marian. "See? I didn't miss. This arrow passed through something that skinned off this fletch. That made it hook sharp to the right."

Marian pricked a chicken strung over the fire. "I see, Rob. I was wrong to think you'd missed. Yet the villain inside the Jack was dead. No arrow could stop him." She crossed her breast.

Robin grunted, but added, "Still, I didn't miss."

"Here. I've found something queer too. I tried sorting herbs and seeds, but without Rocana's knowledge, they might as well be oak leaves. Yet I discovered this." She fetched a small stone crock that held a pale yellow dust. "Mandrake root."

"So?"

"Mandrake's rare, Rob. It only grows in the Holy Land. Rocana, may she find peace, claimed to have only a single whole root that she never cut. Yet here's a handful ground fine."

"Why would she lie?"

"I don't know. We all have secrets. Wash your hands."

They sat down to chicken roasted with sage and onions and a pitcher of goat's milk. "Drink up. It's the last. The bailiff collected the heriot and the mortuary, the death taxes. The best goat went to the lord and the second-best to the priest. We get the cat."

"She'll hardly make a meal."

"At least we don't need the milk. Serle hasn't returned for his bowl since the witch died. He must scent death, like a dog."

"Or else he misstepped in the marsh and sank. Or was also killed by the vengeful dead man." Robin stopped chewing. "Do you suppose Serle might've killed Rocana, may she rest in peace? A madman can do anything."

"Why should he harm her? She fed him milk every night at the stoop. Even mad, he'd remember kindness."

"Poor dead Willa, may she rest easy, was his wife. She must have fed him when they were wed, but that didn't spare her beatings."

"I'd offer that Alwyn, the priest, killed her out of spite." Marian threw chicken skin to the cat. "'Like people, like priest', and he's the most hateful man in the village."

"Why should Alwyn kill her?" The outlaw plied his knife. "They feuded, but that went back years. And Alwyn wouldn't have wrecked the cottage."

"He's almost mad as his brother. The whole family's cursed by bad blood. And Alwyn has a temper. Once he saw that mandrake root, he turned vicious as a mad dog. He struck Rocana and bellowed about women birthing demons. The filthy hypocrite. Remember how he accused Rocana of bedazing women to be ravished?"

"I think so." Robin scratched his beard with a knife point. "He ranted about many things."

"What do you always say? 'A man accuses others of what he practices?' A thief is quickest to say he's robbed, a cheat to say he's cheated?"

"So... you think the priest bewitches women and ravishes them?"

"No, I think he promises Heaven and threatens Hell until they lie down."

"A woman shouldn't listen to a man," mumbled the husband mumbled. "Some reckon it's no sin to sleep with a priest. Some women think it's lucky."

"How long has Serle been afflicted mad?"

"Huh?" Robin's mouth was stuffed with chicken.

"More than a year, according to Rocana." Marian waved a drumstick. "Yet Willa bore only seven months. Serle didn't get her with child. And neither did mandrake root."

"So... Wait. The priest bedded Willa? Christ on the cross, he can't do that. She's his brother's wife. That's incest."

Marian nodded. "Another sin that he laid at Rocana's feet. He accused her of luring father to lay with daughter, and brother with sister, and mother with son?"

"While Father Alwyn was lying with his sister-in-law." Robin shook his head. "Pitiful Jesus, an incestuous priest. What would a bishop do? Castrate him?"

"Nothing. No one would tell. This village is like a family. It keeps it secrets close."

"Hang on. Everyone knows Alwyn fathered his brother's sister's child?"

"All the women know. 'Who's the father?' is the first question a woman would ask."

"Incest?"

"It's thick as fleas in this village, Rob. See you, how they all look alike? See the harelips and webbed toes and simple minds? Poor Willa, may she rest in peace, thought a dark angel visited her by night. Rocana, may she lie quiet, let her believe it."

"Still," Robin sighed, "men need a priest, same as they need a king."

"Men, yes. Women, no."

"Marian."

"It's true. Men need a priest to absolve them of sins, but what can they do for women? When a woman's screaming in childbirth, can a priest put a knife under the bed to cut the pain, or brew a broth of asparagus and chestnuts and fennel? Men work women harder than oxen. They kill them slowly with too many babies. The graveyards are full of three wives for every dead husband. Women cherish the old ways, because women don't need God. They need other women."

"Jesus, Marian, you'll draw down lightning. I'll agree if you wish 't. But a priest should tend spiritual matters and the witch secular ones. A wise woman shouldn't interfere in God's plans —"

"It was God who made me barren! And with Rocana dead, I'll stay that way." Suddenly Marian was sobbing. Robin reached to comfort, but she pulled away. "Just... leave me alone..."

Robin took his bow outside. The moonlit sky was strung with wisps blown from the north. "One way or another, we each dig our own grave."

Days later, Robin slogged knee-deep through tea-colored water after a dropped pintail. He stumbled against something lodged in duckweed.

A dead man bubbled up, gurgled, and belched gas. He had no head, just a gnawed stump tipped with the white dice of a spine.

Retching, Robin Hood slopped from the water and stumbled up the hill. The hell with ducks. He wanted out of this ghastly village. He and Marian had sought new life and found only death.

And nightmares that repeated. In back of the cottage, the madman Serle raided his smoking racks. The outlaw barked, "Hoy, get away!"

The madman clawed hair from his eyes and croaked, "I'm hungry. A man's got a right to eat."

Robin stopped cold. Serle was filthy and ragged, but upright, pouty, and arrogant. His old self. "You're sane."

"What of it?"

Marian came to the doorway. Serle turned. Robin plucked a fleck of red from his coarse smock. "My hen feather. It was you in the Jack. You bent over and ran with it, so my arrow skinned your back. Why'd you do it?"

"The Jack saved Rocana from the trial by ordeal." Marian was breathless. "Was that why, Serle? Because she'd been kind to you?"

"Hardly," retorted Robin. "He dumped the Jack on the path to her cottage. My, God. You killed her!"

"I din't kill no one!" Dizzy and dazed, Serle sputtered. "I din't —"

Something flickered on the path to the gallows tree that caught Robin's eye. He saw Alwyn drop a sack and run. Wondering, Robin fetched the sack and found bread, cheese, and a jug of ale.

"'The guilty flee where none pursueth.'" Robin ran after the priest. Marian caught up, loping like a deer.

Robin yelled, "That Alwyn is a two-faced lying hypocrite. That night, when everyone scattered before the Jack, he went searching for Serle and found he'd strangled the witch. He couldn't let his brother take the blame, so he dragged the Jack across the path to the gallows tree. He ripped down Ingram's body — popped the head right off! — and stuffed him in the pond to make him disappear. Then he shooed Serle into the marsh to hide. He's been taking him food, which is why Serle doesn't come sniffing for milk at the stoop. Alwyn blamed Rocana's murder on a dead man."

They found the chapel barred and shuttered. Villagers clustered around twittering. Marian nodded at the door. "Break it down."

"What? A church?"

"Quickly, Rob."

Robin Hood handed Marian his bow. "Some men put faith in God, others in their wives." He ran shoulder-first and smashed the door, backed and bashed again until the bracket tore free.

Inside, Robin and Marian gasped. Another hanged man dangled, but this one wriggled and writhed.

Marian thrust the longbow at Robin. "Shoot him down!"

Alwyn, parish priest of Skegby Moor, swung by his neck. His hands clawed at a hemp rope sunk deep into his throat. A wooden cross lay tumbled on the dirt floor where he'd jumped off the altar.

The greatest archer in the England nocked,

drew, and loosed. The arrow sliced the jerking rope.
The priest crashed with a bone-jangling jolt. Robin
and Marian knelt and tugged loose the noose, yet
Alwyn remained blue. His hands flapped. Robin
cursed. "His windpipe's crushed. He's finished."

"Strangled same as Ingram, same as Rocana."
Marian called loudly, "Alwyn. You're dying. You
needs confess. You killed Rocana, didn't you?"

The priest's eyes bugged at the ceiling, or
Heaven beyond. He nodded.

"What?" Robin barked. "He killed Rocana?"

"And has hanged himself as punishment. Serle
could tell the truth now. Alwyn made Serle hide in
the marsh because Serle witnessed Alwyn strangle
Rocana. But why did you kill her?"

"She drove −" a harsh whisper "− my brother −
mad with − her witchments. Plucked − mandrake −
when he was − nearby. The scream − drove him
mad."

"But now he's sane again."

"I − saw."

From the doorway where villagers gaped, the
scruffy brother shuffled up. Crying, he said,
"Wyn..."

The childhood name tugged tears from the
priest. His lips formed the word. "How?"

Marian began to cry. "It was mandrake root that
drove Serle mad, but not by its scream. By milk.
Women sip drams of mandrake when birthing
because it fogs the mind and dulls pain. Rocana
ground some root fine and fed it to Serle in goat's
milk. One strong taste masks another. The potion
banished Serle's reason."

"But why did she?" asked Robin.

Marian flung out a hand. "Serle terrorized his
poor wife. He beat Willa without mercy. But he was
shielded from justice by his brother's office.
Rocana was just an old woman, but she had
potions, so dosed him daily at her stoop. It
rendered him harmless as a dog. But since
Rocana's been dead these nine days, Serle's mind
has cleared. You killed Rocana for the wrong
reason, Alwyn, but it brought your brother back,

damn him."

The priest sagged. "God — forgives."

Half-dazed by events, Robin Hood fetched a bowl of holy water. He knelt over the priest and dipped his finger to absolve the man —

Hissing, Marian slapped the bowl away. Holy water splashed and soaked into the dirt floor.

"Marian!" Robin was shocked. "He'll die unshriven."

"Let him."

"He confessed."

"It's not enough. Look at him." Tears spilled down Marian's cheeks. "He has no remorse. Never a word for poor Willa, his own sister-in-law, raped and deceived and degraded. Not a word for his bastard child, killed by his own words that made a deluded mother rip open her belly. No regrets for a harmless witch strangled. No regrets for the child I'll never have. Let him burn in Hell."

Robin Hood stood tall over his wife, the back of his hand to his mouth. "God help us all, then."

Flyting, Fighting

"I didn't want to dance with her, but she clung like a leech!"

"Ah, so you had to prop her bottom with both hands?"

"No! I – I don't know what I did."

"I do. You acted a perfect pig!"

Robin Hood stifled a groan. His head throbbed, his stomach churned, his ears rang, his vision blurred. Worst, Marian yammered like a woodpecker to drill his wooden head full of holes. Even the late spring sun hounded him, searing his eyes as he stumbled along the forest path. "It was – quite a dance."

"You outstepped Saint Vitus, you vulgar swine." Marian was dressed like her husband in a green shirt and deerhide tunic and soft hat sporting a pheasant feather. Like her husband, she wore a quiver and an Irish knife and carried her longbow ready in her left hand. "You clutched that saucy tart as tight as any tankard."

"Folks give me drinks. 'S rude to deny 'em."

"Such chivalry. My mother warned me not to marry an outlaw."

"'N the one time she was right, you didn't listen."

"Take my soul. Now you'd defame my mother?"

"No. Ow, my head! I – What the hell?"

The trail intersected another wending east-west. Eastward lay the Greenwood, but Robin blocked Marian from stepping. Dropping to one knee, and gurgling inside, he squinted through a headache at the muddy track.

He studied the track for a number of yards. Twice he put his hand alongside a footprint, then laid his head to peer sideways. He measured the length of strides against his bow, then traced a small scuffed print.

Rising, he pronounced, "The king's foresters have made off with a girl."

Arms crossed, Marian asked, "What?"

"Look. Poison Hugh has a crippled toe that turns out. He's head forester. These other two must be foresters, because their stride glides like ours. This'n must be Osborn because it's his bailiwick and he's big. They drag a girl against her will. Her feet are tiny and toed-in in doghide slippers. See how she stumbles? Here she dug in her toes but got yanked along, likely bound by the wrists. Why else would a girl travel with loutish foresters except by force?"

Marian looked at the jumbled tracks of men and deer marring the mud, then snorted. "You made that up."

"Made it up?" Robin's jaw dropped. He spread his hands at the trail. "It's plain as a page of Scripture."

Marian gazed at treetops. "I suppose it might rain."

"I — I disbelieve this. You doubt my word?" Robin trotted a dozen feet down the tail and pointed. "Look. She planted both feet and went to her knees, but here she's dragged again."

Marian turned a beech leaf to study its underside. "Be time to pick mugwort soon."

Robin Hood pinched the edge of a footprint to find it still sharp-cut, not yet crumbling. He pressed a callused thumb and watched dampness recede. "An hour agone. Let's get after them." Eyes on the trail, bow bobbing in his left hand, Robin Hood trotted.

Skipping, Marian caught up. "If you think this excuses your boorish behavior, you're dead wrong."

Thumping along, skull throbbing, Robin snapped, "I've half a mind to let these kidnappers keep the girl just to spite you."

"So?" Marian sniffed. "If a helpless girl is abused, what matter? What's the suffering of one more woman in this man's world?"

"It's men suffer the vexations of women. Ask Adam."

"Ywis. Blame Eve. 'T'was her done it, Lord. She made me eat of the fruit. I never had a thought for myself, nor will I shoulder the blame, so help me Almighty God.'"

Bile bubbled in Robin's throat, but he refused to slow. "You concede there is a girl in distress?"

"I concede no such thing."

Robin suddenly halted. "She's gone."

Marian piffed.

"No. Someone's hoisted her on his shoulder. Osborn, probably. His tracks deepen and shamble. She must be a handful." Moving on, Robin nodded. "Here she is. Too much trouble to lug. I hope she doesn't resist too long. They might find it easier to knock her on the head." He resumed trotting.

"That's men for you." Marian puffed alongside. "Cruel. Unkind. Liars, cheaters, gropers."

"I wonder if this girl gives them an earful like some I could name. I wonder if she was at the wedding. Everyone in Nottinghamshire was there. If she left early —"

"For a secret rendezvous with a dashing outlaw?"

"Eh? No. I just wonder if —"

"If she exists? Likely you hope 't so. Dozens of girls fell over their feet to dance with you."

"Is that knavery?" Robin jog-trotted, watching the trail but the woods too, as always, for oddities or ambush. "You circled young men laughing gay as a lark."

"Would you have me pine under some arbor? A weeping willow, mourning unloved and unattended?"

Robin paused as the tracks swerved towards brush. "She broke away. But they caught her again." The outlaw swiped at a bush and found a long hair, held it against the sky, then a tree trunk. "She's blonde."

Raven-tressed Marian sniffed. "Surprise."

Watching his wife, Robin Hood ran the hair through his mouth. Tasting, he mused, "She's... fourteen, this high, blue-eyed, dressed in red... Her name is Mary."

Marian frowned under dark brows. "You are such a liar. An evil, low, lying blackhearted dog."

"A goodly gazehound, let's hope." Robin trotted. "Come, before they hurt her."

Panting alongside, Marian groused, "Behold who speaks of hurting. I can't believe I married you. I should have bid the huntsman sic the hounds when first you sniffed round my door."

"Wouldn't w-work." Robin belched thunderously and gasped, but felt better. "Dogs like me."

"Foul. Like likes like. I should have had my brothers thrash you."

"When I was sneaking in by day," Robin laughed, "or sneaking out at dawn?"

"Don't you besmirch me, you malkin-trash." Marian's dark eyes smoldered as her hair bounced around her shoulders. "I never let you stay the night. And I never shall again."

"As I recall, your brothers begged me on bended knee to take you off their hands."

"They did not."

"Picklepuss, they called you. Shrew-tongue. Hammer-fist, too."

"You lie. They'd never slander me. They daren't."

"I told them, 'I don't understand. Marian, my sweet poppet? She's gentle as a milch cow and tender as a lily.' Oh, Lord, they laughed to split their spleens. I thought they'd never stand erect again. They offered me the Rushcliffe wapentake to marry you because it's the farthermost fief and they reckoned to only suffer you at Christmastide."

"Lies, lies, lies."

"Did you really push Galliard out a window? And set Marshall's clothes on fire? And lock Sidney in a tower?"

"I'll kill them," Marian growled. "As God is my judge, I'll make them suffer."

"Marry them off. That'll do it." Robin Hood stopped abruptly. "No hope. An hour'r more ahead. They could harm the girl grievously before we catch them. If we catch them."

"If there's a girl."

"Yes, if." Robin scanned the forest. "Advise me..."

"Why think?" snapped Marian. "Why not indulge your basest instincts? Just do as you will, heedless of consequence. Such you've always done. Why change now?"

Stroking his head, Robin mapped trails in his mind. "Too true. Plunging into marriage has been the ruin of a good woman. The poor creature's wasted the prime of her life on an undeserving cad..."

"God wot't. A woman's a fool to marry."

"Hmm? Softly, now... If Osborn drags the girl but not the other two, 'haps only Osborn has designs on her... Yes, we'll essay. Come, Marian."

Leaving the trail, bearing south, Robin cut cross-country. Nimbly he and Marian dodged beech and oak trees, then startled a herd of fallow deer dappled yellow and white. Marian panted, "Where do we go?"

"Osborn has a croft at Elmsley. I doubt he'd take her there. Even a forester can't drag a girl about like a balky calf. But there's a hut near the old iron mines at Black Hill. We'll diverge to the path to Brown's Covert and cut their trail."

"And if we don't?" asked Marian.

"I'm proved wrong and you can gloat. And an innocent girl suffers. Any road, it wasn't my idea."

"What wasn't?"

"To marry. I had no say. Ever since I could walk I tripped over this skinny girl with dark hair who'd tell me, 'We're going to be married, Robert Locksley.' Crass to take advantage of an eight-year-old. Still, it saved me seeking a betrothal."

"Lackaday. You needs practice for your next

wife."

"Never. I'll abstain. I'll take the cowl and tend sheep."

"Much like the women you prefer. Fluffy and brainless and clinging for protection." In falsetto, Marian warbled, "'Ooh, Master Robin, you're so powerful strong you crush me like a rose blossom.'"

"Better the blossom than the thorns," muttered the husband. "And I can think of a few rosy buds I've nipped that delighted the gardener."

"Don't be crude."

They saved their breath for running. The shortcut was short only because it vaulted hills. They chugged upslope around ash trees towering like columns in a cathedral. Before long Robin raised his hand. They skipped across open heath, then crept through a scatter of silver birches on to a narrow trail of polished roots and rocks. Frustrated by lack of sign, Robin dashed along the path until he found a muddy wallow. Rising, he waved Marian behind a cuckoo oak, an ancient hollow trunk stuffed with saplings.

"They haven't passed," whispered Marian. "Even I see that."

"Never yet." Crouching in the scrub, Robin Hood slipped off his quiver and laid it atop his bow, as did Marian. He plied his Irish knife to cut and whittle a sapling. Too, he pointed with his knife to green shoots. "Adder's Tongue. Good omen."

Marian puffed and watched. "You'd attack three foresters with just a club?"

"What fear I to die if my Marian rejects me?" Robin's only sign of anxiety was to whittle the club obsessively. "Pray you're lucky and I'm killed. Men love to comfort a widow."

"Likely you'll fly off the handle and flounder. Besides all your other faults, you've a filthy temper."

"I can't indulge it today. We needs get the girl back."

"I remember that fair where the boor

manhandled me. You half-killed the man. It took the entire Merry Men to pull you off. A horrid display."

"Good thing I'm the only one in the family with a temper."

"Jape. Mock me." The Vixen of Sherwood tisked. "Why didn't I see your cruel streak? Why was I blind? What did I that God punished me with a vindictive vengeful louse for a husband?"

"Serves you well for not taking the veil. Decent women dedicate their chaste bodies to God, not bawdy pleasures. Do you want a stick?"

"Dare you tell me how to fight?"

"Never. You wouldn't listen anyway."

"Ro-bert Lock-sley —"

"Hark."

Silently they waited, hearing only their breathing. Then a small cry like a kitten's. The tramp of heavy feet. A girl whined and sobbed. A man growled. Creeping, without touching, Robin Hood peered through leaves. Came three foresters in brown with the king's arrow stitched on breast or hat. They wore quivers and weapon-knives, and one man carried two bows. Poison Hugh was unshaven and jowly and red-eyed. A second forester Robin didn't know. Osborn was a big brute dragging by rawhide thongs on her wrists a skinny girl in a bright gown and kirtle now tattered.

The Fox of Sherwood drew his long Irish knife and tucked it alongside the club in his fist. He hissed, "Make noise as if all the Merry Men. Here we go.

"*Yah! Have at them, me hearties! John, Scarlett, kill them all!*"

Just past, the foresters had their backs turned. Surprise was complete as Robin and Marian leaped out roaring like lions and swinging weapons.

The unknown forester bolted headlong. Poison Hugh fumbled his bow to draw his sax-knife. Osborn whirled the wrong way and tangled with the bound girl. Robin Hood walloped Osborn's knee so he crashed to earth. Marian charged Poison Hugh with her long keen blade laid along her forearm. As Hugh shrank back, Marian slashed the villain's sleeve and tunic straight across. Blood welled. Hugh shrieked and stumbled.

With both felons down, Robin Hood chucked the club, snipped the girl's thongs an inch above Osborn's fingers, caught her arm, and half-pitched her at the scrub. Snatching up quivers and bows, making sure Marian followed, he gasped, "Run like the wind!"

Hard they pelted past trees and through bracken, not letting up until they were half a mile from the path. Only then did Robin collapse to his knees. And laugh and laugh, sobbing for breath.

Marian crumpled too, gasping and giggling. "Benedictee. Did you see – their faces? Lord – we showed them. Oh, dear – oh, dear, what's your name?"

Still in the grip of terror, the girl hiccuped, "M-M-Mary."

Robin Hood hooted. Marian tried to glare, but rubbed her nose and smiled. "A lucky guess. Don't fret, honey, we'll see you safe."

"God's fish and teeth," gasped Robin. "That'll teach those foresters to cross you, Marian. You half-dressed Poison Hugh like a prize pricket. Oh, you're wonderful. The most boon companion a man could want. Come to my arms, turtledove."

"Ooh, you're so aggravating. You really are impossible." But Marian scuffed on her knees into her husband's embrace. Passionately they kissed, though their noses ran and they lacked breath. Coming up for air, Robin squeezed Marian so hard she grunted.

"See, Marian?" laughed Robin. "You're the only woman I could desire. And so beautiful when you're angry. Far more stunning and exciting than any scrawny minx from Clipstone."

"What?" Marian shoved free of her husband's clinch. Dark eyes hot, she snarled, "You still think of her? And dare compare her to me? You swine. You cur. You lowly stinking toad!"

Robin Hood's Treasure

"– almost defiled me! The indignity of it! The
nerve! Burned my barn and my castle! Laid hands
on me! And stole – stole – the last of the money I'd
planned for my old age! A pittance to you, no
doubt, good Sheriff, but the only bulwark I had
against the cold and the wolves of the forest! And
now it's gone! I say to you, I demand of you, what
are you going to do about it! What? Tell me!"

"Good lady, I –"

"You don't care! Why should you? You have
money! You have wealth! You have silver enough
and gold too to last the winter! What care you? Eh?
Tell me!"

"Good lady, we –"

"Oh, it's all very well to talk! That's all you men
ever do! Here I am, practically naked as a virgin
before the world, and you can only boast of
catching these ruffians and bringing them to
justice! But any real help? No! Where am I to get
it? Needs I take myself to the forest and beg help
from some scurrilous outlaw? He's a friend of the
poor and the sick and elderly and the widowed! He's
not sitting here in a silver chain swilling wine
while –"

"Madame, I'll get your money back!"

Nicholas, High Sheriff of Nottingham, was
reminded of that Greek king who could never eat
his meals for the harpy women who swooped from
the skies and shit on his plate. Even his wine
tasted sour. The Lady Amabillia, formerly of Three
Oaks above Derby (would she be willing to sell her

land cheaply, he wondered?) hung over him like a gallows tree, alternately wringing her scrawny hands or sketching in the air the horrors she had suffered. Her sleeves brushed against his forehead time and again, no matter how far back he leaned. The Blue Boar's patrons peeked and chuckled. The lady's sleeve dipped in the mustard sauce on his plate, then striped across his forehead. Nicholas clambered to his feet and upset the table. His breakfast, barely begun, landed on the floor.

"Will you, good Sheriff, will you?" Lady Amabillia cried with joy. Her hands hooked as if to caress his cheeks. He jerked back and tripped over his stool. "Yes, m'lady, yes, I will. I'll have your gold back by tomorrow."

"Will you start right now? Right away? Now?"

She swayed back enough that the sheriff could scuttle upright. A boy had come to clean the mess. He held up the sheriff's slice of mutton. It was speckled with straw and dirt and dried dog shit. "Will you take this with you, milord?"

The sheriff's hands shook as he fumbled out a silver penny and threw it at the boy. He scampered for the door with the widow right behind.

Out in the sunshine his men snapped to attention. One let go a milkmaid's waist. One lobbed a tankard behind a tree. Three got up from dicing in the dust. They tightened cinches and untwisted reins.

The sheriff squinted in the light. Nicholas of Nottingham was a short man with flat black hair and beard. He was dressed in a silver-chased doublet and satin-lined cloak and new hose, all in the blue of Nottingham, with the silver-antlered chain of office on his breast. His matching hat had a short peacock feather that constantly intruded on his side vision. The widow clung to his tails like a swarm of hornets. He grabbed at his saddle pommel and jerked himself astride.

"Which way did they go, milady? I want to get after them as soon as possible."

"Which way? I don't know. I had to flee. But they'll likely come this way, so you go that way."

The sheriff followed her finger. Through Sherwood Forest. Of course.

The widow raised her voice. "One hundred ten marks it was they got. Almost all gold, except for the silver. Good Roman florins. There were four of them — don't you want to know how many? Sheriff, are you listening?"

The sheriff was not listening. He rode as fast as his mount and sour stomach would go.

"We could give more to the crippled ones that crawl in here on hands and knees."

"And more to them little parish churches that have to give to the bishops."

"And more to the orphans. We could do a lot more, Robin."

"A lot more with what?"

"Money."

Robin Hood opened a sleepy eye and fixed it on his cousin. Green-tinged shafts of light and silver birch pillars gave the greenwood a cathedral air. The morning forest hummed with spring noise. They had to raise their voices above bird song. "What would you do with more money, Will?"

Will Scarlett intoned, "I would give it to the poor."

Everyone hooted.

"Then they wouldn't be poor no longer." Old Will Stutly recited the old joke. "And we know what you'd do with it."

Scarlett laughed. "And what would I do with it?"

"You'd spend it on lust."

"And malmsey," added Little John.

"And you'd gamble the rest away," added Hard-Hitting Brand.

"And buy food," added Much. He'd been turning the deer on the spit over the fire pit.

"And he'd waste the rest," muttered Robin Hood. "Aren't you supposed to be on watch, Brand?"

"This is more interesting."

"Must be powerful boring out there, then."

Will Scarlett nodded. "You're right. I'd spend the money on them things and more. I'd spend it right."

"And that's wrong," Robin finished. He sat up straight and stretched his arms. He scratched both armpits and then his beard. Robin had been up since yesterday, visiting Marian who'd slipped out of the nunnery, and they'd spent the night wandering the woods, gathering spring flowers, kissing and hugging, talking. He didn't know if he were ready for the day or not. "When we steal, it's not for us. It's for the poor and anyone else as needs it. We're not the receivers. We're just the vessels, carriers for Our Lady."

"I know some ladies in Nottingham would love to receive some money," said Scarlett.

"You never knew a lady in your life," Little John told him.

Robin picked up his great bow and stretched the string, taking imaginary aim. The weapon fairly hummed. "Gold can't buy anything important."

Will Scarlett clucked his tongue. "But really, Rob. Why can't we keep some of what we steal?"

"You know the answer to that, Will. Because it wouldn't be right. We didn't become outlaws to steal money. We became outlaws and that's why we steal money. Don't get things backwards. You're always doing that."

Little John rumbled, "But you know, Rob. He's right about one thing —"

"Ach." Robin Hood let his bowstring twang, something he never did. "All this talk about money. I don't remember Jesus talking about getting rich. I seem to remember just the opposite. All we ever talk about is money. How many times a week do I have to dig up our treasure chest? Eh?"

Little John rocked his quarterstaff across his lap so the ends thumped on the ground. "Last time you opened it you frightened a mole."

Robin Hood swung his bow in a great sweeping arc. "Would you look at this glade? Would you look at that lime tree? This cave? These oaks, that were saplings when Our Savior walked on water? This glade, this forest, yon brook, this way of life we have here — sitting around a tree and lazing the day away and watching the sun come up and talking about nothing at all — we might's well be steeped in emeralds —"

"In what?" asked Brand.

"— when we could be chained to some plow scratching a furrow across rocks, or hobbling crippled a leper on a pilgrimage to Jerusalem, or lost, or alone, or hurt or unloved or without families — all this, and you lot want money?"

The outlaws looked at one another. They looked at their camp, which showed no sign of human life other than the fire pit and Will Scarlett's spare shirt hanging on a bush. They looked at their leader. Robin Hood's shirt and trousers were worn through at the knees and elbows. His leather tunic was scuffed almost white, his belt cracked. Only his deerhide boots, tall and greased, were presentable. Even the feather in his hat drooped. The King of Sherwood was the poorest-dressed among them.

Little John cleared his throat. "If we did keep more of the money, Robin, we could build a chapel."

Robin grunted, his voice tight from pulling his bowstring. "I could build a chapel without leaving this glade. From stone below and trees above."

"We could have a gilt cross."

"Jesus hung on a wooden one."

"What about our arrowheads, eh? You don't find them growing on trees."

"No, I find them hiding in the pack of ironmongers from Kent."

Scarlett said, "Rob, all we're sayin' is —"

"Enough." Robin Hood hopped into the air and landed facing them. "I'm for a walk. Good day."

He strode off for the woods, the arrows in his back quiver clicking rhythmically. They watched him go.

Will Stutly sucked one of his few teeth. "Much, that deer done yet?"

Scarlett poked his chin with a long finger. "Too bad you mentioned malmsey, John. That's got me thirsty. If we had a few pennies we could walk to the Boar."

"Oh, shut up, Will."

"No, there's nothing like it, Ned, nothing at all. We rise when we please, we hunt the king's deer, we sleep when we're tired, visit whom we please when we please — there's just nothing like it at all. I'd not trade places with King Henry. No king's treasure could amount to a hundredth's part of mine."

"Tell us more, pray." The challenge came from a shadow that filled the doorway. Dust motes whirled around the stolid figure. In a blink the doorway darkened with two more men, then another. Long tapers hung from black hands. They shooed a few peasants past them and shut the door and slammed the shutters. Sunlight and fairy dust were banished outside.

The Blue Boar was quiet. Robin Hood had several bowls of ale under his belt by now. He enjoyed talking to the innkeeper Ned, who'd been the cook in Robin's father's household in the old days. Robin loved to hear stories about his father's careless Saxon tastes and his mother's refined French ones. And of how Ned would make him a berry duff if the boy Robin pestered him enough.

The outlaw chief squinted as the men advanced. Ned the innkeeper moved slowly down the bar, but froze as a man barked. Ned and Robin Hood and the inn's boy, Cnut, waited.

The gruff men were knights, dusty from the road. The four wore leather hauberks with rusted iron plates, scratched Norman helmets and broken shoes. They carried long knives at their belts and slim swords in their hands, and faces stern from recent sin. A tall thin knight dropped a leather sack onto the planks of the bar with a clank.

The four surrounded Robin where he leaned on

the bar. The outlaw stood as straight as he could.

"I said," growled the knight, "tell us more."

Robin squinted again. "More about what?"

The knight used his free hand to punch Robin in the chest.

Quick as a snake Robin's right hand came off the bar and slammed the knight's jaw shut with a *clack!* His left swung wide for the second knight's face or throat — Robin didn't care which, as long as the man fell back. He did, and Robin smashed his shoulder into the man who'd hit him. He clawed for the man's sword. Robin had only his long Irish knife: his bow and quiver hung from a peg on the wall. The outlaw grabbed, but the man clutched his sword tight. Robin had the disquieting thought this plan might not work.

With a toe-popping lurch, he ripped the sword free. It was just in time, for a silver blade swung at his neck like an executioner's blade. Robin shoved his steel into the air and even managed to back the flat side with his other hand. The knight's sword struck his with a muffled clang that hurt to hear. It was a solid blow, too solid. Off-balance and clumsy, Robin was knocked sprawling. He tossed the sword rather than cut his face open.

Somewhere along the way he hit the dirt floor with his back, then his head. Someone kicked his foot. Someone kicked him in the ribs. He rocked forward to get clear and almost ran onto a sword blade.

"Ouch."

The tip was dull. It did no more than puncture his tunic and bruise his breastbone. But it stopped him cold. He sighted along the shimmering blade. It seemed to go on forever, like a one-color rainbow. The tip of the sword skipped from Robin's breastbone to just under his chin.

"Don't kill him, Wycliff. He said treasure."

Treasure? thought Robin. I said that? His thoughts jiggered like tadpoles in a pond. Treasure?

A third knight shouted. "Where is this treasure

you spoke of, lout? It means your life."

"Umm... Yes, milord."

"It's 'milord,' now," said a man. Robin couldn't see any of them well, up there in the dark of the rafters. "He's scared."

"Hush. Talk. Who are you, anyway? Why are you in devil's green?"

"He looks like a beggar."

"Not with them boots, he don't."

Ned spoke from behind the bar. "He's Robin Hood, the famous outlaw. He robs the sheriff and others on the road. Rich folk. He's got a lot of treasure hidden away, back there in the forest."

"How much?" Someone kicked him. "How much?"

"Oh —" Robin's croaked and tried again. "Oh, some. Gold marks, a double fistful at least."

"No."

"Aye. Some stamped with William's head. Some with Harald's."

The sword at Robin's throat backed an inch. "What else?"

"German pennies. Ecus. Florins. They're all the same, same size and weight. Lots of silver. Fifty marks if it's a penny."

Ned asked, "Would you lords like a drink while you plan? My ale's fresh-brewed in new vats."

"Aye. That's good." The greedy man, the leader, sheathed his sword. "Rufus, watch him. Don't let him up."

The knights stepped to the bar and took jacks of foaming ale. Rufus spilled ale out the corner of his mouth as he tried to stare at Robin. The outlaw laid his head back on the cool earth and rested and listened. His eyes burned.

Ned talked as if the knights were his best customers. He topped off their ale and asked whence they traveled, what they'd seen, what the news. They bragged about their latest coup. "We've gained a small fortune just this morning. Robbed a widow down Derby way. Fired her house and barn. Cooked one of her sucklings for dinner. And got that." He pointed with his jack to the leather sack on the bar. "Sixty marks if it's a penny."

The man with the sore jaw and fiery temper, Wycliff, laughed. "We left her her son and her virtue. How's that for a bargain?"

The leader choked on his ale. "I wonder where she'll sleep tonight?"

"Not in the barn, nor the house neither." One knight, an older man, wheezed so hard he snorted ale through his nose.

Ned chuckled with them. He hunted back of the bar, then nodded to his boy. "Cnut, run to the house and fetch that cask of special brandy I've been keeping. Let me know if you can't find it."

"Yes, father." The boy put down his broom and left. A few minutes later he stuck his head in the door. He squeaked, "I can't find it, father."

"Gah. You useless sop doll." He banged down a pitcher. "I'll be right back, milords. I've something you'll like."

The leader of the knights nodded. The men drained their jacks and refilled them from the pitcher. It was quiet in the room. Robin stared at the blackened beams. He thought it curious no one else came in: someone must be steering people clear. The Blue Boar sat by the road by itself, halfway between Edwinstowe and Nottingham. Ned liked to be alone. They waited some more. The inn's cat, a piebald, slipped into the room and rubbed along the hearthstones.

Wycliff banged his fist on the smooth oak planks. "Where is that fool?"

The leader put down a pitcher. "Hey. I bet he's run off."

From the floor, Robin Hood said, "He's gone for the sheriff. He told me Nicholas was here just this morning, with eight men-at-arms."

Wycliff threw his jack at the fireplace. "Bugger. Let's burn this place to the ground."

The outlaw said, "The smoke'll attract attention."

Wycliff walked over and peered down at him. "I haven't forgotten you punched me in the jaw."

Robin told him, "Please forgive me that, lord.

But 'tis better you slip off quietly into the woods — with me — to fetch that gold. That or fight the sheriff's men."

Rufus gulped the rest of his ale and tossed his jack. "He's right there."

The leader frowned. Wycliff kicked Robin in the side. "There better be lots of gold. A double handful for each of us. You better not be tricking us."

Robin rolled his eyes. "Me? Trick you? I don't think I could. There's plenty. I took it from the Bishop of Hereford himself."

"That's a sin," said Rufus.

"May I get up now?"

The leader grabbed the sack from the bar. He bounced it to feel its weight. "Aye, get up, you scut." He jerked Robin's knife out of his belt and threw it across the room to thud against a wall. "Lead us to this gold. And no tricks."

Robin pushed the door open to blinding sunshine. "Follow me."

"Where're you bound, lad?"

The voice came from the trees. Alphonse jumped like a rabbit struck with an arrow.

One of Robin's foresters had appeared from nowhere. He was tall and broad, Saxon blonde, with a crooked nose and large bony fists. He wore forester's green and a tunic of chain mail scraps, with a bow taller than himself and arrows half as long, and a staghorn knife in his belt. In the green wilderness Alphonse found him more terrible than a dragon.

"A-are you Robin Hood's man, Little John?"

The man reared back and laughed. "Me? No, I'm just a little titch compared to Little John. He's big. Come along and meet him. Are you bearing news or asking for help? You don't act smug enough to have news, so you must need help. Am I right? And stop shaking. Your teeth chattering will scare the deer."

Robin's camp was only a meadow at the base of a tall hill. A lime tree filled the sky and shaded the glade. Oak trees loomed so high they could crush a boy and never notice. A cave mouth in the hillside beckoned and repelled Alphonse at the same time. Caves led to hell.

Robin's band of Merry Men (as Alphonse had heard them called in songs) lay around the cows in a paddock. There was an older man with a head gray and white like a badger's, a squat and ugly and snaggletoothed idiot, a smiling rogue in red, a peasant fresh from the plow. Most noticeable of all was a man who covered too much grass. And as he stood... Alphonse found himself staring up at the giant's face, silhouetted against the sky like the face of God. The giant had a blonde beard cut like a spade and a long braid down his back. His hand was bigger than the Bible in the parish church.

The man with the crooked nose called, "Someone looking for help."

"Looks more like he's after food," said the man in red. Alphonse had smelt roasting deer. "I'll cut him a haunch before he faints and we don't get our news."

"None of the deer you shoot are ever edible, Will," put in the gray man, "You always gutshoot the poor things and let 'em run. Makes 'em bitter."

"You're just cranky 'cuz you ain't got the teeth to chew 'em with, Will."

"Least when I shoot 'em, they go down and not long."

Robin's cousin cut away a long wide slice of golden-brown venison and juggled it as he rolled it into a tube. He handed it to the hungry boy, whose eyes shone with appreciation.

The man with the crooked nose, Hard-Hitting Brand, poked Alphonse with a finger. "Your news, boy?"

The boy spoke around a mouthful. "I'm Alphonse, son of Amabillia, widow of Richard of Three Oaks near to Derby."

"Widow Amabillia. We know of her," said the giant. His voice rumbled as if from under the ground.

"We was attacked early this morning. Before dawn. There were four knights tried to get into our manse. They stayed the night in our barn, and when they couldn't get inside this morn, they fired the barn. Then they fired the door and broke in. They took mother's treasure."

The man in red, Will Scarlett, asked, "How much treasure?"

Little John pointed a finger like the short end of a club. "Tha's none of your business, Will. Go on, lad."

"That's all there is to tell. They took our money. That's what Mother told me to tell y'."

"And she expects us to get her silver back?"

"Gold, it was, she said. Near to ninety marks. All we had in the world, and now us thrown out in the cold to starve."

Will Scarlett scratched his head. He signaled to old Will Stutly and Little John to move away. He whispered, "I've seen this Widow Amabillia before, and heard more of her. She's the one loses her cattle all the time. Has six head and loses thirteen or more a year. She thinks the pindar works for her. I'll bet if she says she lost ninety pounds it's closer to forty-five. Or thirty."

"You're daft, Will," Little John told him. "Not everyone's a thief like you."

"And she couldn't conjure up four wastrel knights from the ground." Will Stutly scowled, "Still, I don't believe anything until I see it with my own two eyes. We'll set out on their trail. It's what Robin would do."

THey walked back to the boy.

Alphonse, skinny and dirty and fifteen or so, gulped down a hunk of venison a dog couldn't have swallowed. Little John carved off another piece. Will Scarlett sat on his heels across from the boy. "All right lad — you're a bright looking type, you know that? I hope my little Tam grows up as sharp as you — why don't you tell us everything that happened? Let's start with descriptions of these knights, their weapons, and their mounts..."

The boy's throat tired from answering questions. Finally Will Scarlett said, "That's all very well, but these knights could have gone anywhere."

"But probably they'll go to Nottingham," said Will Stutly. "With that gold weighin' 'im down, they'll be wanting to spend it, and town's the place to waste money. Just ask Scarlett."

"It's as good as any," Little John agreed. "We can take the Black Brook Trail to the Salt Road. Maybe we'll get there before 'em."

"'Specially if they stop at the Boar," added Scarlett.

"You've yet to pass it by, tha's true," replied John.

"This'll be grand. If we collect the robbers and the money too, that'll do Rob in the eye."

"This ain't a contest. Be sensible. Now let's go. Much, you stay here in camp. To tell Robin where we are, or in case anyone else comes. Where are we going?"

Much furrowed his black brows. "Af-ter knights. To Nott'in'um."

"Good." The giant slapped the idiot on the back. "We'll be back tonight, or maybe not. Rob'll understand."

He caught Alphonse under the arm and picked him clean off the ground, then set him down. "Come on, son. Let's catch these marauders of yours. Maybe we can collect their heads to adorn your mother's gate."

Alphonse choked on his meat but stood ready as the foresters shouldered their quivers and picked up their bows. He stepped out after them, then found himself running to keep up with their long woodsmen's strides.

Will Stutly called over his shoulder, "Where's your mother now, boy?"

"Oh, she's safe. She's asking the sheriff to help."

Before Will Scarlett could say anything, Little John poked him.

"How much farther?"

Robin stopped and turned. Any time they addressed him he stopped, and was slow to start again. "Eh?"

"I said, how much farther?"

"Farther?"

"To camp, you oaf!"

Robin Hood leaned against the bole of an oak tree that reared to the sky. This was climax forest, where the trees had almost ceased to grow. The lowest branches were fifty feet off the ground. The ground was carpeted with oak leaves and nothing else, as clean as if overgrazed by goats. The only moving things were brown moths. High overhead a green woodpecker laughed, the sound eerie.

Behind him had come the four robber knights on their horses. The beasts' hooves were silent on the dead pliant leaves. Only an occasional thud of iron on root sounded in the cathedral of forest. That and the knights' grumbling.

The leader, whose name was Roger, kicked his mount to crowd Robin. He slapped at him with the end of his reins. Robin Hood took it on his shoulder. "How much farther to this stinking outlaw camp of yours? And the gold?"

Robin rubbed his chin. "Oh. To camp, milord. Let's see now..." Robin pretended to think. He yawned.

Roger's face turned bright red. He scrabbled off his horse and ripped his sword from its sheath to level it at Robin's belly. "Yes, you goddamned yellow scurvy outlaw bastard mongrel whoremongering fool. Yes, to the camp and the treasure you spoke of, you idiot. And why are you yawning, you dick-headed harlequin? Aren't you afraid?"

Robin waved an apologetic hand. "Of course I'm afraid, milord. Terrified. But I was up all night and I drank my breakfast — we outlaws live to carouse, you know — and — I'm tired."

In truth, Robin Hood had planned to lead these

men on a little farther, past this stand of oaks and down a slope to the edge of a fen. There, in the holly and hawthorn, cattails and bullrushes, he had planned to run away from them. Horses couldn't penetrate that swamp without sinking, even if a rider could force them onto the deer trails. But if he did lead them to the fen... There would be mosquitoes down there – he and Marian had had to avoid some of their favorite places because of the clouds. It was a warm spring. And the fairies might still be abroad, since they stirred in the spring along with everything else, and their first thoughts were in discomfiting humans. And Robin didn't himself like that fen. There were barrows back there, and probably barrow wights. And he was hungry and thirsty and tired, and he didn't feel like running...

"No, I'm addled," he said. "T'will be quicker to cut up north and come to camp that way. The trail should be dry by now."

Roger waggled his sword. "So how far?"

Robin scratched his elbow where it protruded from his shirt. "Oh, not an hour's walk."

The knights looked at one another. Clearly, they didn't know what to make of this rogue. Roger jabbed at Robin's chest, scarring his tunic again below the fresh cut of the morning. "Well, let's get to it. We're tired of wandering these damned woods for nothing."

"Me, too," Robin replied. He pointed. "That way."

The men mounted and Robin took the lead. He turned for a slight detour so he could drink from a brook.

He pondered his new plan. He would lead the knights towards camp. He'd make noise to alert the lookout, sing a signal, and his Merry Men would ambush these knights. They were begging to be killed anyway.

He hoped the lookouts weren't asleep.

"'West by northwest. West by northwest.' What kind of directions are those?"

Cnut, the boy from the Blue Boar Inn, had almost given up hope of finding Robin Hood's camp when he saw the smoke. It spiraled up in the middle distance, white and thick. A cook fire full of grease, he guessed. Didn't it seem unwise to make so much smoke if they were hiding from the sheriff's soldiers?

Cnut came to the clearing at the foot of a hill. The smoke came from an animal carcass — it must be a deer — that had ignited from too hot a fire.

A man beat at the flames with a stick. His mad flailing broke the spit and dropped the meat into the fire. More beating whipped up flames and ash and set the stick afire. In flailing the stick about, he set fire to the back of his tunic.

Cnut ran up, snatched off his filthy apron, and whapped at the flames on the forester's back.

Much the Miller's Son spun around. Someone was hitting him. He struck back with the charred stick. The boy tried to get behind him. Robin Hood had told Much never to turn his back on an enemy, so the idiot danced in circles. The boy followed, shouting. Much hit him with the stick and left black streaks on his hat and face.

Cnut finally just pushed the forester over to crash on his back. Then he backpedaled out of range.

Much got up slowly, like a turtle. He tried to remember what all the excitement had been. He studied the boy, a young boy from town. (Anyone not a forester was "from town.") "Hail," Much told him, in Robin's voice. "Wel-come to camp. What do you want? Why you wear a skirt?"

Cnut panted as he tied his apron back on. "I don't know. It's not. We need help. Or you do. Not us, you. There are robbers and they've got Robin Hood. They knocked him down and kicked him —"

Much remembered. "You knocked me down."

"Y-yes, I did. You were on fire."

"Oh." Much frowned. "What do you want?"

"These robbers, knights, false knights, with

horses. They've got Robin Hood. They took him away."

"Where they take him?"

"Uh, to camp." Cnut looked around. Some crows had landed on the lower branches of an oak tree to investigate the meat smell, but that was the only activity. "To here, we thought. To get Robin's treasure."

"Rob-in's trea-sure? What trea-sure?"

"Uh, I don't know. Don't you know about his treasure?"

Much shook his head gravely. "You hungry? Boys are always hungry."

"N-no, I'm not hungry, thank you, milord."

"I'm no man's lord. I'm Much the Mill-er's Son. I get you some food."

Much drew a slim knife and dragged the smoldering deer clear of the fire. He poked around, hacked with his knife, used his hands and tore a bloody chunk loose. He dropped it on the grass, speared it, brushed it off, finally presented it to the boy with black fingers. "Eat. Sit. Wel-come to camp."

Cnut took the meat and sat cross-legged on the grass. He tried to nibble at the lump. He wondered how it could be raw and burned black at the same time. He closed his eyes and bit deep, tried not to spit it out.

Much sat across from him, too close. He dandled the sharp knife in his hand. "Why you come here?"

Mouth smeared with blood, Cnut started, "I'm the slops boy at the Blue Boar Inn. This morning —"

"Boars are black," Much told him. "With gray —" he plucked at his hair and pulled it around to look at it. "— hairs."

Very slowly, not eating his meat, Cnut explained what had happened to Robin Hood. It took a long time. In the end he said, "So Robin Hood is coming here — I think — with the bad men — here. No, not yet. They're coming — to steal your treasure. Robin's gold."

"Gold!" Much exclaimed. He got up and ambled

off towards the cave. Cnut threw his meat into the
bushes, wiped his hands on his singed apron, and
followed.

The boy crept into the cave after the idiot. The
inside of the hill was very dark after the sunshine.
He waited for his eyes to adjust. He smelt water
and dry stone. The cave was surprisingly large,
the ceiling higher than he could have jumped.
Some bulky objects — barrels and sacks and a chest
or two — were stacked at the back. That was all.
This was an outlaw's life? Living with idiots in
caves in the woods?

Much knelt at the far side of the cave without
any light. Cnut heard digging. Much moved
something aside, stomped dirt flat, picked up the
something and headed out. Cnut got out of his way.

Back on the sunny spring grass of the clearing
Much brushed dirt off a small wooden box. It was
ironbound, riveted to be strong, with a hasp but no
lock or even peg. Much pried up the lid and
something sparkled brighter than the sun.

It was silver and some gold, more than Cnut had
ever seen, even working in an inn all his life.
There were fat Norman coins with Stephen and
William's heads, and older coins with faces he
didn't know. There were coins stamped with city
walls. The silver was black with tarnish, but thick
and round or cut square. When Much closed the box
it seemed like sundown.

"Robin's gold," said the idiot.

"Well, sir Much, I don't know what you should
do with it. Except hide it, maybe. Those robbers are
coming soon. They should have been here by now."
Cnut gulped. The sight of all that money and the
thought of marauders coming to steal it unnerved
him. "I have to go, milord."

Much stood up and picked his nose. "You hungry? Boys al-ways hun-gry."

The boy shook his head. "No, no thank you. I'm
full from that venison I had. Really."

But Much headed back towards the fire pit.
"Non-sense. Boys always hun-gry. Can't send you
'way emp-ty." He shooed crows away from the

scorched wreck and ripped another hunk loose. He picked up the deerhide from the grass, shook off the ants, wrapped it up and gave it to the boy.

"Thank you muchly, uh, Much. Will you hide that treasure? It shouldn't be left out."

The idiot stood over the box. "Hide it. Hide it. Hide it where? Hey, where you go?" Cnut had made his getaway.

Eventually Much picked up the chest, set it on his sloping shoulder, and settled it into place.

He marched off into the woods.

"I know you lot don't appreciate the forest. You'd rather a town. Bright lights, alehouses, painted women. But it's a lovely place to be. There's no other spot on Earth like it. Not a one. Why just look at those trees, would you? Just look at them. Other men see only the wood in them, that they'd fell and cut out the heart of, but I say they're beautiful, God's finest works —"

"Would you shut up with your drasty speech? You'll drive us all mad. You talk and talk and talk and say nothing!"

Robin Hood turned in complete innocence. The four knights scowled at him. Or three did. The fourth, the old man, clung in the saddle and panted. Robin calculated. They were past the lookout's post, so the Merry Men knew they were here. He hadn't hailed or blown his horn, so they expected trouble. A signal would cap it. He asked, "If I mayn't talk, may I sing?"

"No!"

Robin had already launched into *"Pour Mon Coeur"*. *"At-tend-ez moi, les pe-tites —"*

The lead knight spurred his horse and swiped at Robin with his fist. The outlaw sidestepped by moving close to a tree trunk. The knight cursed him. "Shut up and move!"

Robin Hood shrugged and walked. With every pace he expected the *zip!* and *thop!* of an arrow hitting a man or horse, and he tightened his belly

231

for the dash for cover. But one step followed
another, and eventually he could see the bright
green-yellow of the camp clearing. Then he was in
the open and the horses were snorting behind him.

The King of Sherwood stood and stared at the
empty camp. The only thing out of place was a
misshapen burned deer on the grass. Nothing
moved. What the hell?

Roger walked his horse beside Robin. "Well?
Fetch out the treasure."

Robin Hood scritched this beard with his
thumb.

"Go!"

"Yes, milord." Robin hitched his belt and
started for the cave. Oh, well. He'd give them his
gold and bolt for the woods if necessary. If he could
find the Merry Men, they could maybe hunt the
knights down. Or maybe not. And he could always
steal more gold.

Robin chirped as he crept into the cave, but
there was no answer. Roger bustled in behind him,
leather-and-iron armor creaking and squeaking.
The tall Rufus came after and thumped his head
on the entrance. But that was all. Wycliff the
Quick-Tempered stayed outside, as did old Tomkin.
Wycliff said nothing, but Tom carried on about
"caves ain't no fit place for men. Devils' territory,
that. Y'u'd be mad to venture in there..."

Robin Hood reached for his belt and found his
sheath empty. "Borrow your knife?"

Roger squinted in the dark. He'd drawn his
sword. "D'ya think I'm a fool?"

Robin didn't answer that. He poked around and
found an iron spoon. "Never mind."

He felt with his hand for the spot. There it was,
tamped down in the shape of feet in deerhide soles.
He dug. The earth seemed looser than it should be.
He hadn't been at this chest in weeks...

His spoon scraped hard dirt. The hole was deep
now. He stopped. He felt around. He poked the soil
on either side of the hole. It was tough,
undisturbed.

Robin Hood sat back on his heels. He scritched

his beard.

Behind him stood Roger and Rufus. Their sword blades shone dimly in the yellow light of the cave mouth.

"So where's this gold?"

"Christ, what a day. Bloody woman."

The Sheriff of Nottingham rode the skirt of Sherwood Forest, going west. He had more taxes, more rents to collect, more business to transact. He smiled at the thought. And if he should meet the robber knights, well and good. His men could capture them, and he'd impound their money. "But it would be just my luck to meet bloody Robin Hood and his bloody Merry bloody Men —"

He heard a *zip!* and *thop!* and blinked. An arrow shaft stuck out of his horse's breast just in front of his foot. How did that —

His horse took another three steps, died, and collapsed. His nose banged the dirt road, his neck twisted, his body slumped at an angle. Nicholas of Nottingham followed, tumbling out of his high Norman saddle. He landed on his back knowing his clothes would be filthy. Then the sky darkened.

A hand came down and caught the sheriff by the doublet. Nicholas was plucked up off his feet as he hadn't been since a child.

Little John propped the sheriff on his feet. The forester was impossibly tall, making Nicholas feel even smaller. He grinned. "Hail and well met, good Sheriff. Master." The giant laughed, then laughed some more. "How your home and your lovely wife? Hired a new cook, or any more servants?"

Nicholas scowled. It was not so long ago that Little John, then unknown, had entered his service, cleaned out his kitchen, and lured away his cook. Later he'd tricked the sheriff into attending a feast in the greenwood. Nicholas had eaten off his own plate, been served his own wine by his own cook, and then been robbed for dessert.

More foresters held bows with arrows nocked

and pointed at his soldiers. Nicholas found his temper rising. Here was Robin's cousin, the laughing Will Scarlett, who prowled Nottingham as a cutpurse named Badger. Here was Hard-Hitting Brand, a tall man often mistaken for Little John (by anyone who hadn't seen the real thing). And here was old Will Stutly, whom the sheriff had tried to hang, but whom Robin Hood had snatched from under his nose.

Brand pointed. "No word for Reynold Greenleaf, Sheriff?"

Will Scarlett laughed, "Isn't it Reynold John?"

Little John smirked. "Or Little Greenleaf?"

Will Stutly grinned a gapped grin. He rasped, "And have you reconsidered joining our band?"

The foresters laughed, Brand and John and Simon and the two Wills. Little John finally wiped his eyes. "You ought to teach your men proper archery, Nick. Them crossbows are too slow to engage, and they look so helpless."

The soldier at the forefront burst out, "Only cowards strike from cover."

Simon darkened. "Cowards?"

Little John waved a hand. "Don't be touchy, Simon. They always say that. We're forever killing the sheriff's men, and they're sensitive about it."

Nicholas brushed at his cloak. "Did you have to kill my horse? They cost more than the soldiers, you know."

The giant shrugged. Besides his quiver and bow across his back, he held a quarterstaff taller than himself, thicker than the sheriff's wrist. "All you lot do is complain. Next time we'll knock you out of the saddle and spare the horse."

Nicholas shuddered, then froze as the giant continued. "Now hand over the gold."

"G-gold? What gold?"

"Or silver."

"I, uh, I haven't any —"

Little John shook his head.

Nicholas sighed. "It's in the saddlebags."

Little John waved. "Scarlett, fetch it." Will untied the saddlebags and bounced them on the road. They gave a muted chink. Little John stuck out his hand. The sheriff produced his purse from inside his shirt.

Nicholas asked, "How did you know I had money?"

Scarlett laughed. "You always have money."

Little John added, "And you're not supposed to even be in Sherwood. This ain't sheriff's territory."

"I can ride the roads."

Will Scarlett slung the saddle bags over his shoulder. "You gonna do like Rob does? He always splits it and gives half back."

"Robin ain't here."

Stutly croaked, "Besides, he lied. He said he didn't have no gold."

"Oh, that's right." Will nodded at the soldiers. "Do we rob them?"

Little John answered. "No. We're too cowardly to go near fighting men. Besides, anyone takes up soldierin' needs money bad." The sheriff's eight men fidgeted in their saddles, but said nothing. He told the sheriff, "That's all. You can go. Oh, did you hear about four knights robbed the widow of Three Oaks? We're hunting for them."

Nicholas grit his teeth. "I heard. I met her. We're hunting too."

"Oh, good."

The sheriff's eyes blazed at the foresters. "One of these days... I'm going to catch you lot and hang you all."

Simon was stunned. Stutly was smug. Will Scarlett nodded. "Fair enough."

Nicholas, High Sheriff of Nottingham, stalked back to the last man in line. "Get off that animal, you idiot. I need it." The soldier got down and the sheriff mounted. "Start walking." Head high, he led his troop down the road. The dismount soldier walked around the outlaws and the dead horse, swinging his arms.

Little John laid his staff down in the road, broke the laces on the saddle bags, and dumped out the money. He whistled at the bushes. "Alphonse. Come here."

The widow's son crept out of the bush. He looked at the retreating entourage. "Is that always the way you rob people? The sheriff?"

Scarlett stacked coins in piles of ten. "No. Sometimes we make fun of him. Look at this, son. How much did your mother lose?"

Alphonse gulped. "Near to ninety marks, is what she said to say."

"But how much did she lose?"

"Uh..."

Scarlett glanced at Little John. The giant shrugged. "Count out ninety and give it him. Near enough is close enough."

But when it was counted out, there were only eighty marks in gold and its equivalent in silver.

Little John straightened up. "Eighty's almost ninety. Good." He squinted at the sun, scratched the base of his braid. "Not yet noon and we've recovered most of the widow's money. Robin will be pleased."

Scarlett grinned. "We're one up on Rob."

"This ain't a contest, I tell you. Alphonse, why don't you get along home? Your mother'll be frantic over the loss of that money, and glad to see this. We'll chase after those knights, but they could be anywhere. We'll send word if we get lucky."

"What will you do if you catch 'em?"

Little John kept pulling at his braid where it caught on the bowstring. "Depends what they do. If they surrender, we'll... march 'em into Nottingham for the sheriff, I guess. If they act up, we'll stack 'em by the side of the road for the wolves. You lot ready?"

Scarlett said, "You're the one talking and fussing with your hair."

Little John frowned. "I see what happened. Robin was born first and got all the brains in the family."

Will grinned. "That's right. I got all the looks."

"Must be one ugly family. Let's walk."

Alphonse went west, and they set off south. Simon asked, "You think Robin's back in camp yet, so we can tell him what we did?"

Little John reached for his braid and turned the gesture into another shrug. "'Less he stopped for a nap."

Robin stood up in the dusky cave and brushed off his trousers. Because of the holes in his knees, most of the dirt fell inside his pants legs and down his deerhide boots.

"Well?" demanded Roger. "Where's the gold?"

Robin turned around slowly. "I forgot. I had one of my men fit it into a niche here."

Rufus asked, "What's a niche?"

"Up here." In the gloom Robin walked to a wooden rack suspended from the ceiling by pegs. As the robbers pressed behind, he caught at something and brought it down. It was long and wrapped in deerhide. Robin tussled with the wrappings, turning around in the process.

Rufus pressed closest. "What is it?"

"This!" Robin spun around and shot his arm. Rufus gave a grunt and dropped his sword.

Roger slapped his shoulder. "What are you doing, you fool? Pick that up."

Rufus merely clutched his middle. Robin Hood danced backwards and tossed the wrapping aside.

Robin Hood laughed. "Roger, you false pig. Let's see you use that sword!"

In the half-light, the knight could see Robin Hood facing him down a length of steel. He bore a long tapered sword with a wheel pommel and wire-wrapped handle. It was a Norman sword, Robin's father's. Robin Hood shuffled forward and swiped at the knight, who only just jerked out of the way.

"I was trained by Will Stutly, who fought in the wars of Wales and taught King Henry a thing or two." His voice was gravely from a bellyful of adrenaline. He took another swipe and Roger jumped again. Rufus coughed, face down. The outlaw chief had punched a hole through his midriff. The scent of hot blood, like iron ore smelting, filled the cave. Roger turned and bolted.

He popped out of the cave and pelted for his horse. Dismounted, Wycliff and Tomkin were caught by surprise. "What's happened?" "Where's Rufus?"

Then Robin Hood appeared in the cave mouth waving a bloody sword. "*Yah! Git! Git! Hyaah!*"

Spooked, the two knights snatched at their cantles. Roger and his mount were already entering the forest, going much too fast. Wycliff slammed into the saddle and rammed home his heels. His horse banged Rufus's, who whinnied and shied aside to trot into the woods.

Robin shouted and waved. He had no plans to fight them all. But as the last knight, the old man, finally got mounted and moving, Robin spotted something. Tied behind his saddle was the leather bag from the Blue Boar. That would be the widow's money.

"Oh, no, you don't." Robin caught up to the horse before it set its back hooves. He swung the sword wide and cut a back leg to the bone.

The horse screamed and reared. The man screamed too. Robin swung again and chopped the beast's leg below the fetlock. The horse slewed sideways, stumbled, and crashed to the earth. Old Tomkin crashed along with it. He was quick enough to pull his leg clear so the horse didn't pin it.

The horse shrieked and kicked. It chopped the forest loam into powder. Robin Hood skipped to its front and chopped the windpipe, then jumped aside to avoid the spray. The beast thrashed and fell still. The round brown eyeballs glazed over.

Robin Hood stood back and signaled with his thumb at Tom. "Can you get up?"

Tom was shaky but upright. He nodded, his mouth open and dry.

Robin waggled his thumb again. "Then drop your belt and get out."

He was gone in a moment, hobbling off down the trail after his companions.

Robin Hood stood for a while, breathing deep

238

and wiping his forehead. Eventually he cleaned
his sword on the dead horse's tail. He unstrapped
the saddle and tugged it clear. The leather bag
contained gold, right enough, though not more
than twenty marks by a quick count.

Robin wondered about that: hadn't they bragged
there was sixty-some? Could they have spent some,
or hidden it? He thought about carrying the gold
into the cave, but he'd had a treasure there and it
was gone. He stashed the bag under some bushes
instead.

He hauled the dead knight out of the cave and,
for lack of a better place, stacked him with the
dead horse. "What a waste," he remarked to the air.
"Can't eat either."

He fetched out his scabbard and baldric and
hung them on. He strung his old bow, found a
spare quiver and filled it with arrows. He catfooted
after Rufus's horse, crooned and cooed to it.
"You're a valuable piece yourself, aren't you,
hmm? That's right. Good fellow. Animals are
smart. They don't chase after money, do they?"
After some nose-patting and neck-rubbing, he got
mounted and settled.

"And where do we go?" Robin asked his new
horse. He yawned. "I thought I wasn't sleepy. Well,
let's see what transpires on the road. It can't be
any more busy there than it's been here."

"Hello? Hello?"

Alphonse had found his way back to the camp
largely by luck. Robin Hood's camp was far from
the road, but all trails seemed to lead there.

The camp was a riot. The deer he'd partaken of
earlier was a scorched heap on the grass. Nearby
was the carcass of a horse, slashed in several
places, its saddle torn loose. A knight lay dead
next to it. Crows picked over both, but flew off at
his approach. With his heart pounding to burst,
Alphonse came close enough to recognize the man.
It was one of the wastrel knights who'd burnt his

mother's barn and home.

The boy's hands shook as he opened the saddlebag full of gold. He had carried it first in one hand, then the other, then behind his back, then in front. It worried him terribly to be carrying this much money. It felt obscene. Especially since he didn't deserve it.

Alphonse had a good heart, inherited from his deceased father. The boy knew well his mother hadn't lost "near ninety pounds" but more like thirty. She'd hoped more would somehow find its way home. It might have, except that Robin Hood's men had thought Alphonse dishonest. With a pride that can only come from poverty, he'd prove them wrong.

The widow's son counted out stacks of ten coins each, as he'd seen Will Scarlett do, then piled four stacks back into the saddlebags. His mother would be pleased enough to receive ten extra marks.

The rest of the gold stood stacked on the grass, glittering in the sun. Alphonse hunted for inspiration. The crows circled overhead. Flies thickened. The forest glade was oppressive. Where to hide the money? Not the cave. Caves led to hell.

He spotted the saddle. He scooped up the gold and swept it underneath, covering it completely. Then he grabbed the sheriff's saddlebags and scampered for the woods.

"The rats. The shits. The bastards."

Old Tomkin had run for most of a mile before his breath gave out. He leaned against a giant oak and clutched his chest. Cool air burned his lungs. He tugged off his heavy helmet and threw it in the bushes. A hell of a thing, running. No wonder God invented horses. They'd run off and left him, all of them. He started as a covey of quail raced by on invisible legs. Christ, what a place, this forest. "The dogs. The pigs —"

He squinted at his back trail. There was no one in sight, but there could be any second. Best to keep moving. That Robin Hood was a killer. Teetering from tree to tree, he stumbled off down the path.

And stopped. Up ahead — damn! — was another of Robin Hood's outlaws, dressed like the devil in green. One before, one behind, no way to leave the trail without getting lost...

But that one was carrying something on his shoulder. A chest. A small one for gold.

Tomkin wiped his face and checked his back trail again. No sign of Robin Hood. No sign the fat forester before had heard him. Tom drew his long knife.

Much the Miller's Son rolled down the trail towards the road. He had a walk all his own, like a crippled duck, but he covered ground quickly and never tired. Get to the road, he thought. Find Robin... and then... do something... Robin would know.

A thumping sounded behind him, feet on the forest floor, coming fast, and he stepped out of the way.

Charging like a demon let loose from Hell, knife held high, on his last breath, Tomkin sailed towards the idiot. Much discommoded him by sidestepping, and further so by leaving his foot in the path. Tom stubbed on it and crashed full length on the ground. His knife flew away and slithered under the oak leaves that lay everywhere.

Much the Miller's Son helped him up.

"You hurt?"

Tom was surprised at the idiot's strength. "No, no, I'm not hurt. Uh, are you?"

Much checked himself slowly. "No."

"Oh, good. I was afraid you'd fallen."

"No."

Tom pointed. "Uh, what's in the chest?"

Much turned halfway around peering at it. "Trea-sure."

"T-treasure? Real gold?"

The idiot frowned.

Tom brushed at his clothing. "I, uh, lost my

knife. D'ya see it?"

With his free hand, Much drew his own knife and pointed it at Tom. "Knife like this?"

"Uh..."

Much suddenly jerked the knife sideways, just missing Tom's arm. "'Point that damned thing some-where else.'" Then he jerked it back in Tom's direction. "You take mine. Every-one needs knife."

Tom gingerly took the blade away and shoved it in his own empty sheath. "Right. Thanks. That's better. Uh, if that's really treasure — I mean, uh, Robin's sent me to take that treasure from you — for you."

"Oh." So Robin had known what to do. Much shoved the chest at the robber, who caught it awkwardly.

Tom grunted. The box was heavier than Much had made it look. It must be chock full of gold. He scouted the trail again, then set the box down. No harm in checking...

He pried back the lid and had to shield his eyes. Even under the green roof of leaves the sun jumped around in the box. Tom grinned so wide his face hurt. "It is. It's gold." Then he remembered Robin Hood's man.

Much grinned too. "'Gold can't buy any-thing 'por-tant.'"

"What? Never mind. Let's... lighten the load some. No use hauling the box."

He was hot anyway. He shucked off his hauberk and his shirt. He laid the shirt on the leaves, then dumped the coins onto it and pitched the box. He stirred the treasure with his hand. The coins made a lovely liquid sound, a friendly chuckling noise. He stuffed some into a pouch to spread the load, then gathered the corners of the shirt, made sure there were no leaks, and slung the sack on his back. He staggered as it hit.

Much asked, "I help carry? I strong. Strong as Lit-tle John at arm wrestle."

"No." The old man shook his head and staggered again. "No, thanks, lad. I'll manage. You run along back to —" Wait. He couldn't point him towards camp. He'd run right into Robin Hood. "You better come with me for a while, lad. Keep out of trouble. What's your name?"

"Much the Mill-er's Son. 'Sher-wood ain't much with-out Much.'"

"Much. Good. I'm... Peter. Come along now."

So Tom, or Peter, hunched now and rolling like Much, set off down the trail. The unencumbered idiot followed, happy as a dog after its master.

"If you'd gone into the cave we could have killed him there."

"And if you hadn't gone into the cave there'd still be four of us."

"Afraid of a cave."

"Stupid enough to be taken in the dark."

"Idiot!"

"Fool!"

"Coward!"

Wycliff jerked his tired horse to a halt. He grabbed for his sword. "No man calls me coward."

Roger clutched at his own hilt. He had to drag his horse backwards, for there was no room to swing. The Nottingham road was very narrow here, overgrown at the sides from neglect. "No man calls me fool. Defend —"

His horse snorted.

From out of nowhere, Little John said, "You're both fools. And loudmouths. Let's call it even."

The giant — he was the biggest man the knights had ever seen — filled most of the road. He held a quarterstaff lightly across the horses' throats. He smiled at their discomfit.

Roger was furious at the impertinence, Wycliff blind with anger. They both raised their swords. Roger snarled, "You scut. I'll —"

A cord snagged his throat. His Adam's apple was wrenched out of joint as an irresistible force tugged him backwards. The knight tumbled out of the saddle and landed hard on his head and shoulder.

Sprawled in the road, Roger and Wycliff rubbed their throats and gagged curses. Facing them were more outlaws in green. Their bows had been slipped over the knights' heads while the giant distracted them.

Will Scarlett examined his bow, then used it to rap Wycliff on the helmet. *Tonk!* "You cut my string with your blade."

Snarling, Wycliff dove for the outlaw. Scarlett skipped aside and let him pass. The mad knight plowed into old Will Stutly and both went sprawling.

Will Stutly growled on his own as the knight pummeled him. Will didn't bother to call for help – he knew better. He tossed his bow and jammed both thumbs into the knight's eyes. Hard-Hitting Brand crashed a fist onto the side of Wycliff's neck and knocked him loose. Brand stamped on the man's back and snatched away his knife. The outlaws tied his hands with the broken bowstring.

Roger felt a rap on his helmet. He looked up, and up.

Little John pointed at the saddles. "Where's the widow's gold?"

Roger swore. "We lost it. One of our men – old Tom – ran off with it." He watched Wycliff thrash on the floor like a suckling pig. Why had he taken up thieving with these three: one mad, one stupid, one decrepit? Next time he'd enlist real men-at-arms.

The giant rested his quarterstaff on the ground and rolled it between his hands as if drilling. "Hmm..."

Scarlett grinned. "This puts us up even more on Robin. We've robbed the sheriff, paid back the widow, and now captured two of the knights."

"This ain't a contest, I tell ya. Where'd the old man get to?"

"I don't know. Away."

"Where's the other one, then? There was supposed to four of ye."

"He ran off too."

"Is that so? But no widow's gold, eh?"

"No. And I don't care anymore. Damn you all."

"Hmm..." Little John sped up his drilling. "I don't think I believe you. But this can work out fine. Robin didn't get any gold yet, but we will."

Scarlett laughed. "I thought this wasn't a contest."

"Hush. Let's pack up this baggage. We'll take 'em to Nottingham."

Stutly grunted. "Nottingham? What for?"

"We're going to stuff 'em into a wine press and squeeze out gold."

Scarlett grabbed Roger by the shoulder. "That makes sense."

Roger gasped as his shoulder was wrenched. Wycliff chomped grass. "Are all you bloody outlaws daft? What's wrong with you? What are you talking about?"

"You'll see. Get up. I'm thirsty."

Will Scarlett slammed the knight belly-down across his own saddle. "See? He's not daft at all."

"Mother! Look what I have!"

Amabillia, the Widow of Three Oaks, poked a maid in the shoulder as the girl stirred an iron pot over a fire. All around stood the burned wreckage of her house. She stopped in mid-poke as the boy held a bag aloft.

Alphonse trotted to a halt. He panted, "Here, mum. Here's the gold. From Robin Hood's men." He thrust the bag into her hands, glad to be rid of it.

The widow blinked at the heft. She set the bag on a fallen timber and counted the coins.

"This isn't our gold. There are no florins. It's someone else's. Though we'll keep it. Where did they get it? Was it Robin Hood did it?"

Alphonse nodded and wiped his cheeks. "Aye. His Merry Men..." He told her about their intercepting the sheriff.

Amabillia smiled a cold smile. "That's fun. I set the sheriff on the knights' trail, but I knew he'd slough it off and run for Nottingham." She cackled some more, then turned to the cook. "Never mind that. Dump it out. We'll leave now."

For the first time Alphonse noticed the two pack horses hung with sacks and ironware. "Mother, where are we going?"

"Where do you think? Use your head, Alphie." The widow circled the horses and tugged at knots. Three servants watched her with slack hands. "We're going to live with your Aunt Alditha in York. There's nothing for us here. Now that we have the gold."

Alphonse looked about at the ruins of the manor and barn, at the tumbledown cottages, at the weedy fields. He pointed to things at random. "We're leaving? But I've lived here all my life. What about our home? What about the land?"

Amabillia struggled to mount a horse already piled high. "Oh, for heaven's sake, Alphie. Shut up. It's only land. Nobody wants that. It's not worth anything. Now come on."

She kicked the horse with her skinny heels, and the beast lumbered forward. The servants trailed, leading the other horse.

Alphonse took one more look around, then followed.

"After we get the money, can we spend it on wine and debauchery?"

Little John pointed to the robber knights trussed on the floor. He answered Will Scarlett. "Are you sure you shouldn't be on the floor with those two?"

The Merry Men waited in the dust-speckled dimness of a barn on the outskirts of Nottingham. They ate and rested, lazy with the long day and spring warmth. Barn swallows turned circles that brushed the rafters and skimmed straw from the floor. The knights' horses chewed hay. One kicked his hoof regularly against the outer wall.

Scarlett carved his initials in a post with a wicked knife. "Those two don't know anything about debauchery. I can tell 'em about debauchery. When I go out to debauch, I have a good time. They probably just get drunk and beat up someone small. By the time they get to a whore they'd pass out. Did you ever see two more sour faces?"

From the loft Hard-Hitting Brand called. "Here he comes with the blacksmith."

"Anyone else?" asked Little John.

"Nope. Just a smithy and two apprentices."

"Well, keep an eye out all around. He may have told the sheriff's men to come later, when we're negotiating hot and heavy."

"Right."

Scarlett brushed away shavings to see his handiwork, yellow etched in brown. "You doing the negotiating?"

Little John rumbled, "No. I'm goin' to leave it to Simon here, only because we don't have Much to talk for us." Simon blinked, but the giant waved a hand at him. "Just joking, lad. I'll do the hagglin'."

Scarlett touched up his graffiti. "You sure you don't want me to?"

"I'm sure."

"Fine. You handle it. I'll keep quiet."

Little John snorted.

The owner of the farm, a merchant, knocked at the door and then crept in. With him was the Nottingham blacksmith, a short solid man whose long tunic had burns in the front. He carried an iron box. His two apprentices, a thin boy and an older journeyman, carried steel pokers.

The Merry Men shuffled about in the tight barn to make room. Little John signaled to shut the door, and for the blacksmiths to put down their pokers. "You won't need those. We're not here to rob you." The boy breathed easier. The journeyman seemed disappointed.

The blacksmith set down the box and put one foot on it. "So what have you?"

The giant forester squatted and unfolded a hauberk. On it lay all the knights' accouterments. The knights themselves wore only gambesons and rope.

"Two swords, two long knives. Baldrics – this one ain't got a crack on it anywhere – scabbards and sheathes. Tooling, here. Their shoes, one pair with double soles. Hauberks, one with copper, one iron squares, good solid rivets. Norman helmets. Some kind of a locket here, must be silver, and a cross of whatever this metal is – bronze, is it? Someone's been to a shrine, though it din't do him any good. Plus them two nags. And their tack."

The merchant, the owner of the barn, cleared his throat. The giant gave him a gold mark for fetching the blacksmith.

There was a very long space as the blacksmith checked over the booty. He unsheathed the swords and tested their edge. He rapped them together to hear them ring. He picked at the handles to learn what kind of wire wrapped them. He scrutinized everything the same way. Then he checked the horses. He counted their teeth, stared into their eyes, pressed his ear against their chests and bellies, poked their frogs, peered under their tails.

Finally he rocked back on his heels and rubbed his throat. "All of it?"

Little John nodded. "We can't use it."

The smith probed the barn with his eyes. "Forty marks."

"Forty marks?" Will Scarlett bounded off the stall railing and landed in front of Little John. "Forty marks? Are you mad? God's fish and teeth, one of those damned helmets alone is worth forty marks. Where in the hell did you get a figure like that? Forty marks! Christ's sweet tree, it'd take you three months to make one of those hauberks, and you'd be glad to charge some idiot fifty marks for it alone. Did you hear the ring on those swords? One of 'em's got to be Milanese or Damascan, and you're offering us forty marks for it? The knives would be worth forty marks even without the sheathes. You Jew. You Saracen pirate! You tax-collecting, wine-nipping, cheese-paring, gold-shaving –"

Little John interjected, "We'll take it."

Red-faced but silent, the blacksmith twirled

the barrels on the lock and opened the chest. Shielding it with his body, he extracted forty thin marks and stacked them on the floor. Little John packed them into his purse. All the while Will Scarlett ranted and raved and waved his arms in the air. "... call us thieves. Simpletons, maybe. Fools. Children wandered to the woods. But thieves. You need a town man to teach you about thievin'..."

The blacksmith ordered his apprentices to tie everything onto the saddles of the horses. Then he led them out, not directly towards the town gates, but along some oblique route. He didn't say goodbye.

Will Scarlett wasn't through. "... can't believe you let it go at forty marks, John, and clipped ones at that. Have you lost your mind? We were robbed, plain and simple, same as we hoist the sheriff. We could've shopped around. We could've gotten three smiths here, pitted 'em against one another, gotten a fair price. But no. You had to give the stuff away. We could've gotten two hundred marks −"

Little John grinned. "It's worth a hundred to see you hop like a frog in a pot."

Scarlett glared. "Forty needs a hundred sixty to make two hundred."

Little John picked up his quarterstaff. "Does it? I never was one for numbers. Get over twenty sheep and it might's well be a thousand and one, and half of them wolves. Get you up, you lot, we're for the woods."

Will Stutly creaked upright. He rubbed the small of his back. "What about them?"

The giant regarded the knights. Through the exchange, as their worldly goods had been auctioned away, they had glared and chomped on their gags. John scratched his jaw in imitation of Robin Hood. "Can't sell 'em. Can't eat 'em. Can't leave 'em here, 'cause that'd get Paul in trouble. Hmm..."

A little later the Merry Men approached the tall broad towers that were the gates of Nottingham. Slung from Little John's quarterstaff, between

John and Hard-Hitting Brand, were the two
knights. With hands and bare feet in the air, their
gambesons hung slack. Their rumps shone in the
sunshine. Women in the fields pointed and
laughed.

The foresters stopped in the road outside
crossbow range. The sheriff's guards, in blue
gypons and soupbowl helmets, had already
gathered at the gate — they could spot Lincoln
green a mile off. Little John dropped the knights in
the road and slid his staff clear. "Hoy! Captain of
the guard!"

The captain cupped his hands around his
mouth. "What d'ya want?"

"These here are the false knights robbed the
widow of Three Oaks by Derby! Give 'em to the
sheriff with our compliments!"

"Compliments of who?"

"Don't be thick!" the giant retorted. He pointed
with his thumb at the guards and asked Will
Scarlett, "Relations o' yours?"

Robin's cousin snorted. "Maybe. My father went
into Nottingham a lot. But none of them — thick as
they are — would trade away two liveries and
horses for forty marks."

Little John shrugged and started down the road
towards Sherwood. His quarterstaff on his
shoulder stuck out six feet behind him. "I suppose
not. Next time, you do the negotiating and I'll be
the one to keep quiet."

Old Tomkin sat down by the side of the path to
rest. He kept the gold in his lap with one hand on
it. He grimaced at Much, who had followed him for
miles. "Awful hot today, ain't it?"

Much pointed up. "Sun's out."

"Aye. Makes it hot. But my hands are cold.
Funny." Tom wheezed and rubbed his chest. "Can't
get my breath neither. Not as young as I used to be.
M' ribs feel squashed."

He tried to shift the gold in his lap, but it was

too heavy. He shifted himself instead and winced. "You don't need to keep me company, lad. I can fend for m'self. You just run along now. I'm going to just rest here, maybe take a nap... Awful hot. Makes me chest..."

His head sank back and he lay still. Much sat down beside him to wait.

He waited a long time.

Much grew hungry. He poked the old man gently on the leg. He was stiff. The idiot poked the man in the eyeball. He was dead. Much knew what death was.

He scratched his upper lip for a time.

Eventually he picked up the shirt full of money. He started walking towards the Blue Boar.

"Because we still owe the widow ten marks, that's why."

"We don't owe her nothing. You know and I know she lies like a flounder —"

Little John walked fast and everyone struggled to keep up with him. The deep woods were warm and buzzy with late-day heat. Pale green translucent leaves unfolded almost as they watched. Lizards basked in sandy patches. Digger wasps bored by, heavy with eggs. "No, we don't know that. She's supposed to have ninety marks and we only gave her eighty. That leaves ten we owe her, if my countin' is right, and you'll probably tell me it ain't."

Will Stutly croaked, "Slow down, John. For Christ's sweet mercy."

The giant stopped altogether. The five foresters stood in the middle of the road and felt they should have been walking.

Little John explained, "We're giving her ten marks, and that's all there is to it. If you want to argue, take it up with Robin. You know he's funny about honorin' women. Are you going to tell him we shorted a widow in need?"

Scarlett sliced at the iron-red head of a foxglove

with his knife. He said nothing.

"Right then. Anyone doesn't want to go with me to Three Oaks can return to camp. Well? Right then. Let's go."

"Slowly," said Stutly.

"Slow it is. I'm easy."

Another two hours' of shortcut brought them to Three Oaks. The ruins stank of damp ashes.

Simon said, "There's no one here."

Will Scarlett said, "No. There isn't."

Brand pointed. "Fresh horse turds here."

Little John scratched his beard. Then stopped.

The Sheriff of Nottingham and his men stood up from behind the wreckage of the hall. Four soldiers covered them with crossbows. The other four were behind.

Nicholas grinned like a wolf. "The tables are turned. I took your advice, Little John. Our crossbows are cocked and nocked this time."

Little John frowned. "Where are your horses?"

"Far down the road, west. I didn't bring them anywhere near here. Shall I shoot you now?"

Little John drilled his quarterstaff into the ground. "Shoot as you please, just don't tell Robin we walked into your trap."

Will Scarlett asked, "How did you know we'd come here?"

The sheriff put his hands on his hips and puffed out his chest. "I knew it because — Stay there, Will Stutly! I like you in a covey. It makes a smaller target. I came here —"

The giant stopped his drilling. He thumped his staff on the ground. "Do you want your purse back?"

"That and my eighty marks. I —"

Little John dragged out his purse and hefted it, making it look heavy. Will Scarlett snatched it away. "Let me give it to him."

Robin's cousin dumped the contents of the purse into his hand. Coins spilled into the blackened grass.

"Here now," called the sheriff, "you fool. Give me that —"

252

Will Scarlett whipped back his hand and flung the coins. Gold and silver sparkled in the air and pelted the sheriff and his men. The sheriff ducked. His men grabbed at the air with one hand.

Little John spun around and slung his huge quarterstaff by one end. Crossbows thunked. The staff hummed through the air and slammed into two soldiers behind.

Will Stutly hopped backwards into Simon, jostling him out of the way. Another crossbowman shot. The bolt sizzled overhead. The other took aim, too late. With arthritic hands Will nocked an arrow, half-drew, and loosed before the man could pull the trigger. The long arrow caught him in the upper chest. He cried out and folded, dropping his crossbow to clutch the shaft.

Will Scarlett followed his gold-throwing with a knife. He aimed for the one man who'd kept his head. The soldier ducked. By that time Hard-Hitting Brand was over the wreckage and among the soldiers. He slung his fists and bowled men over. He made sure their crossbows went flying.

"That's it!" Little John cried. "Run!"

The giant grabbed Simon by the shoulder and spun him around towards the road. Scarlett was already there with an arrow nocked. Will Stutly looked for a ready victim. Brand caught at the old man as he ran past. "Come on, Will!"

"Always hurryin'." He pegged his arrow at the most alert soldier and scuttled along.

Ten minutes later and many trees deep into the forest, the outlaws stopped to catch their breath. They were built for walking, and not running.

"Fine thing," Scarlett gasped. "You get robbed selling the knights' tackle — and then robbed by the sheriff."

"If you hadn't been arguin' about money —" wheezed Little John, "— we would'a spotted the sheriff hiding."

"If you had listened to me — we wouldn't have come — in the first place."

"You came along. I gave you a choice."

"I don't care about the money anyway — I just

like arguin'." He grinned. "You still going to give the widow – ten marks when you see her?"

Little John huffed. "No, I'm going to give her you. If she's traveling the roads, she'll need an ass. Let's get back to camp. We've done enough today."

"What have we done?" Simon asked.

The giant snorted. Lacking his quarterstaff, his hands clasped and unclasped. "We'll figure it out later. Let's go."

Stutly cursed. "Always hurrying."

"If you lot could shoot better, we wouldn't have this problem. Damned slippery outlaws. Cowards. Why didn't you pot them? We'd be out a few headaches, or I'm a fishmonger."

The sheriff berated his men in a flat uninterested monotone. His soldiers clutched their wounds and grit their teeth and said nothing.

"We'll have more practice, I can assure you that. Up before dawn, now that the days are longer, out there in the sun until you can knock a mosquito off a squirrel's ear. Eighty marks down and only thirty-five back, and – Who's that up there?"

Much the Miller's Son plodded down the road with a sack of treasure over his shoulder, the same as when he'd carried grain and flour for his father, the same as when he'd met Robin Hood. He waddled along and thought about... about... wherever he was going...

Whiff! Something plunked in the road alongside him. He stooped slowly and picked it up. Was it a snake? A bird? No, it was... a crossbow quarrel. Another slapped the earth nearby and spattered dirt in his eyes. Who was?..

Much saw the sheriff's men thundering towards him. He knew these men. They were bad. What would Robin do? He heard his leader's voice. "Run, Much! Run!"

Much dropped his sack and ran for the deepest,

most tangled bushes he could find.

Moments later the sheriff dismounted in the road, exulting. "It was one of Robin Hood's men. Look at this silver. No, get away. I'll get it." Nicholas scraped the muddy coins together onto the filthy shirt that had carried them. "Well, it's not such a bad day after all. Robin's treasure come home. We might even celebrate when we get to the Boar."

The sheriff remounted, the money on his lap. "Now, let's —"

There came a *zip!* and *thok!* The sheriff's horse gave a grunt and stumbled, squealed, fell.

Nicholas grabbed at the beast's mane as it collapsed in the road. This time he got clear without tumbling in the mud, but he dropped the money.

"Sheriff!" the voice echoed all around.

Nicholas raised his arm. There. Down the dappled leafy tunnel of road sat a lone rider. Long arrows at his back and a long bow held ready marked the silhouette. The sheriff tried to crab behind his men's mounts. His men were already in the bushes. Another arrow thudded into the horse carcass. The arrows were impossibly long, as if hurled by God. "Hold still!"

Nicholas stood still, alone. His mount twitched, then sighed with finality. The sheriff sighed too. "Twice in one day."

He brushed back his brocaded sleeves and called down the road. "Who are you?"

A laugh.

"Goddamn him." In the brush his men cranked their crossbows — those who could. The sheriff cursed some more. Robin Hood was outside crossbow range, but not, obviously, longbow range. "Keep still."

The sheriff cupped his mouth. "What do you want?"

The distant figure bobbed. "Today? Money! I've something to prove!"

"I don't have any —"

Ziiiiip! Something snatched at the sheriff's

255

sleeve. He could see the red satin lining of his doublet where there should have been only blue. Sweat broke out on his forehead. But this was gold at stake. He tried once more. "Your men have already robbed me once!"

"I believe you!" Another laugh. "Truly!"

"Then why do you think I have any money now?"

"You always have money!"

The sheriff wanted to cry. "Goddamn you, wolfshead! You've no right!"

"You don't like it, become a shoemaker! Now I've had a long day, Sheriff! Leave your money and go! Your men can keep theirs!"

Nicholas shook his head. He tugged out a purse (Little John's) and set it on the saddlebag. He pointed. "It's all here!"

The archer waved a long bow. "Our Lady thanks you!"

Unable to go forward, Nicholas of Nottingham mounted yet another horse and turned back towards nowhere. It didn't make any difference which way he went today.

Robin Hood dismounted and tied his horse to a branch. He moved away, crouched, and waited for thirty minutes. Finally he walked around wide, back to the road. He watched for soldiers, but they couldn't hide in his woods. He took the purse, the saddlebags, and a shirt full of mostly silver.

He took the saddle as well. "Should be able to sell this to someone."

"Hoy!"

Little John and the rest sat under a tree, just lolling, not talking, when Robin Hood staggered into camp. He came up to them and dropped several loads: saddlebags, a pouch, a shirt full of money, Little John's purse.

Little John frowned. "Where have you been?"

Robin went for a drink at the stream. "Out and about. Adventuring. Where have you been?"

"Nowhere."

"You've sat here all day?" No one answered. "Surely that's not possible. The sheriff told me you robbed him once."

Little John and the others just stared at the pile of loot. Robin Hood went behind some bushes and produced yet another bag to throw on the pile.

The giant said, "Well... we did that."

Robin flopped down on the grass, but grunted and reached into his shirt for more money. "I forgot. I sold a knight's horse and saddle to Ned for forty marks, and threw in the sheriff's saddle." He slapped his friend on the knee. "Now come, John. Tell me what you did. Please."

"Well... we captured them robber knights."

"Oh. Good."

"We delivered them to the sheriff."

Robin plucked up a blade of grass to chew on. "Good."

"And we recovered the widow's money and gave it to her son."

"Good. Very good."

"Is that all you can say? 'Good?'"

"No. Tell me the rest."

They did. Robin listened, then said, "You want to hear what I did?"

No one answered, so he told his story. He finished with, "And on the way back, on the Meadow Trail, I found the oldest robber dead. Just fell over, I suppose. He had a purse on his belt. So that's it. I must have been picking up after you all day."

He laughed, alone. Everyone else was quiet. Robin asked, "How much money did you get?"

It stayed quiet.

Little John rocked his makeshift staff to thump the ends on the ground. "I wonder if anyone else is forming an outlaw band in this forest this year."

Robin laughed. "What? What are you talking about?"

Stutly lay on his back with his eyes closed. "I'm hungry. Do we have to eat that horse? The meat'll be bitter."

Robin Hood went on. "You don't have to fret

about anything you did, John. Getting the widow's money was wonderful. Selling the knights' tackle in Nottingham was a very clever idea and an apt punishment. And the sheriff robbing us is a great joke. Getting away safe is even better." The way he said it, so jolly and gay, made the Merry Men feel much worse. "By the way, how much did you get for the tackle?"

Will Scarlett piped up. "You won't believe, Robin. This one here only got —" He stopped, shriveled under a murderous glare from Little John. "Uh... John got near to a hundred marks for the knights' gear. Just the gear alone. The horses we — uh — gave to the boy to give to his poor widowed mother to keep her from the cold."

"Horses to keep her from the cold? What are you babbling about? And hadn't you already sent the boy on his way with the money? No? Well, it doesn't matter anyway..."

Simon called, "Here's Much."

The foresters watched as their idiot friend rolled out of the woods and up the small slope towards them. Much the Miller's Son walked right by the dead horse and knight without blinking. He sat down with a thud. He greeted everyone by turn, as if he hadn't seen them for weeks. "Hul-lo, Robin. Nice to see you back."

"Thank you, Much, thank you. It's good to see you and good to be back. But where have you been?"

The idiot pointed towards the woods. "Out."

"What were you doing?"

"Walk-ing."

"Good. Walking is good. But Much, did you dig up our treasure?"

"Trea-sure?"

"Gold?"

"Gold."

"Yes, Much. Gold. Did you take it?"

Much nodded. "No. Dead man took it. In a skirt."

"What? You mean a shirt? This shirt here?"

Much patted his thighs. "Skirt."

"Who was he?"

"Peter."

"A dead man – named Peter – wearing a skirt – dug up our treasure?"

"Yes."

Simon shuddered. "Maybe he met a saint. Maybe it's a miracle."

Robin grunted. "It'll be a miracle if we figure this out."

They talked some more, but eventually gave up. Robin Hood said, "I'm sure – fairly sure – part here is our treasure. I think I recognize this cracked sovereign. And I know some of this is the sheriff's money and some is the knights'. And we've paid back the widow, so that's fine. It's all fine. But where's the lesson here? What have we learned from all this?"

It was as quiet as it would ever be in the Sherwood glade.

Robin laughed again. "What? So quiet? Will, you're never at a loss for words. Where's the lesson here?"

Will Scarlett stood up. He looked at all that gold and silver, then at his fellow foresters. "The lesson, Rob? The lesson... The lesson is this. That money just isn't important –"

"Good, Will. Finally."

"– because it's so damned plentiful in Sherwood it practically grows out of the ground."

The Merry Men laughed.

Robin Hood frowned. "I give up. You lot are hopeless. Let's go get some ale. I'll buy."

Will Stutly let out a groan. "Walk to the bloody Blue Boar? Again? After all the walking we've already done?"

Scarlett told him, "It's for a drink, Will. You won't have to kill any soldiers along the way."

Robin caught Will Stutly by an arthritic hand and hauled him up. "But before we go, let's get that saddle into the cave so the foxes don't chew on it. Later on we'll –"

Simon shouted. Underneath the saddle lay a pile of gold coins that sparkled in the late evening sun.

Robin Hood blinked. "Where did this come

from?"

No one knew.

"Aha! Sheriff! Here you are! Drinking in a tavern when you should be on the road!"

Nicholas, High Sheriff of Nottingham, wrapped his hands around his tankard and dropped his head on the grimy table. He knew that voice. It was Amabillia, Widow of Three Oaks, above Derby.

"Is this where you've been all day? Sitting here, a disgrace, while robbers ride the highway free as the air? Haven't you been after them? Answer me! Talk to me! Where's my money?"

About the Author

Clayton Emery is an umpteen-generations Yankee, Navy brat, and aging hippie who grew up playing Robin Hood in the forests of New England. He's been a blacksmith, dishwasher, schoolteacher in Australia, carpenter, zookeeper, farmhand, land surveyor, volunteer firefighter, and award-winning technical writer.

He's the author of the Robin & Marian Mysteries and Joseph Fisher Colonial Mysteries in *Ellery Queen Mystery Magazine* and elsewhere, twenty fantasy-adventures, kids' books, and other tales.

Read more stories at www.claytonemery.com.

More Mysteries

Royal Hunt
A Robin & Marian Mystery

In a forest verging on Stonehenge...
The Wild Huntsman and his Hellhounds ride the night, chasing down innocents and snatching their souls – and their heads.

Forced to act as Royal Forester, Robin Hood and Marian hunt for the truth behind kidnappings, arson, forgery, rape, and betrayal.

From a fear-choked forest to the lonely wastes of Stonehenge, from King Richard's court to a sacred cloister, from a freewheeling forest eyre to a bloodstained temple, the legendary outlaws fight ghosts and greed, phantoms and fire, witches and wickedness – and uncover a secret grievance planning the ultimate sacrifice!

Pale Ghost
A Joseph Fisher Colonial Mystery

Amid the flames of frontier war, one man spies murder...
1703 New England is ravaged by flintlock and tomahawk. Mohawk warriors and French Marines kill, loot, and burn, then drag captives away to slavery and torture.

Yet Joseph Fisher tracks an evil worse than war. For a murderer has used the raids to cover a trail of butchery and betrayal. Travelers vanish, soldiers muster, fanatics rail, and pirates ply the waves. Even dead men walk as a killer strikes again and again.

Raised by Indians, schooled by Jesuits, trained by Puritans, Joseph is a man of three worlds who belongs to none. Condemned by society and crippled by consumption, his only weapons are an iron will and a keen mind.

"Let justice be done, though the heavens fall." No one will stop Joseph from digging up the truth.

Order them today from Amazon!